Doctor Rebel
Mercy Emergency Medical

A Novel

by:
Grace Maxwell

Copyright 2024 Blind Date Publishing

All rights reserved. No part of this publication may be reproduced, distributed or transmitted in any form or by any means, including photocopying, recording or other electronic or mechanical methods, without the prior written permission of the author, except in the case of brief quotations embodied in critical reviews and certain other noncommercial uses permitted by copyright law.

This is a work of fiction. Names, characters, places and incidents are a production of the author's imagination. Locations and public names are sometimes used for atmospheric purposes. Any resemblance to actual people, living or dead, or to businesses, companies, events, institutions or locations is completely coincidental.

Mercy Emergency Medical: Doctor Rebel/Grace Maxwell — 1st edition

CHAPTER 1

Chance

The rumble of my Harley echoes off the hospital walls as I cut the engine outside the emergency department. My boots hit the pavement in front of the sliding glass doors with a solid thud. Standing next to my bike, I pull off my helmet and shake out my hair, feeling eyes on me—some wide with fear, others narrowed in what might be appreciation. The beast between my legs might as well be a fiery stallion for all the attention it commands.

I stride into the emergency department, leather creaking with each step, and rather than checking in at the desk, I find a corner seat in the waiting area to observe. I watch, silent and still, as the scene unfolds around me.

A few minutes later, a man bursts through the sliding doors, his face swollen and contorted in pain. His cries are primal, unfiltered by the stoicism expected of grown men. I can't help but assess his condition. Wasps seem the likely culprits, and based on the swelling, anaphylaxis is a threat. He begs for relief as the staff springs into action and whisks him into the back.

Not far behind him comes a woman cradling her abdomen, flinching with each movement. A darkening bruise mars her left eye, giving voice to a story she refuses to tell. Her pain is two-fold, part physical, part deep within. She avoids eye contact, her shame a shroud around her. But the domestic abuse is not her fault, no matter what the abuser tells her.

She, too, has been swept off to the back when a young boy, no more than eight, is ushered in by frantic parents. His lips are tinged blue, and his chest heaves in a futile quest for air as he wheezes. *Asthma* — a thief in the night, robbing this child of the breath most take for granted.

The team once again springs into action, and I nod in approval. Patients are quickly triaged and moved out of the waiting area. This is a good sign.

Then the wail of arriving ambulances cuts through the hum of activity, a reminder that trauma never sleeps. Outside, red and white lights flash while, inside, nurses and doctors move with hurried efficiency. But there's a tightness in their shoulders, a brusqueness in their voices.

It's clear they're stretched thin, worn down by a system pushed to its limits. I sit back, my gaze sweeping over the controlled chaos, already diagnosing, planning. This is where I'm meant to be — where I'm needed. My purpose here couldn't be clearer. They just don't know it yet.

I step back out the doors of the ED and wander the other parts of the hospital, watching. People eye me everywhere I go, probably unsure about my leather attire. Mercy Hospital is the largest in Vancouver, and as I move past the information desk, I watch the receptionists give directions via the vividly colored map behind them.

On down the hall, I push open a door that reads *Medical Staff Only* and step into the doctors' locker room. It's a quiet sanctuary away from the bustle of the hospital and the emergency department. A faint echo of voices catches my attention as I head for the bathroom.

Two doctors converse, their words muffled by the row of lockers between us. "...can't keep switching like this," one gripes. "Eleanor Thompson finally left; whoever takes over had better put an end to these night-day flips."

"Agreed," chimes the other. "It's killing our circadian rhythms."

A smirk tugs at my lips, unbidden. They have no idea that their potential savior stands just a wall of lockers away. Eleanor's shoes are big, but I'm ready to fill them — and stabilize their schedules too. I shake off the amusement and make a mental note — figure out what's up with these rotating shifts and see what we can do to change them. And I should let the staff think this is their idea. I can do that.

I finish in the bathroom and emerge to sit on the cool metal of a bench, still observing. The two doctors pass, deep in conversation about hospital politics. Their white coats are pristine, names embroidered over their hearts. Dr. G. Martin and Dr. K. Johns. They embody the medical profession as I know it — dedicated, weary, hopeful.

"This is the men's staff locker room. Though you're welcome to use the restroom." Dr. Martin nods toward the hallway, mistaking my presence for confusion. He looks me over briefly, an outsider intruding on sacred ground. "But it's really meant for staff, so don't linger."

"Thanks," I reply with a nod, my voice low and even.

Alone again, I turn to the row of lockers and find one unclaimed. Methodically, I strip off my heavy leather jacket, the vest, and the bulky chaps that have been my armor against the road's bite. Once they're stowed away — a symbolic shedding of skin — I'm left in black jeans and a T-shirt. I feel more like the doctor I am.

With a glance at the mirror — a stranger's reflection staring back, dark blond hair, blue eyes, a new beginning — I square my shoulders and step out into the fluorescent-lit corridors. There's work to be done, changes to be made, and lives to save. Mercy Hospital doesn't know it yet, but its new chief has arrived. And I'm ready to make my mark.

"Major MVA coming in!" The nurse in charge's voice cuts through the din as I turn back toward the ED. "Eight cars involved. Helo en route, six minutes with criticals."

The room tenses, bodies and minds shifting gears. The staff braces for impact as they prepare to receive the wounded.

From my vantage point outside of triage, I watch Dr. G. Martin and Dr. K. Johns and the teams that assist them spring into action—fresh paper gowns, rubber gloves, goggles, and for some, bands to hold hair tight from the gusts of wind created by the helicopter. They anticipate the worst, ready to offer their best. The helicopter's distant whir—the herald of what's to come—grows louder, more insistent.

The double doors burst open, with gurneys rolling in. The doctors are immediately on their feet, dealing with the broken bodies. "—two majors, two minors. Sideswiped by a semi skidding on Highway One and crashed into the concrete barrier," the paramedic reports.

"What do we have?" Dr. Martin commands, his voice steady as he assesses the damage on the first gurney off the helo.

"Head, neck, and chest. Possible pelvic injury. He's had three liters of O-neg. Blood pressure sixty-three. Pulse one-forty and thready."

They move to one of the triage rooms.

The next victim is pulled off the helicopter. "She's been unconscious the entire time. Pulse one-fifty. Sharp laceration and fracture of the right femur," announces the next paramedic.

"Let's get vitals, people." Dr. Johns directs the team with a calm authority that belies the adrenaline undoubtedly rushing through him. There's no hesitation in his touch as he begins his examination, fingers trained to find fractures beneath the skin.

I stand back, itching to join the fray. But this was only supposed to be a peek at how the team works and what I'll be walking into in a few days. For now, I commit every detail to memory, each movement and decision cataloged for future reference.

The accident victims continue to arrive, and I can't hold back any longer. I slide into a paper gown. My gaze locks on a head injury first—a laceration that's more bark than bite—but the abdominal swelling whispers of deeper problems.

"Merde," I mutter under my breath as my hands probe gently, expertly, feeling what shouldn't be there. My guess is the spleen has ruptured, unnoticed by paramedics too overworked or too rushed to catch it. A life-threatening mistake, hiding in plain sight.

"Hey—" I snag the nearest nurse, urgency sharpening my voice. "We need a surgeon, stat!" No time for niceties; there's blood pooling where it shouldn't, life ebbing away with every delayed second.

The nurse nods, reaches for the phone, and calls surgery to tell them they have someone on the way. She moves like she does this every day—swift, decisive. They're good here; I'll give them that. And I look forward to making them better.

But there's no rest for the weary, not today. Another body rolls through the doors, this one with pale skin and pinpoint pupils—a drug overdose, young, too young. I reach out to steady the gurney as they transfer him to a bed. The ambo driver reports having administered Narcan three minutes ago, yet he's not coming around. But if we're quick enough, we can still save him.

"Let's get more Narcan," I call. This dance is familiar, even if the floor is new. "Keep pressure on that wound!" I shout back at the other patient's bedside as I pivot to face this new challenge. Two lives hang in the balance, and I'll do anything I can to get them through this.

"Stay with me," I urge the boy as his eyes flutter. I spray another dose of Narcan into his nose. "I need an IV kit." The kid's veins are collapsed, likely due to his addiction, so I need to keep pushing Narcan every two or three minutes.

I'm murmuring instructions in French under my breath, a habit from years of trauma work, when a nurse rushes past. She's got a look on her face that spells trouble, and I catch the tail end of her words as she nearly collides with a man in scrubs. "—speaking French and working on patients." My hands don't stop—they can't afford to—but my attention splits as Dr. G. Martin approaches, his brows knitted together.

"Excuse me, you can't be back here," he says, firm hands pressing against my chest. His voice is authoritative, brooking no argument.

"Je suis fine," I respond, catching myself midsentence and switching to English. "I'm fine. I'm where I need to be."

Dr. Martin isn't convinced. He's already motioning for security, clearly not used to being disobeyed. Three broad-shouldered men approach, the air around them crackling. The radio squawks, a dispatcher's voice calling for police backup.

"Wait," I say, and thankfully, something in my voice gives them pause. I reach into my back pocket, fingers closing around the familiar edges of my old business card. It feels like another lifetime, but it's the key I need right now. I present it to Dr. Martin, who takes it with a skeptical frown.

"Chance Devereaux, Le Directeur, Salle d'Urgente," he reads aloud. Then his eyes flick up to the header. "Santé Montréal Hospital?" He looks up at me. "We appreciate you stepping in, and your emergency room experience, but you're a long way from Montreal."

"I'm the new chief of the emergency department here at Mercy," I tell him. The weight of those words hangs heavy in the air. Silence falls, broken only by the beeping of monitors and the distant sound of ambulance sirens. Everyone around me seems stunned, grappling with the reality that the stranger in black jeans and a T-shirt is more than just an interloper.

"Chief?" Dr. Martin repeats, the skepticism in his voice giving way to something akin to respect—or maybe just surprise. "Why didn't we know you were starting today?"

"Because I don't start until Monday. I just came to observe today."

Dr. Martin nods as a nurse calls him away. "Carry on, then, I suppose," he says as he vanishes behind a curtain. The tension in the air diffuses slowly. Staff return to their stations, and I find myself fading into the background once again. I return my attention to the patients in front of me. Bleeding seems under control on one, and I administer more Narcan to the other. As I finish and hand off the patients, I hear my name called.

"Dr. Devereaux?" I turn to see a woman extending her hand, her grip firm and sure. "I'm Jessica Scott, nurse in charge on this shift." There's an edge to her tone, not unkind but weathered by years of triage and decisions made under pressure.

"Nice to meet you, Jessica," I reply, taking in her alert eyes and the set of her shoulders — ready for whatever comes through those doors.

She guides me through the controlled mayhem, pointing out the key players on her team. We stop first at a young woman with honey-colored hair tucked under a scrub cap. "This is Dr. Cordelia Johns. We call her Dr. Cordelia because her brother and father also work here. She's one of our hospital pediatricians."

"Dr. Cordelia." I nod, noting the gentle way she speaks to a small boy clutching a stuffed bear. Her eyes are kind, the sort that see pain and offer solace without words.

"Her brother, Dr. Kent Johns, you've already met," Jessica continues as we pass a man whose focus doesn't stray from the chart in his hands.

Siblings in the same battlefield, I muse.

"Dr. Harlan Mitchell," she announces next.

The surgeon looks up from stitching a wound with a grunt, his hands never pausing in their intricate dance.

Nina Jacobs, a staff nurse, offers a weary smile as we

pass, her scrubs splashed with the day's labor. And then there's Dr. Christian Bradford, whose gaze flicks to me with disdain.

"Don't take it personally. He's always an asshole," Jessica says dryly.

"Best cardiologist in the country," I add. "Comes with the territory."

The shift stretches on, a blur of faces and names, ailments, and whispered stories. I'm able to help out here and there, and when it finally winds down, I feel exhaustion in my bones. But it's the good kind, the kind that comes from diving headfirst into the fray.

I return to the locker room and redress in my leathers, ready to return to the quiet apartment I've rented across town.

"Dr. Devereaux!" Dr. Griffin waves me over as I step out into the cool, late-July, Vancouver evening. Beside him, Dr. Kent Johns offers a half smile.

"Barney's Pub is right across the street, and it's a staff hangout," Griffin says, jerking his thumb toward the warm glow of neon on the other side of the road. "Care to join us?"

"Sure," I agree. I don't have anywhere to go, and I'm curious about these men outside the sterilized confines of the emergency department.

"Welcome to Vancouver," Griffin says as we jaywalk to the pub. "When did you arrive?"

"Yesterday, and I'm just getting the lay of the land," I tell them. "My first day isn't until next week." New beginnings, new challenges—Mercy Hospital is already shaping up to be more than just a job. This blank slate is mine to color, and I'm here to make it the best it can be.

We settle into a booth, the wooden seat groaning beneath our collective weight. The air smells of malt and spirits, with a hint of fried food lingering. *Céline would hate this place.* That thought comes to me unbidden. I hate that I'm thinking about her, but I'm still adjusting to not having her as part of my life. I do like getting to make my own choices. She'd have me at some expensive restaurant or club. This is pure comfort.

The server places three pints in front of us — all black and tans. Griffin picks up a glass. "This is our usual, but if you want something else…"

I lift the glass, and we clink them together.

Kent eyes me over the rim of his pint, foam sticking to his upper lip. "So, Devereaux," he says, wiping his mouth with the back of his hand, "how's Mercy stacking up against your old stomping grounds at Santé Montréal?"

I take a slow pull from my drink, the cool liquid settling my thoughts. "So far, it's not too shabby. But back in Quebec, we had the West End Gang, Montreal Mafia, and Hells Angels to keep us on our toes." I shrug as their eyebrows shoot up. "Keeps the job interesting."

Griffin chuckles, shaking his head. "You're not in Quebec anymore, that's for sure." He leans forward, elbows on the table. "Got a place to crash? Vancouver's rental market can be brutal."

"Found myself a legal basement apartment in a West Van neighborhood," I say casually, tracing the condensation down my glass. "Good view, quiet enough."

"Ah, but the Lions Gate Bridge during rush hour is a nightmare," Kent interjects, his tone almost cautionary.

"That's why I ride a Harley," I reply. There's freedom on two wheels that you don't get behind a steering wheel.

"Ever treat someone with road rash?" Griffin asks.

"Of course," I answer, my voice even, recalling the gravel-embedded wounds, the smell of antiseptic battling with the iron tang of blood. "But I like my odds."

Griffin shakes his head. "Motorcycles are donor cycles."

There's a moment of silence, and then the conversation shifts to the men's partners. They're both in committed relationships, and after they've finished their drinks, they need to get to them.

After they leave, I lean back against the wood of the booth, a half-drained pint of black and tan in hand, and scan the room with casual interest. Barney's is alive with the energy of unwinding. I'm new here, but not unwelcome. I like this place. I like it a lot.

A group of nurses, still in their scrubs, huddles at the bar, stealing glances my way. Their laughter is a melody that rises above the noise of the room. Eventually, one of them breaks away from the pack, her hair the color of autumn leaves, and approaches with a confidence that speaks to more than just a few casual encounters.

"Dr. Devereaux, right?" Her voice wraps around my title like she's trying it on for size. "My name is Mandy Howard. I heard you made quite the entrance today." She touches my bicep.

I offer a tight smile. "Just doing what needs to be done."

She leans in, close enough that I catch the hint of her floral perfume, and her hand grazes mine—a deliberate touch hidden as an accident. "Well, if you ever need a tour of Vancouver beyond the hospital walls, I'm your girl."

"Appreciate the offer," I say, tilting my glass toward her before taking a sip, keeping the exchange light, non-committal. Even if I was interested, I'm not ready to date. I was with Céline for ten years. And who knows, maybe she's going to realize she made a mistake not moving with me to Vancouver...

Mandy lingers, her body language an open invitation, but after a moment more of flirtatious banter, she rejoins her friends, sending me a look over her shoulder.

I turn back to the room, my mind not on the offers or the allure, but on the lay of the land—of Mercy Hospital, of this city. Every place has its rhythms, its secrets. From the thrum of motorcycle engines beneath me on the open road to the pulsing heartbeat of an ED, it's all about learning the patterns, anticipating the next move.

I finish my black and tan and signal for another. As the night stretches on, I stay rooted in my corner, once again a silent sentinel, watching the ebb and flow of the bar and the hospital staff that come and go.

CHAPTER 2

Lucy

The intercom's static crackle pierces the classroom's hum, and I straighten, ready for what's to come.

"Attention!" Principal Bishop's voice echoes through the tinny speaker. "We've had a bear sighting on school grounds. Please follow lockdown procedures immediately."

My grade-five students all run to the window and spot the three-hundred-pound black bear that's munching someone's lunch that got left outside this morning. *Oops.* The bears eat well around an elementary school. Despite the concrete jungle surrounding us, nature has a way of reminding us of its presence, usually in the form of a bear following discarded lunch items or the scent of fresh salmon from the stream by the greenbelt that edges our campus.

"Okay, everyone," I say, clapping my hands for attention, "we'll go to the gym for recess." The children line up, though fidgets and shuffles betray their pent-up energy. No outdoor recess means we'll have a surplus of wiggles to contend with indoors.

The kids have lunch at their desks, and I navigate a small food fight and a juice box being stepped on, which sprays the wall with pink juice.

Once we clean up, we march toward the gym, joining the throngs of other classes funneling into the echo chamber of squeaky sneakers and high-pitched voices. Controlled chaos is a lofty goal we fall short of achieving; the reality is screams of young children that make my temples throb. I scan the sea of heads for familiar faces, spotting my friend Tiffany Reynolds corralling her own grade fives with a forced smile.

"Hey, Tiff," I shout over the din, sidling up beside her as she directs her students to sit cross-legged on the floor.

"Lucy! A black bear again?" She rolls her eyes, annoyance and amusement in her gaze.

"Yep, I just want to go home, pour myself a glass of chardonnay, and soak in the tub until I prune," I confess.

"Ha, sounds like a plan. If only…" She sighs, glancing at our charges, who are now engaged in an impromptu game of silent telephone, giggles bouncing around the circle.

"Keep dreaming, right?" I chuckle, but my mind is already drifting to the quiet comfort of my apartment, the liquid gold of wine swirling in a goblet, steam rising from hot water — a sanctuary far removed from this raucous gym.

But for now, duty calls. I turn back to my kids, mustering enthusiasm. "All right, fly. Be free. But let's not be too loud, okay?"

Eventually, we return to our classroom, and fortunately, the bear has ambled away by dismissal time. We collect backpacks and jackets, and the students' laughter echoes out the door at the end of the day, their energy undiminished. I sigh, absentmindedly stacking papers into a neat pile on my desk. The enticing image of bubbles caressing my skin fades as my phone buzzes from the drawer. Dad's picture flashes on the screen as I pull it out, a smile tugging at his lips, eyes crinkling with mirth. No chardonnay for me tonight.

"Hey, Dad," I answer, slipping into my coat, a resigned acceptance settling in.

"Lucy, love, Beatrice has called in sick. Can you cover her shift tonight?" His voice is hopeful yet apologetic, an Irish lilt dancing through the line.

This is not shocking news on a Monday. Beatrice often has an illness related to the start of the work week. "Of course. I'll be there," I assure my dad. The words tumble out before I can consider the mountain of worksheets and projects waiting to be graded.

"Ah, you're a lifesaver, my girl. I owe you one," he promises.

"Sure, Dad. See you soon." I hang up, my previous hopes dissipating like steam on a mirror. I grab my purse, keys jingling a familiar tune as I lock up my classroom.

The drive over to Barney's is automatic, muscle memory guiding me through the streets. With each passing block, anticipation builds, replacing the weariness. At least I'll see Janelle tonight. She and Tiffany are my best friends, but with her in nursing school full time and working full time for my dad, it doesn't leave a lot of room for us to hang out.

Pulling into the familiar parking spot in the alley behind the bar, I cut the engine and take a deep breath. The pub's warm glow beckons. A night at Barney's might not be the quiet evening I'd envisioned, but with friends and family, it won't be so bad.

I push through the creaking back door, the familiar scent of hops and wood polish greeting me like an old friend. The pub is bustling with the pre-dinner crowd, locals unwinding after a long day's work. The hospital gang isn't here yet, though. Mercy's Hospital's day shift ends a bit later. I immediately find Janelle, her arms crossed as she leans against the bar, her expression stormy.

"Can you believe it?" she huffs as I approach. "Your dad calls you in again because Beatrice can't show up? She's about as reliable as a chocolate teapot. He should just let her go at this point."

A shrug lifts my shoulders, the weight of resignation pulling them down just as quickly. "Well, when would we ever see each other without this?" I tease.

Janelle's lips curve into a reluctant smile. "True. Between your teaching and my nursing school, it's a miracle we can still recognize each other."

We share a chuckle before the conversation turns, as inevitably as the tide, to her weekend date. "So, come on then, spill," I demand, leaning on the counter next to her, eager for the diversion.

She hesitates, fiddling with a coaster, her face scrunching in thought. "He's a radiologist from the hospital. Nice guy, really. But..." She trails off and sighs, the thought hanging unfinished in the air between us.

"But?" I prompt, nudging her with my elbow.

"No spark. No fireworks." Janelle shrugs. "It was like going out with a really friendly Labrador—pleasant but no excitement."

My heart sinks. Janelle's romantic pursuits are always roller coasters, thrilling rides that often end in spectacular fashion. I'd been hoping this time might be different, more...stable. "I'm sorry, Janelle. I was rooting for this one," I admit.

"Me too," she murmurs, tucking a stray lock of hair behind her ear. "But hey, life goes on, right? And who knows? Maybe Mr. Right is just around the corner."

"Or standing at the end of the bar," I quip, nodding toward a group of newcomers filtering in.

"Maybe," Janelle concedes. "But for now, let's focus on getting through tonight without dropping a tray or murdering Beatrice in absentia."

"Agreed," I reply, rolling up my sleeves. "Let's get to work."

A little while later, as I slide a pint across the bar to an eager patron, I lean in closer to Janelle, my voice barely cutting through the din. "The other night, this guy came in, right off a biker mag cover."

"Trouble?" Janelle asks, her eyebrows arching as she fills a pint and turns to deliver it.

"Big time." I pause to pour another drink, watching the foam crest just below the rim. "He was hot, though, in a bad-boy way. Blond, six-three, built like he tosses kegs for fun. Black leathers, head to toe." I make a show of pulling at my black apron. "Way more *Sons of Anarchy* than Friday-night happy hour."

"Sounds charming," she says drily, returning for another round.

"Charming and dangerous. I got this vibe... He's Irish mob. I'm sure of it." My hand grips the tap a little tighter. "They've been sniffing around Dad again."

"Lucy..." Concern softens Janelle's features for a moment before she masks it with her work face, the one that's all smiles and efficiency.

"Keep an eye out, okay?" I ask before we're swept up in the current of customers, orders, and clinking glasses. "I'm sure he's some kind of enforcer."

"How can we figure it out?"

I think for a minute. "What if we serve him bad food with lousy service? That'll show him we aren't afraid, and if he comes back, we'll know he's here for other reasons, right?"

After a moment, she nods. "As long as you're sure he's not a restaurant inspector."

"Definitely not."

"Let's do it."

Hours blur. The pub is alive with the hum of Mercy Hospital post-shift chatter and laughter spilling as freely as the beer. Despite the ache in my feet and the stickiness clinging to my skin, there's a comforting rhythm in the frenzy.

"Lucy, table six needs their check!" Dad calls from the other end of the bar.

"Got it!" I yell back, whisking up the bill and weaving my way through the crowd, dodging a group of nurses with tales wilder than any Friday night.

"Sorry for the wait." I smile, setting the check on the table. They wave me off with grins, clearly in no hurry to end their revelry.

"Another Guinness, Lucy!" hollers Christian Bradford, a doctor from the hospital and a regular.

"Coming right up!" I shoot back, already anticipating the next three orders in line.

The ebb and flow of patrons is relentless; the lull I'd hoped for never arrives. Instead, it's a constant stream of faces. It's well past eleven when I glance at the clock for the umpteenth time, the hands inching toward midnight. The Irish mob enforcer hasn't shown tonight, but my nerves haven't untangled. Every leather-clad figure makes my heart skip, wondering if he's here for more than just a pint. But Dad's laughter rings out as he shares a joke with some firefighters, and for a moment, I let myself believe everything will be okay.

"Last call!" Dad announces, and the collective groan is almost drowned out by my sigh of relief. I start collecting empty glasses.

"Hey, Luce, you did great tonight." Dad's hand finds my shoulder. "I'll handle the rest. You go on home."

"Thanks, Dad." I flash him a tired smile, stripping off my apron and heading for the door, the promise of rest now a tangible thing. Tonight was just another Monday at Barney's. My feet ache in protest with every step I take to my car, but the thought of my bed propels me forward.

"Lucy, wait up." Dad's voice carries from the doorway.

I pause and turn back, finding his silhouette framed by the warm glow of the pub. He crosses the distance between us, his coat flapping slightly in the night breeze.

"You sure you don't want me to drive you home?"

I shake my head. "I'll be fine. I drove from school. I'm tired, but I'm good."

"You work too hard." His brows knit together in that way that tells me he's both proud and concerned.

"Learned from the best," I quip, attempting to ease the wrinkle from his forehead. It works, partly; a smile tugs at the corner of his mouth.

"All right, go on then. But text me when you get home, yeah?" He pulls me into a hug, brief but fierce, and I'm reminded of all the times his strength has been my shelter.

"Will do," I promise, smiling up at him. "Talk to you tomorrow. Love you."

"Love you, too. And thank you for helping out and always being there, love." There's a glint of something more in his eye—gratitude, maybe a touch of guilt for asking so much of me.

"Always, Dad." And I mean it.

He watches me a moment longer, then nods and retreats into the pub as I pull away.

My thoughts drift to the day ahead tomorrow, the eager faces of my grade fives waiting for me, their energy boundless. I smile, my physical fatigue momentarily forgotten.

CHAPTER 3

Chance

When I was hired, hospital administration expressed concern about turnover and the morale of the emergency department. I've observed for the past six weeks or so, and it didn't take long to identify — well, confirm — the biggest obstacle for the staff. Now, I'm standing at the head of the table in the staff conference room, my new mantle as Chief of the Emergency Department weighing heavy on my shoulders. The morning shift is over, and the night shift is here, so we have just enough overlap to meet.

I look around at all of them. Nights, days, nights again — the constant flip-flop is battering my internal clock. I knew from the beginning that the rotating shifts were an issue — at least for some of the staff. Now, I've experienced them, and they have to be on everyone's list of things they hate. So we need to work through this, but I have to build consensus. I think this nutty schedule was an attempt at fairness, so we need to be sure people have a voice in where they end up.

"Okay, let's talk schedules," I say, getting the meeting underway. "I'm curious to hear your thoughts on this rotation thing—one month nights, next month days. How's that working for you?"

A sea of fatigued faces greets me, and Melissa Lewis, a lead nurse, speaks first. "The changing routine is very hard for childcare," she notes, and a murmur of agreement ripples through the room.

I can see the dark circles under her eyes, helping make her point. "Thanks, Melissa. That makes sense." My gaze shifts to Dr. Mitch Henderson, whose posture seems to have deflated a bit more than usual. "Mitch, what about you?"

"Trying to maintain any semblance of a personal life is near impossible when you bounce back and forth like this."

"I could see that," I say as I nod, trying to encourage others to talk. If I can get their buy-in on the change in scheduling, they'll be more cooperative about other changes I want to implement.

Kent, sitting beside Mitch, chimes in before anyone else can. "Come on, Mitch, when was the last time you had a date anyway?" he teases, his smirk softening the blow.

"Hilarious," Mitch shoots back, but there's no real heat behind his words.

I lean forward, resting my hands on the back of an empty chair. They all hate it. That's good. "What I think you're telling me is that this schedule isn't working." I tap a pen against the notepad in front of me. The murmur of the staff meeting quiets as I roll my shoulders back to ease the tension that's built there. "I'd like to propose that starting next month, we switch to a fixed schedule of day and night shifts." I pause to let that sink in, watching brows rise and heads tilt with interest. "We'll add overlapping shifts for midday and midevening to cover peak hours."

I scan the room, noting the tentative smiles and nods. "I've spoken with HR," I add. "There'll be a pay differential for the night shift."

Now, the smiles turn genuine, relief palpable in their tired eyes.

"We'll start with volunteers," I continue. The room falls silent. "If there aren't enough volunteers, the more senior staff will get their preferred shift choice first." I look at the nurse in charge. "Jessica, let's work together tomorrow and set up the schedule. Everyone, please give your preferences to Jessica. She'll also have the pay structure for the night shift. And I don't want any of you to put pressure on your teams if they don't want the same shift. This may take some shuffling things around. Hear me?"

I get a few nods. I won't let them bully the staff.

"Okay, let's move on to other matters." I look down at the agenda. "We've got medication shortages to discuss and some weird drugs popping up on the market." The conversation picks up again, turning technical and detailed, but my mind is drawn to the people behind the issues—stressed parents, exhausted doctors, burned-out nurses. I think this scheduling change could make a real difference.

"Anything else before we wrap up?" I ask.

Jessica raises her hand, and I nod. "What are we doing about the Prometheus Health Solutions drug trial?" she asks. "I don't know who to send the documentation to."

"Ahhhh... Give it to me, and I'll chase it down," I say. This is news to me, but I want to help, and I should be informed anyway.

She smiles. I'm winning them over one at a time.

When the meeting wraps, I push away from the conference table feeling like I've accomplished something tangible. My day is over.

I shrug into my leathers in the locker room and head across the street to Barney's. Even on a weeknight, the place has a pulsing energy about it. As I enter, my mind shifts gears from Chief of ED to just Chance, who's in need of some good food and maybe a beer. I scan the crowd and find a booth tucked away in the back. Settling in, I lean back and exhale slowly, letting the noise wash over me.

From here, I can watch without being too obvious, a habit I've picked up from years in the ED, always observing. The pub is alive with stories I don't know, dramas unfolding at every table. For now, I'm content to just sit and take it all in, anonymous in my corner, far from the pressures of schedules and staff complaints.

A server comes over with the kind of efficient grace that speaks of long hours on her feet — Lucy, according to her name tag. My gaze lingers appreciatively for a moment. She's got curves that draw the eye, dressed in jeans and a form-fitting T-shirt. But it's her hair that snags my attention — the rich auburn hue twisted up into a bun, professional yet hinting at some untamed spirit beneath. A fleeting thought crosses my mind, a curious wonder about how that hair would look falling loose around her shoulders, soft and wild.

"Evening," I say, attempting a smile. "What's the special tonight?"

"The special is on the board," Lucy replies curtly, pointing to a chalkboard by the bar without meeting my gaze. Her voice is clipped, businesslike, leaving no room for pleasantries.

"Right." I nod, chastened, feeling a flicker of irritation. It's been a long day of managing crises and placating staff. I'm not in the mood for games or attitude. "I'll just have the burger. Salad on the side, please."

She scribbles down the order, already halfway to her next table. "Sure thing."

As Lucy walks away, I watch her exchange a quick word with another server. They glance back at me, their expressions unreadable. I feel a prickle of annoyance. Have I somehow upset her? I run a hand through my hair, second-guessing my every move, but come up empty. Maybe it's nothing personal; maybe it's just been a long shift for her too.

All I want is to eat something that didn't come out of a

hospital cafeteria, to enjoy the anonymity of this booth before I retreat to the solitude of my ride home. I lean back, letting out a slow breath, trying to shake off the disquiet of the exchange. The night outside beckons with the promise of a cool wind and the purr of my Harley, but for now, I watch Lucy navigate the pub with an air of detached professionalism, hoping for a quiet end to an otherwise eventful day.

I glance up as she returns, balancing a plate, and my stomach growls in anticipation. But as she sets the plate in front of me with a clunk that lacks any hint of care, I immediately sense something is off.

"Enjoy," she says flatly before turning away, not waiting for a response.

I stare at the charred disc masquerading as a burger, sandwiched between what has to be a stale bun, its texture reminiscent of day-old bread left out on a kitchen counter. The side salad sits limply next to it, its leaves wilted and uninviting. This is a far cry from what I've had here before.

With a sigh, I muster my courage and take a tentative bite of the burger. It's like chewing on a hockey puck. My jaw works overtime trying to break it down, and I quickly realize no amount of ketchup will rescue this culinary disaster. Reluctantly, I abandon the burger and begin foraging through the sad excuse for a salad, plucking out the few cherry tomatoes and strips of carrot that still cling to life.

As I'm picking through the greens, I find myself wishing for a cold beer to wash down the disappointment. My eyes flicker around the room, searching for the server who seems to have disappeared into thin air. When she finally reappears, she scans the room, deliberately avoiding my table. And when our eyes do meet, there's a chill to her look that sends a shiver down my spine.

"Excuse me, could I get a beer?" I try, but she's already flitting away, lost in a sea of customers, her attention pointedly elsewhere. I sigh, resigned to the fact that this meal is one I'll have to endure rather than enjoy.

I brace myself and take another bite of charred burger, the rubbery texture fighting back against my teeth. The taste — or rather the lack of it — sends my thoughts spiraling away from the culinary catastrophe to the staff meeting earlier today. Jessica was a godsend afterward, her organizational skills shining as we pieced together an outline for next month's schedule. Now, we just have to fill everyone into the slots tomorrow. Despite my dinner, I smile as I imagine the coming month free of scheduling fires to put out.

But the new scheduling plan also points to a glaring problem. We remain understaffed, a gaping hole that won't be patched by clever scheduling or wishful thinking. As I spear another wilted leaf, this salad reminds me of our nursing roster — both lacking necessary substance. Our nurses are stretched thin, doing the work of two people, sometimes more. They're not to blame; they've been nothing but dedicated. But plain and simple, there is a nursing shortage.

We need more hands, more hearts in the trenches with us. I push the plate away. How many more shifts can they pull before the strain shows? Not just in tired eyes, but in potentially costly mistakes?

My jaw clenches. I need to find a solution, and soon. For their sake, and for the patients'. I push my plate away. This problem won't be solved tonight. But it's on my list, a challenge I'm determined to tackle head-on, just as soon as I can escape this gastronomic purgatory. Maybe there's a drive-thru I can hit on my way home.

With a sigh, I scan once again for the server, hoping to settle up and make my escape. She's nowhere in sight. Impatience skitters through me as minutes tick by, but then resignation sets in. I fish out my wallet, laying enough cash on the table to cover the meal and then some. It's more than this dismal experience warrants, but I'm not one to let a bad night sour potential future visits. After all, Barney's is the hospital's hangout. You never know when you'll need to have a beer or relax with the staff.

I stand and head for the exit. The bell above the door jingles sharply as I step into the cool night air.

"Chance! Hey, man!" Griffin waves as I step outside. They're just arriving.

"Finished already? Come back in, grab a beer with us," Kent suggests, gesturing toward the entrance.

Part of me—a very small part—is tempted by the offer. But the weight of the day and the tragedy of my meal presses on my shoulders, reminding me of the tasks still ahead and tomorrow's early start. "I appreciate it, guys, but I need to get home."

"Another time, then." Griffin claps a hand on my shoulder. "By the way, the new shift plan is solid," he enthuses, his face animated in the soft light. "It's exhausting bouncing back and forth. Genius move. And bonus money for working nights is spot on. It will play to the needs of the staff."

Kent nods in agreement. "It's already a game-changer for morale. And honestly, getting to pick our poison will make those twelve-hour shifts feel less like a death march."

"I'm glad you think so," I say, my spirits buoyed by their approval. "I've got more ideas brewing. We're going to turn things around in the emergency department, make it a place where people don't just come to work, they come to thrive."

Griffin nods. "That's why you're the boss, man. You actually listen—and act on it."

"Thanks, guys," I say with a wave. "Let's keep this momentum going."

Focus on the positive, I tell myself. Despite that dinner, things are looking up around here.

CHAPTER 4

Lucy

It's Friday night, and I'm covering for Beatrice for the third time this week. Supposedly, it's only for a few hours while she does something for her work visa. But we'll see.

The door chimes jingle, and heads swivel almost in unison toward the entrance as he strides in, leather jacket creaking with every confident step. It's the motorcycle-club guy, the one with the eyes that miss nothing. I hate that his disheveled blond hair draws my curiosity. His eyes catch mine, and the corners of his mouth turn up. My heart races, like the traitor it is, and my grip tightens on my rag as I watch him saunter to his usual spot in a booth at the back of the bar, where he can look over everything. Why does this man turn my insides into liquid? And why is he back?

I keep wiping down the counter, trying not to think about what he does to me or how the hospital staff at the other end of the bar are eyeing him warily. They're good customers, always polite, and they tip like clockwork. But their shoulders are tense now, laughter dying to uneasy murmurs.

His last visit made it clear. He's not some biker looking for a greasy meal; the forty-percent tip he left screamed *mob enforcer*. And after the meal I served him last time, there's no way he's here for our pub food.

What did Dad get himself into?

I steal glances at him and Dad, who seems to ignore him. Is it money or maybe something harder to come by — a rare whiskey, perhaps — that's got us caught in this mess? I can feel my mind beginning to spin. Soon, our little pub will be labeled a hot spot for bikers and organized crime alike. We'll lose the regulars, the decent folks who just want a pint after a long shift.

A little while later, as the crowd thins, I spot my chance. Dad's at the other end of the bar, laughing with one of our neighborhood regulars about something or other. I toss the rag aside and make my way over, my heart drumming a nervous beat against my ribs.

"Dad?" I ask. He turns, his smile lingering until he sees my face. "Can we talk?"

"Sure, love. What's on your mind?" He wipes his hands on his apron and excuses himself from his friend.

"Is it... Did you take out a loan from them?" There, I've said it. The words hang between us.

"What?"

"Did you borrow money from Frankie Ryan?"

His brow furrows. "No, no loans. Frankie Ryan and I, we go way back. Why are you worrying about something like that?"

His reassurance feels hollow, like he's brushing away cobwebs while ignoring the spider lurking in the corner. *Frankie Ryan*. A name from stories I heard growing up, tales of wild youth and narrow escapes. It's supposed to comfort me, but the knot in my stomach only tightens. I force a smile, hoping it looks more convincing than it feels. Frankie "The Weasel" Ryan is head of the Irish mob, and I'm sure he has this enforcer here for something.

"I've just been wondering about that guy," I say, pointing with my eyes. But Dad just waves his hand. I don't even think he looked. "Okay, Dad. If you say so," I murmur, turning back to the emptying bar.

I want to believe him; I really do. But as I watch the guy order another round, fingers drumming an idle rhythm on the countertop, I can't shake the dread that's settled in my bones. Frankie Ryan or not, trouble has a way of finding my dad.

I look over at the framed photo of Mam behind the bar, next to the good whiskey, her smile a bittersweet reminder of better days. Dad's words about Frankie Ryan and their shared history in Dublin do little to ease my mind. Every time that motorcycle-club guy saunters through the door, my heart squeezes a little tighter. And *not* because of how he looks.

The bar is Dad's lifeline, his anchor since we lost Mam. If anything were to happen to it… My fingers tighten into a fist. There's Officer Singh, one of my students' parents. Maybe I should talk to him? No, that could make things worse.

"Lucy, you're off." Beatrice's voice cuts through my worry as she bustles through the door. "Go have fun."

"Thanks." I can hardly believe she's here, but I keep my snotty comments to myself. I manage a smile, tossing my apron under the counter and shrugging into my jacket.

Outside, the crisp evening air clears my head as I stroll to meet Janelle and Tiffany. Tonight, I need the escape, the laughter, the promise of something that isn't steeped in anxiety.

"Lucy!" Tiffany's familiar cheer greets me as I spot them waiting outside the bar.

"Hey, girls." I approach with open arms, embracing each in turn. I pull my stiletto sandals out of my bag and slip them on. "Ready to forget about the week?"

"Absolutely." Janelle nods, her eyes bright with anticipation. "Let's find a place where the music drowns everything else out."

We weave our way through Vancouver's nightlife and

land at a hipster bar, The Alibi. As a teacher, it's rare for me to let loose, but tonight is different. We've all felt the grind — Janelle with her nursing studies and Tiffany, who matches my teaching challenges step for step.

"First round's on me," I declare as we settle into a booth.

"Only if we race you to the dance floor later. It's girls night at Glimmer," Janelle counters, her competitive streak peeking through.

"Deal." I laugh. We always say we're going to go dancing, but mostly, we use our time together to hang out and catch up.

"Okay, what are we drinking?" I ask, ready for something stiff.

Tiffany waves down the server with a confidence that only a woman who has tamed classrooms of ten-year-olds can possess. "Lemon drop martini for me," she announces.

Janelle scans the menu before pointing triumphantly. "I'll try the Australian Johnnie & Ginger highball."

"The what now?" I lean forward.

"Johnnie Walker, highball style, with spicy and sweet ginger ale," Janelle reads.

"Sounds adventurous." I'm sold. "Make that two, please."

A few minutes later, glasses clink and we sip, the alcohol warm and the ginger zesty against my tongue. It's new and rather delicious.

"Tell us about this date of yours, Tiffany," I prod.

"Ugh, where do I start?" She rolls her eyes, but I spot a smirk playing on her lips. "He took me on this epic motorcycle ride out to Hope. Three hours one way!"

"Three hours?" Janelle's eyebrows shoot up. "On a motorcycle? That's insane."

"Tell me about it," Tiffany groans, sliding down in her seat. "By the time we got there, I couldn't feel my hooha. Completely numb!"

"That's the last thing you want to be numb!" I exclaim.

Our laughter erupts. The image of prim Tiffany, disheveled by the wind and robbed of sensation, is too much.

"Thought about hitchhiking back," she continues, shaking her head. "But I stuck it out. And he had the nerve to be disappointed when the date didn't end...favorably."

"What did he expect?" I ask, still chuckling. "But seriously, how was the pizza?"

"Average!" Tiffany throws her hands up in exasperation. "All that, and the pizza was average!"

We laugh again, caught up in the moment. For now, the shadows of worry are banished to the fringes of my mind.

As we drink, we talk about everything and nothing—work, dreams, the ridiculousness of reality TV. It's effortless, this camaraderie, and I can't remember the last time I felt so...normal.

"Who needs to dance when we've got the best company right here?" Tiffany raises her glass, and we all echo the sentiment with a toast.

"Besides," Janelle adds, "I'm pretty sure my dance moves would only attract the kind of guy who thinks grinding is an acceptable form of communication."

We erupt into laughter again. The thought of sweaty strangers invading our personal space has no appeal tonight. This, right here, with these two incredible women, is where I want to be.

Hours slip by without notice, and it's only when the bartender announces last call that we realize how late it's gotten. We gather our things, still chatting as we spill out onto the busy street. Hugs and promises to do this again soon are exchanged before we go our separate ways.

The chill of the night air hits me as I start the walk home, the streets eerily silent. As I near my apartment, the stillness is shattered by a sound that sends a shiver down my spine—the deep, rumbling growl of a motorcycle. Instinctively, I know it's him, the motorcycle guy from the bar.

My pulse quickens, and I fumble for my keys, casting

nervous glances over my shoulder. Why is he here? What does he want with me—or worse, with my dad? I finally open the door, slipping inside and darting up the stairs to my place. But even the safety of my apartment isn't enough to ease the knot of anxiety tightening in my stomach.

From my window, I watch as the red glow of the motorcycle's taillight fades into the distance. I crawl into bed but toss and turn, unable to find comfort. Each time I close my eyes, the roar of the motorcycle fills my ears, reminding me of the threat lurking beyond the safety of these walls.

I need answers. What is my dad mixed up in? What could possibly be worth inviting the attention of the Irish mob?

CHAPTER 5

Chance

I toss my reading glasses on the stack of paperwork on my desk at the hospital and rub my eyes. I came in early before the night shift to figure out what the hell my predecessor was doing with Prometheus Health Solutions. As near as I can tell, she's signed us up for a drug trial targeting the unhoused. She was doing all of the tabulations and reporting herself, but it's still an additional load on our staff, and the well-being of my team and the quality of care we provide takes precedence. Even after reading this stuff, I'm not sure what the drug is supposed to accomplish. Frankly, I can't see how the funds are worth the strain.

Maybe I'm missing something. I need a copy of the contract. I pull up legal in the employee directory and dial. It's late in the day, but hopefully, someone is still in.

"William Long," the deep baritone voice says in answer.

I introduce myself as the new head of the emergency

department. "Sorry to bother you so late. I'm looking for a copy of the contract we have with Prometheus Health. It's for a drug trial?"

There is silence on the other end of the line.

"Hello?"

"I'm here." Clicking of a keyboard fills the silence. "Are you telling me your department is working on a drug trial?"

"It seems so. Eleanor Thompson was my predecessor, and the nurse in charge handed me a stack of data a few days ago. I don't know what to do with it. I don't even have a contact to ask, so I thought I'd look at the contract. Is that possible?"

"I don't know. It doesn't look like it was run through my office."

"Is that normal?"

"It's not supposed to be. Department heads don't have authority to sign contracts. Have you brought this up with Dr. Johns?"

"Not yet. I'm just trying to understand it. It seems like she was doing all the work herself to process the numbers. I'm just trying to get caught up."

"I don't see a copy of it here."

I sit for a minute. *What the hell was she doing?* "I have the reams of paperwork she's submitted in a filing cabinet. I haven't gone through it all. Maybe it's there," I tell him. "I'm sorry. I just assumed legal would have the contract."

"We should. If you find it, let me know."

"I will."

I disconnect the call. Eleanor moved out of the province, but maybe someone has a way to reach her.

"Code Yellow. Code Yellow," blares over the ED speakers.

I groan. We have a missing patient.

I walk out of my office and look at Jennifer, the nurse in charge. "What happened?"

"It's a regular. He was walking around naked, and a woman is upset. He took off running as soon as the woman shrieked."

I try very hard to suppress my smile. We have a streaker. In the hospital. And the moon is full. It's going to be one of those nights.

Fortunately, the wild and craziness decreased as the full moon set and the sun peeked over the horizon. Nights like last night are no fun, but it meant the twelve-hour shift went quickly. I'm exhausted, and I've dumped my scrubs into the laundry. I shrug into my jacket, muscles aching. The last of the adrenaline that carried me through has evaporated.

"Hey!" Griffin's voice arrests my trudge to freedom. "Got plans?"

I turn, finding his eyes searching mine, reflecting a purpose I recognize too well. He's dressed in scrubs like they're armor, staving off the exhaustion I'm sure gnaws at him too. "Sleep," I answer, though my voice is more hopeful than certain.

"Before you crash..." Griffin leans closer, lowering his voice. "There's this safe-use clinic nearby. We could use an extra hand today."

My eyebrows knit together. Volunteering at these clinics isn't exactly encouraged by the hospital. But what they stand for—giving drug users a safe place without worry about overdosing or violence—couldn't be more important. And it always comes with a soft reminder that when they're ready, we'll find them a bed in rehab.

"Sure." The word slips out, decisive, before doubt can creep in. "Where?"

"Ten minutes from here. Follow me?" he asks, already

moving toward the exit with an energy I envy.

"Lead the way."

We navigate the quiet streets, the city still asleep. When we arrive, the clinic is nondescript yet somehow inviting. Inside, six beds line the room, each one occupied, a sanctuary in the midst of personal storms.

"Here." Griffin hands me a clipboard with a rundown of protocols. "Just sit with them, keep an eye on their vitals. Step in if things go south, and holler if you need help."

I nod, sitting beside the first bed where a man lies, his breaths shallow but even. His face, etched with lines of a hard-lived story, seems peaceful. I monitor his pulse, the steady beep of the heart monitor a comforting refrain.

This is medicine, raw and real. No barriers, no judgment, just care. My gaze drifts over the occupants, every one of them fighting battles unseen. It's a far cry from the sterile, controlled mayhem of the ED. Here it's about connection, about being present in the most human way possible.

And as the morning light grows brighter through the blinds, I know I'll come back. This clinic, a haven in the heart of the city's darkness, strikes a chord with me. Medicine should be about presence, about ensuring that even the most marginalized get a chance to see another day.

"Thank you," Griffin murmurs as we wrap up a few hours later, his gratitude genuine, his smile weary but satisfied.

I nod and return the smile, feeling oddly rejuvenated despite the lack of sleep. "This is what we do."

I ride home, grateful that the traffic is busy coming into the City and easier leaving it. I trudge up the walkway to my basement apartment, my body aching with every step. Shadows cling to the edges of Ginny's well-kept garden as I slide my key into the lock of the basement door, my private entrance to what I've come to call home.

"Chance?" Ginny's voice cuts through the silence. I hadn't expected her to be waiting for me.

"Hey, Ginny," I mumble, stifling a yawn with the back

of my hand.

She stands on the sidewalk behind me, wrapped in a robe that's seen better days, her hair disheveled. "I'm sorry to bother you, especially after your night shift, but I need your help."

"Of course," I say, my words more automatically than consciously. It's hard to switch off the doctor in me, the part that responds to calls for aid without hesitation.

"It's the hot water in the shower. It won't turn off. I've tried everything." She wrings her hands. "The plumber can't make it until tomorrow, and I don't know what to do."

"Let's have a look," I offer, following her into the main house.

Ginny leads me to the bathroom, where the sound of rushing water greets us, relentless and unforgiving. I reach for the faucet, hoping for an easy fix, but reality is never that kind. With a sigh, I realize it'll take more than a twist of the wrist to solve this problem.

I twist the knobs again, harder this time, but they're not stopping the water. A quick inspection of the water heater and its natural gas flame shows it's burning steadily—no issue there. I scan the area for leaks, anything that could give me a clue. It's something more complicated, beyond a simple fix I can provide.

"Looks like we'll have to wait for the plumber, Ginny," I tell her. "For now, I'll have to shut off the hot water entirely." I try to offer her a reassuring smile, one I've perfected in the ED when delivering unpleasant news. "It's the best I can do until the plumber gets here."

Her face falls. "But what about you? How will you manage without hot water?"

"Cold showers build character," I joke weakly. "Or I'll use the hospital's facilities if need be. Don't worry about me."

"Okay," she says looking down at her hands.

"We'll both be fine."

A wrench gets the job done, and then I leave Ginny with

her plumbing woes and retreat to the sanctuary of the basement. My body hits the mattress, and I surrender to exhaustion.

The moment my eyelids close, sleep ambushes me—a merciful blackout. But then, the piercing trill of my phone breaks the silence. I fumble for it, blinking away the remnants of unconsciousness as I answer.

"Chance?" The voice comes through, rapid-fire French, a familiar cadence that tugs at the corners of my mind.

"Maman?" I croak, struggling to shift gears. Confusion muddies my thoughts before they finally settle into the rhythm of my mother tongue.

"Yes, it's me," she replies in French, her words a comforting melody even as they come too fast for my sleep-addled brain. "How are you, mon chéri?"

"I'm exhausted," I admit. "Just finished a long shift."

"Ah, my poor baby." She clucks sympathetically. "Make sure you rest. You work too hard."

"Always," I promise, though we both know my word is as unsteady as the hands that tried to fix Ginny's shower. I rub the sleep from my eyes and sit up, pressing the phone to my ear. "Tell me what's new at home," I say, eager for a distraction from my own fatigue.

"Your father," she begins, her voice laced with concern that tightens something in my chest, "he has been asked to consult on a friend's case in Quebec City."

"Is he okay?" I ask, picturing my father, his brow furrowed in concentration over legal texts and case files.

"Yes, yes, he's fine. But you know how he gets—completely absorbed. And the roads are icy there…" Her voice trails off, leaving unsaid worries hanging between us.

"Let him know I'm thinking of him," I say, trying to offer comfort despite the miles that separate us.

"Of course," she replies, and then her tone brightens. "And your sister, she is doing well. The children are growing so fast. They miss their uncle."

A smile finds its way to my face. "I miss them too. Tell them I'll video call soon."

"You promise?" she asks.

"Promise," I affirm. "What else is going on?"

"Ah, yes," she continues, "we are planning to give your sister and her partner a little break. We'll stay with the kids for a few days while they get away. A second honeymoon, you could say."

"That's wonderful," I say. I can picture Karine's relief and joy, a precious gift only our parents could give.

"Family is everything," Maman reminds me, and though it's a line I've heard a thousand times before, tonight it grounds me after the storm.

"I know," I reply. "Thanks for the updates. It means a lot."

"Take good care of yourself, my love," she says.

"Always do," I assure her, though we both understand that sometimes "taking care" is a complex equation in my world. But for now, I let her believe it's as simple as a promise.

My thumb hovers over the end call icon, but before I can tap it, she asks another question. "And the hospital? How are things going there?"

I lean back against the headboard as pride swells in my chest. "It's good. Really good. I've been able to implement a few new protocols that— They're making a difference. Every day feels like…like I'm where I'm supposed to be."

"I'm so happy for you," she says. "It's good to be making a difference."

But then her tone shifts, weighted with a mother's inherent worry. "But you take care of yourself, yes? You work too hard."

"Always," I repeat the earlier promise, knowing it'll placate her for now. "Don't worry about me."

There's a brief silence, the kind where unspoken thoughts gather like clouds on the horizon. Then, softly, she asks, "Have you heard from Céline recently?"

The name is a cold splash of reality, yanking me back into a past I've tried to leave behind. I close my eyes, a single blink to banish her image. "No, I haven't. And I don't expect I will." My voice is steady, betraying none of the turmoil that question stirs within me. "She made her choice."

"Ah ..." Sympathy threads through her sigh, a sound I've come to know well in the wake of my broken relationship.

"It's okay, really," I cut in before she can say more. "I came out here for a reason, remember? For the job, for the change. It's just taking some time to…adjust." The last word hangs between us, a stark understatement of the lonely nights spent turning over what-ifs and might-have-beens.

"Adjust," she echoes, her voice a caress against the jagged edges of my heart. "Just make sure you heal too, okay?"

"Of course." I manage a small chuckle. "That's what the West Coast is for, right? Sunnier days ahead." I press the phone closer to my ear, the cool plastic a stark contrast to the heat of frustration simmering in my mother's tone.

"Chance, how can she do that to you? To leave you after all the plans—"

"Hey," I interject, rubbing the bridge of my nose with my free hand. "Nobody's perfect. Like you always say, we can always do better." I force a half-smile, though she can't see it, an old habit from softer conversations.

She tuts, the sound bristling with the protective fervor only a mother can muster. "You're right. We must push ourselves to always do better. But sometimes, matters of the heart are different."

"Thanks. But really, I'm okay."

"Promise me. Promise me you're taking care of yourself."

"I promise." My words are a thin veil over the weariness that clings to my soul.

"Good. And have a good rest."

"Goodnight, Maman," I whisper, and the call ends.

I let the phone slip from my hand onto the bed, the dull

thud echoing in the silence. Leaning back against the headboard, I close my eyes, only to find Céline's face blossoming against the darkness of my eyelids.

Did I make a mistake?

Long ago, our first date was a dance of dreams and laughter. Even then, she spoke of one day leaving Montreal, tired of the endless struggle to find stability as a massage therapist. And I craved the warmth, the promise of a climate less harsh, a respite from the bitter winters that seemed to seep into my bones.

"*Moving west,*" she had said when we finally got serious about it, years later, her eyes alight with hope and uncertainty. "A fresh start."

But when the time actually came, her resolve crumbled like dry leaves underfoot, and I was left holding the remnants of our plan, alone.

Sighing, I rise and walk over to the window, peering out into the day.

"Was it a mistake?" I murmur.

Maybe. Or maybe the mistake was not seeing the signs sooner, not realizing that our reasons for thinking about leaving were as different as the paths we ultimately took—hers to remain rooted in the familiar, mine to seek solace in the unknown.

With a weary shake of my head, I pull the curtains closed, shutting out the world. It's time to sleep, to recharge for my shift tonight—for the patients who need me, for the life I've chosen here.

CHAPTER 6

Lucy

Farida's high-pitched screams pierce the air, a sharp, relentless sound that goes straight to my temples. Kayla's feet pound against the linoleum floor as she gives chase, her laughter mingling with Farida's mock shrieks, but there's no joy in it for me. This headache is splitting my skull in two.

"Girls! Enough!" I call, my voice lost in the cacophony of their play. I rub at my forehead, willing the pain to subside.

Across the room, Aleksander and Mohammad are tangled up in some rough-and-tumble game that's bound to end in tears if I don't intervene. "Boys, we're not wrestling in class," I warn, but they don't seem to hear me. They're in their own world, where the only rule is the one who's strongest wins.

I close my eyes, trying to steady myself. The weekend has left me ragged, sleepless nights filled with the constant growl of Harleys driving past my apartment. And every time I close my eyes, I see him — the man in the black leather coat. He's been haunting my father's bar, a storm cloud of trouble ready to burst.

If he isn't an enforcer with the Irish mob, then who is he? Though he's magnetic to look at, my gut tells me he's bad news. And he seems a permanent fixture at Barney's...

"Miss Sheridan?" Farida's voice cuts through my musings, and I force my eyes open to see her standing before me, Kayla skidding to a halt behind her. They both look momentarily chastened.

"Can we go outside?" Kayla asks, her cheeks flushed.

I nod, letting out a breath. "Yes, let's get our coats." Anything to get out of this classroom, if only for a little while.

As the kids scramble to follow instructions, I worry again about what awaits me after school. I'm headed to Barneys', as I need to talk to Dad, get some real answers this time. Fear twists in my chest.

I shepherd the children toward the door, my head still pounding. The crisp air greets us as we step outside. Farida and Kayla immediately dart toward the swings, while Aleksander and Mohammad make a beeline for the soccer field, already squabbling over who gets to be the striker.

"All right, everyone, let's play nice!" My words are half-hearted at best; right now, I'm just grateful for the relative quiet of the playground. It's always like this on Mondays, like they've bottled their energy all weekend only to uncork it the moment they see me.

I spot Tiffany corralling her own group of rambunctious grade fives onto the adjacent play structure. She catches my eye and comes over to the bench where I've taken a seat, my gaze following the children's movements.

"Rough morning?" she asks.

"Something like that," I reply. "It's been...a long weekend."

"Something come up since Friday that you want to talk

about?" Her concern is genuine, a lifeline thrown across the tumultuous sea of my thoughts.

I hesitate, then decide to confide in her. "It's my dad," I explain, watching as a boy from her class dangles precariously from the monkey bars. "There's this guy hanging around his bar — black leather coat, all-seeing eyes. He's got trouble written all over him." I shudder, the image of the man too easily conjured in my mind.

"Sounds ominous," Tiffany says. "You think he's bad news?"

"I do. I can't figure out why he keeps coming around." But then I sigh. "I don't actually know," I admit. "But he drives a loud Harley, and there's been one driving by my apartment at all hours. I hardly slept a wink all weekend because of the damn noise."

"Have you talked to your dad about it?"

"Not that part of it," I say, tracking a soccer ball that flies dangerously close to the street. "But I asked him about the guy, and he dismissed it out of hand. I still have a bad feeling. He could be Irish mob."

Tiffany nods. "Let me know if there's anything I can do. You shouldn't have to deal with this on your own."

"Thanks, Tiff." As much as I appreciate her support, I know this *is* something I'll have to face myself. I watch the children scatter across the playground, their laughter mixing with the distant sound of traffic.

"But what makes you think he's Irish mob?" Tiffany asks after a moment, casting a sidelong glance at me.

"Barney's is a pit stop for Mercy Hospital staff after shifts," I explain, keeping one eye on Kayla, who's now drawing in the sand with a stick. "We get a few regulars from the neighborhood, and they're coming in for the beer and the medical staff eye-candy. He's different from all of them. There's a vibe about him that doesn't sit right. And he keeps coming back, even after I gave him not so great service and questionable food."

Tiffany's eyes widen. "Well, if he wasn't a problem already, you're going to make him one!" She laughs.

I feel my cheeks heat. That was rather unprofessional, but in that moment, I was so sure…

Tiffany chews on her lower lip. "Want me to come by and take a look? Sometimes, a fresh pair of eyes…"

I look up at her. "Would you? I'd appreciate an outside perspective."

"Consider it done." She gives me a resolute nod. "Just let me know when."

"Thanks, Tiff." I kick at a stray pebble, sending it skittering across the concrete. "I'm just crossing my fingers that Beatrice shows up tonight. I want to talk to my dad for a few minutes and go home. I could really use a full night off for once."

"Beatrice still pulling her disappearing acts on Mondays?" Tiffany's voice holds a note of amusement.

"Like clockwork." I sigh, watching as Mohammad releases Aleksander from a headlock. "Every Monday, without fail, something comes up, and I'm the one covering her shift. It's like she has an allergy to the start of the week."

"Sounds like you need a break." Tiffany pats my shoulder. "Let's hope for your sake she makes an appearance tonight."

"From your lips to God's ears," I murmur, returning my focus to the kids.

The rest of the day is wild but it's manageable. I distract myself with thoughts of my pajamas and binge-watching old episodes of *Game of Thrones*. That's my plan for tonight.

The final bell rings, and the last of my students scampers out the door, their laughter trailing behind them. I'm bending over to straighten a row of overturned chairs when my phone buzzes in my pocket. The screen lights up with Dad's name, and my heart sinks before I even read the message.

Dad: Can you cover for Beatrice tonight?

I want to type back a two-letter reply—No—but my thumbs hover indecisively over the keyboard. Images of the mysterious man in black leather flash through my mind, and despite my exhaustion, anxiety edges out my desire for rest. With a resigned sigh, I tap an affirmative response and slide the phone back into my pocket.

Dad's behind the bar, wiping down the counter with a rag that's seen better days, when I arrive at the pub. He smiles when he sees me.

"Lucy, thanks for covering," he says as I approach.

"Sure thing." I nod, planting my hands on the polished wood. "But, Dad, we need to talk about Beatrice. This is the fourth Monday in a row that she's bailed."

"Fourth?" He looks genuinely surprised, the furrows in his forehead deepening. "That can't be right."

"It is," I insist. "Something's keeping her from working Mondays, and we need to figure it out. Maybe shuffle the schedule around or something."

He shakes his head. "I'll talk to her. But, Lucy, are you sure? Four Mondays?"

"Positive." I let out a breath. "I love you, Dad, you know I do, but these Monday-night shifts are rough on me. It's the start of my workweek, and without proper rest…"

My voice trails off as the door swings open, ushering in a cool draft and a figure that commands immediate attention. The man in black leather strides in, his presence filling the room. Dad follows my line of sight and gives a subtle nod of acknowledgment.

"You really don't know that guy?" I ask.

He looks at me strangely and shakes his head. "He's a customer. I know that."

With my heart thumping against my ribs, I watch as the enigmatic stranger settles into a booth, which is unmistakably in my area. His jacket creaks softly as he slides onto the padded seat, and I steel myself for what comes next.

"Looks like your section just got its first customer for the evening," Dad says, giving my hand a pat before returning to his bartender duties.

I grab a menu and smooth down my apron, my mind churning with unasked questions as I approach the table. This man's presence in the pub is like a pebble in my shoe—uncomfortably noticeable and impossible to ignore. My intuition gnaws at me; I need to unravel why he's become a fixture here.

"You're back," I say, words casual, tone light, but everything within me on guard.

He greets me with a smile. "Yes," he replies, the single word laden with an accent that could melt butter. "I've developed quite the taste for your fish and chips. And a Granville Island IPA, please."

"Coming right up," I manage to say without betraying the inner turmoil his charm ignites. I jot down his order, forcing my hand to stay steady, though my pulse races. This is no time for swooning.

"Fish and chips and an IPA," I repeat back to him, more for my own benefit than his confirmation. He nods, and I turn away before I lose any more of my composure.

I need to stay focused. I'll get to the bottom of this, one way or another. Despite my serving this guy bad food, he keeps coming back. That only confirms that he's here for some other reason. And I can't think of one that's anything good.

I slip into the kitchen, my voice low as I relay the order to the cook. "Make sure it's burned, would you? That's how he likes it." The cook raises an eyebrow, but nods, knowing better than to question a customer's peculiar preference.

I grab the IPA from the bar and pour it sloppy, the foam cresting over the edge of the glass. But then my feet slow and my heart quickens as I return to his table, hesitation creeping in as I spot two familiar faces—Dr. Griffin Martin and Dr. Kent Johns—seated with him. They're regulars here, Mercy Hospital's finest. Their presence with this enigmatic stranger throws everything my mind has conjured out of focused.

"Griffin, Kent," I greet them, though my eyes remain fixed on the third at their table. "Didn't expect to see you with this gombeen." The word slips out, a reflexive snap of suspicion. Griffin's eyebrows shoot up in amusement, and the silence that follows is heavy with awkwardness.

"Lucy," Griffin says after a moment, "meet Dr. Chance Devereaux. He's the new chief of emergency at Mercy."

I look between them, searching for any hint of jest. The idea of someone like him—a leather-clad mystery with a smile that could turn saints to sinners—running an ED is almost laughable. But there's no trace of humor in Griffin's steady gaze, only the truth. I must have heard wrong.

"Chance, huh?" My voice is skeptical as I finally address the interloper directly. "You don't exactly scream *doctor* to me."

He leans back. "And what should a doctor look like?"

My arm stretches out toward Griffin and Kent—mirror images of medical professionalism with their pressed shirts and clean-cut charm. "Like them," I say. "Not...whatever you've got going on."

He laughs heartily, and the sound catches me off guard. It resonates with a sincerity that nudges at the walls I've built around myself since he first walked in. Despite everything, I crack a reluctant smile.

A wave of embarrassment crashes over me as I realize how wrong I've been about Chance Devereaux. I painted him as some sort of nefarious character, and now, here he is, just another professional trying to make a difference. I reach for the beer I set in front of him. "I'm going to get you a fresh one."

"Thank you," he replies with an easy grin that makes my insides twist.

I return to the bar and catch Janelle's attention. "Can you pour him another IPA? Less head this time."

She nods, taking the glass from me as I return to face the table where Griffin and Kent await.

"Griffin, Kent, what can I get for you this evening?" I ask.

"Black and tan," Griffin says. "And I'd like the lamb stew."

"I'll have the lamb stew too, but make mine a lager," Kent adds, folding his menu.

"Got it," I confirm, scribbling the orders before returning to the kitchen to rectify the fish and chips situation. With a quick word to the chef, I place a fresh order for Chance's meal, making sure it's prepared just right this time, along with two lamb stews. Then I grab the charred plate meant for Chance and tip its contents into the trash.

My father, always vigilant, catches the action and strides over. "Lucy, what are you doing? Liam, watch what you're doing. We can't afford to waste food around here," he scolds.

"It's my fault," I admit, unable to meet his eyes. "I got an order wrong."

He sighs, shaking his head, but doesn't press further, instead turning back to supervise the bustling kitchen. I escape back to the floor, the weight of my earlier judgments pressing heavily on my shoulders.

If only the ground would open and offer me an escape. But it doesn't, so I steel myself to face Chance and the doctors again, ready to atone for my mistakes and serve them as best I can.

I weave through the scattered tables, balancing a tray of drinks as my mind still reels from the revelation—Chance Devereaux, not some mob enforcer but a doctor. And here I was, thinking he spelled trouble for Dad.

My panic had me on edge, I tell myself, depositing the tray at an empty table to free up my hands. She's convinced the handsome stranger is bad news. In hindsight, I can't believe I fell for it. But then again, caution isn't unwarranted; Dad's past in the rough neighborhoods of Dublin taught him to be wary, and he's instilled the same watchfulness in me. We've both seen enough to know trouble doesn't announce itself. It sidles up quietly and strikes when you least expect it.

Approaching their table once more, I catch snippets of conversation, the cadence of medical jargon mingling with casual banter. As much as I try to focus on the task at hand, my ears tune in to the dialogue unfolding before me.

"...the new policies are one thing, but staffing is the real issue," Chance says. "We need more nurses, plain and simple."

Griffin nods. "It's the same story all over Mercy. Everyone's stretched thin. Patients are already suffering."

Kent leans forward. "What's the hospital doing to recruit?"

"Nurses have so many options and running around an emergency department is usually a calling, not just a job," Chance suggests, swirling the beer in his glass. "We need to figure out how to fill the gap we have without nurses, and residents are not the answer. They don't have enough experience."

Their voices fade into the background as I retreat into my own thoughts. It's an echo of so many conversations I've overheard while serving—the struggles and triumphs within the hospital walls spilling over into the pub. I'm just the server, the invisible eavesdropper, but each story leaves its imprint on me.

I hover at the edge of their table, waiting for the right moment to interject. The conversation ebbs, and I seize the opportunity. "Kent, my class is working on a unit about the heart. Would you consider coming in to talk about being a doctor and about the heart and how it works?" It's a long shot but worth the ask.

"Ah, I'd love to," he replies with an apologetic grimace,

"but Griffin and I are swamped with night shifts this month."

I nod. I appreciate the honesty and am about to turn away when Chance's voice stops me in my tracks.

"Lucy, what kind of class do you have?" he asks.

I pause, caught off guard by the interest in his eyes, the same eyes I so wrongly judged earlier. "My dad owns the pub," I explain, feeling a strange need to account for myself. "But my real job is teaching at an elementary school. Most of my grade-five students are from low-income families, and many are migrants from war-torn countries." I glance down, a little embarrassed to admit the next part. "They often can't afford school supplies, so whatever I earn here at Barney's... Well, it goes to helping them."

"Really?" He sounds intrigued, not just making idle pub conversation.

"Yeah." I nod, looking back up at him. "It's not much, but it helps."

Chance appears to consider this for a moment, then surprises me once again. "I'll come speak to your class," he says decisively.

My mouth opens slightly, shock rendering me speechless for a beat before I manage a nod. "That would be great, thank you."

"Here." He reaches into his pocket and pulls out his mobile. "Type in your number. You can text me the details, and I'll make it happen."

As he hands me his phone, I feel a twinge of guilt for my earlier assumptions. This man, whom I had pegged as nothing but trouble, is offering to help my students — kids he's never met. It's humbling, and I feel like a real heel for the way I've treated him.

"Thank you, Dr. Devereaux," I tell him. "This means a lot to us."

"Call me Chance," he says with a sparkle in his eyes.
Oh, I'm in trouble now.

CHAPTER 7

Chance

I stride into Dr. Charles Johns' office. I've been summoned, and it feels a lot like going to the principal's office. I hope this isn't about the drug trial. I still don't know enough to talk to him about that yet.

The head of medicine for Mercy Hospital sits behind his desk, a fortress of paperwork and digital screens around him, and he doesn't look up until I knock lightly on the open door.

"Dr. Johns," I begin, feeling the weight of the impending conversation.

"Dr. Devereaux," he greets curtly, fingers steepled in front of him. "I've heard rumors about our staff moonlighting at those safe-use clinics. That is in breach of their contracts. What do you know?"

I take a deep breath, readying my defense. "They're government clinics, and they're volunteering. It's not moonlighting if they're not getting paid."

"Volunteering," he repeats, the word heavy with skepticism. "It's a liability. What happens if someone dies and their family sues the hospital?"

"Safe-use clinics are saving lives," I push back. "They respond to overdoses immediately, prevent disease spread, and connect users to health services. We should be supporting this, not condemning it."

Dr. Johns' frown deepens. He shakes his head. "I can't condone it. They were hired to work here, not there."

I stand my ground, though I sense we're at an impasse. "Look, as long as it doesn't interfere with their responsibilities at the hospital, what's the harm? It's no different than if we come upon someone passed out on a sidewalk downtown. We stop. We help. That's what we do."

He leans back, the leather chair protesting under the shift of his weight. "That's different, and you know it."

"Is it?" I challenge. "Because I see it as an extension of our oath—to do no harm. Whether that's in the ED or as a volunteer in a clinic, it shouldn't matter."

Dr. Johns stares at me, his eyes narrowed. The silence stretches between us, thick and taut, before he dismisses me with a terse nod.

"This conversation isn't over."

I nod, acknowledging the temporary truce, and exit the office. The door shuts behind me with a soft click, sealing away the discord for now.

I stride back to the emergency department. There's no time to dwell on this. Duty calls, loudly and insistently. I'm greeted by three residents. They're clustered around the central desk like chicks waiting for their mother hen.

"Okay, team," I say, clapping my hands to capture their attention, "we've got a steady stream of lacerations today. Head over to the suture room and start stitching up."

They nod, collecting their gear before scurrying off, each one eager to prove their skills. It's a dance we perform daily, them seeking approval, me providing guidance. Turning away from the departing residents, my gaze lands on Mrs. Kim, her small form almost lost in the bustle of the department. She's standing outside my office, patiently waiting, and I can tell she's holding something in her hands. Her husband was in last week. He cut his finger off doing landscaping work. I approach her, mustering a smile despite my fatigue.

"Mrs. Kim," I say in greeting. "How is your husband today?"

She beams at me and nods vigorously. "Yes," she says, the word hanging between us, both question and answer.

"Annyeonghaseyo, eotteohge jinaeseyo?" I try again in Korean, aware of how my accent must butcher the beautiful cadence of her language.

Her reply comes in a flurry of rapid Korean. She speaks far too fast for me, but by her smile I infer her husband is improving. She offers up the casserole dish she's been cradling. It's fogged with warmth, and the aroma that wafts toward me is tantalizing. She tries to articulate her thoughts, the words stumbling from her lips, but the sentiment is clear — *Thank you.*

"Kamsahamnida," I respond, accepting the dish. She certainly owes me nothing, but to refuse would be an affront to her gratitude. I peek inside, and my mouth waters at the sight of what appears to be a perfectly prepared meal of Korean fried chicken. My stomach growls, reminding me I've skipped lunch.

"Thank you, Mrs. Kim," I repeat in English. She smiles once more, her eyes crinkling, then bows slightly and exits.

With the dish now in my possession, I momentarily consider taking a moment for the comfort of food.

Curiosity gleams in Jessica's eyes as she leans over the desk. "What did Mrs. Kim bring you, Dr. Devereaux? Are you going to share the love?"

"Looks like Korean fried chicken," I say, lifting the edge of the top to reveal the golden-brown pieces bathed in a lustrous red sauce, gochujang probably, its spicy aroma taunting our senses. "Sticky rice underneath."

"Ooh, that smells amazing," Tom Spaulding, one of our

EMTs, chimes in, craning his neck for a better look. "You gonna share?"

Before I can answer, the radio cuts through the banter, the squawk urgent. "Incoming helo, ETA two minutes. Skier, compound fracture femur, severe blood loss."

"Damn," I mutter, resealing the casserole. There's no time to eat now. "Secure that ortho consult, stat," I call as I stash the dish in my office. Fried chicken will have to wait.

I'm already moving when a gurney rolls past. The skier, I presume. Dr. Ian McCormick, our emergency orthopod, is here and taking over. Perfect.

Next, I'm at the side of a 72-year-old female with a head injury from a fall. "Dr. Devereaux," I introduce myself.

She looks up at me with eyes clear and untroubled, an odd contrast to her situation. "Nice to meet you," she replies, her voice strong. "I'm Isla Farrow."

With my pen light, I check the responsiveness of her eyes and examine the hematoma on her forehead. It's a doozy. "What happened?"

"One minute, I was standing there, and the next, I was looking into the brightest blue eyes I ever saw. That ambulance driver, you know?"

"Sounds like quite the charmer," I muse. "How are you feeling now?"

"Much better, thank you."

But I'm not entirely convinced. "Good to hear, but we're going to run some tests, just to be sure everything's all right." I turn to my nurse, who is already prepping for the next steps. "CT, EKG, chest radiographs, urinalysis, basic labs, cardiac enzymes."

"Got it, Dr. Devereaux," the nurse confirms before darting off.

"Rest easy, Ms. Farrow," I tell her before pulling away to attend to the unending tide of need washing through the doors.

The wail of the ambulance siren fades into a rush of

activity as EMTs burst in again.

"We've got a thirty-two-year-old woman," one of them announces.

I listen to her vitals and look her over. Her skin pallid and slick with sweat. The driver meets my eyes, his expression grim. "Blood pressure's through the roof, doc—two-thirty over one-sixty."

"Damn it." I'm already reaching for a syringe. "Get me beta blockers, now. We need to bring that down before she has a stroke or her aorta gives out. Three-point-five milligrams of Lopressor, stat," I bark, my focus narrowing to the woman's strained face.

A nurse nods, drawing the medication.

"Jessica," I call over my shoulder, "notify the OR to prep for transesophageal echo on the double."

"Got it, Dr. Devereaux," she responds.

I watch the woman's vitals, willing them to stabilize until she's whisked away.

As the tension in the room pivots to action, I spare a glance at the board—Ms. Farrow's name now sits neatly under the *Admitted* column. She's in good hands, beyond the immediate danger zone.

My shift's end looms, but there's one last task. I find my residents huddled around a lightbox, their faces lined with concentration and fatigue. Their sutures on today's patients are less than perfect, jagged lines that speak of their inexperience.

"Keep practicing," I tell them, slipping past to review their work. "Those stitches could be a lot cleaner. Remember, your knots are what stands between recovery and complication."

They nod, eyes earnest.

"Tomorrow, back here, on time."

"Will do, Dr. Devereaux," they chorus, and I sense their determination, their youth mingling with resolve. It's a cocktail of potential that keeps my blood pumping.

"Good." With that, I leave them to it and stride down the

corridor, ready to shed the weight of the day.

I flick on the light in my office, and there it is — Mrs. Kim's dish. It sits patiently, a reminder of the humanity threaded through the relentless pace of hospital life. The savory aroma seems to wrap around me.

"Better take you home," I murmur to the casserole dish, as if it could hear me. And why not? After today, a bit of whimsy doesn't feel out of place. I scoop up the glassware and secure its cover, my mind already wandering to the flavors locked inside.

I carry it with me to the locker room and peel off the layers of my scrubs. In their place, I pull on the familiar comfort of jeans and a white T-shirt. Boots follow, anchoring me back to a world where I'm just Chance, not Dr. Devereaux.

Outside, the dish finds its place in the spacious compartment of my bike, nestled securely. As I pull out of the parking lot and head home, the bridge stretches before me, a steel ribbon against the twilight sky. I'm halfway across when Célineslips into my thoughts.

I remember the tarte de sucre I was given once at my hospital in Montreal. A gift from a patient, much like Mrs. Kim, who had nothing but gratitude to offer. Céline's nose had wrinkled at the sight of it, her voice laced with caution about unknown kitchens. I'd laughed it off, slicing through the pastry and letting the rich, sweet filling affirm my belief in simple acts of kindness. The flavor had been a revelation, a testament to the warmth found in handcrafted offerings. And now, with Mrs. Kim's dish resting behind me, I feel that familiar tug, a connection to something genuine.

The city falls away as I reach the other side of the bridge, the purr of the engine a solitary companion through the streets of North Vancouver. Pulling up to Ginny's house, I kill the engine and swing a leg over the bike. And there she is, Ginny, her wave as bright as any beacon. She walks outside, holding her sweater tight around herself.

"How was your day?" I ask.

"Every day above ground's a good day," she declares.

I can't help but grin. "Got a dish from a patient's wife," I tell her, extracting the casserole from my bike's saddlebag. "It's Korean chicken. I'm not sure how spicy it is but care to join me for dinner?"

She doesn't even blink, just nods with an eagerness that tells me she values company as much as the food. Dinner with Ginny — it's a plan that feels right, the easy camaraderie of shared loneliness.

"Let's find out together," she says, and I follow her inside.

I ease into one of Ginny's mismatched kitchen chairs, the casserole dish taking center stage on the table between us. Ginny busies herself with dishing out generous portions onto plates she's had since the seventies, floral patterns faded from years of use.

"Smells amazing, doesn't it?" I comment.

"It sure does," she agrees, settling across from me. "Walter would have loved this. He was always trying new foods."

The mention of her husband brings a softness to her eyes, and I lean in. "Tell me about Walter," I say.

She smiles, a touch of wistfulness coloring her tone. "He had a busy dental practice. Our son was in Toronto at university. He passed away quietly one night, right here in this house. It was peaceful, almost as if he was just slipping into another room." Her voice trembles ever so slightly, but there's a peace in her acceptance of the past.

I nod, understanding the sacredness of such moments, though I've only seen them through the lens of my profession. "Sounds like he went the way most folks hope to go," I reply.

"Yes," she says, her gaze drifting toward the window. "He left me with good memories and this old house full of echoes. That's why I appreciate having you around. You living in the rental unit makes me feel safe again."

Her admission tugs at something inside me, a reminder

that what we do for others often carries weight beyond our intentions. I reach across the table, covering her hand with mine for an instant. "I'm glad I can offer you that sense of security, Ginny."

We share a look, an unspoken understanding that companionship and security are precious commodities in our unpredictable lives. Then we turn our attention to our meal, diving into the spicy flavors Mrs. Kim has so skillfully prepared.

I'm scraping the last bits of sticky rice onto my fork when Ginny leans back in her chair, eyeing me with a thoughtful tilt of her head. "Chance," she says. "When you rented the apartment, I thought there were going to be two of you. What happened?"

The question hangs in the air, mingling with the savory scent of Korean spices. I set down my fork and meet her gaze. "My girlfriend, Céline, decided at the last minute not to come with me to Vancouver."

Ginny frowns. "You must not have been in love, then. If you loved her, wouldn't you have stayed?"

I shake my head, feeling the weight of the decision that brought me here. "I had already committed to the job at Mercy Hospital," I tell her. "I've never been one to renege on a commitment."

"Then why didn't you propose?" she prods, her hands folded neatly on the tabletop. "No girl in her right mind would move across the country without a commitment."

"Most folks from Quebec, around my age... They see marriage more as a religious institution. We're not religious," I tell her, trying to convey the cultural nuance.

Her brows knit together. "But can't you see it as a commitment to another person, not just a religious act?"

I shrug, an easy motion that doesn't quite match the complexity of emotions behind it. "You don't need a piece of paper for commitment."

Ginny opens her mouth, then closes it, wordless for a

moment. In that silence, I feel the gap between our perspectives, wide and untraversable.

Dinner wraps up with a quiet that wasn't there before. I help clear the dishes and bid her goodnight.

Back in my own space, I peel off the day's weariness along with my clothes, trading them for the comfort of a well-worn T-shirt and boxers. As I lie in bed, the ceiling fan casting fleeting shadows across the room, Ginny's words replay in my mind. Céline never wanted marriage; we were united in that. But if there had been a silent vow between us, a promise without ceremonies or signatures, would it have anchored me to Montreal? Would she have come with me as she promised? Or was the pull of my commitments — my word, my career — stronger than the bonds of an unspoken pact?

I turn over, the sheets cool against my skin, and close my eyes. Sleep will come eventually, but first, it demands that I sift through the what-ifs and might-have-beens all over again.

CHAPTER 8

Lucy

The classroom buzzes with the anticipation of our impending visitor, my kids squirming in their seats, pencils tapping, and whispers flitting through the air like nervous butterflies. My own stomach even flutters a little as the time draws near for Chance Devereaux's arrival. This is an exciting day.

A distant rumble grows into a roar that vibrates through the windowpanes. Heads turn, eyes widen, and I brace myself. The Harley's growl is a symphony to some, and a stressor to others. I see hands press against ears, faces scrunch up—the loud noises are too much for some of them. But there's also a ripple of excitement, a few kids bouncing on the balls of their feet, eager for the sight of the giant motorcycle that heralds our guest's approach.

"Remember, deep breaths," I remind them, and a few nod, taking in gulps of air, trying to center themselves amid the disruption.

"Miss Sheridan?" Aleksander's hand is raised.

"Yes, Aleksander?"

"Is it time to get Dr. Chance?"

"Dr. Chance?" Farida echoes, using the name he told me they should use as we planned this meeting.

"Absolutely," I say with a smile. "Please go meet him out front and walk him back to our classroom."

They scurry out, and I catch a glimpse of my reflection on the glass of the framed motivational poster by the door — *Never Say "I Can't." Always Say "I'll Try."* My hair could use a touch-up, and I wonder if my makeup has survived the morning. A part of me yearns to dash to the bathroom for a quick refresh, but instead, I turn back to the math unit spread out before me. After all, Chance isn't coming to see me. He's here for the kids, to be that spark of inspiration they so desperately need. Because that's what makes every challenging day worth it, seeing the moment when understanding ignites in their eyes. And I'm here to facilitate that magic, not get a date.

I dive back into the world of changing fractions to decimals, trying to finish today's mathematics lesson before our guest arrives.

My gaze drifts toward the window, where Chance dismounts his Harley as young Aleksander and Farida bounce from side to side. I can tell he's talking to them as he takes off his helmet and gets a box from his bag. He hunkers down and extends his hand in greeting to each of them. They gesture wildly, animated in conversation, while Chance's nods are slow, deliberate — a gentle giant with them.

There is no way this guy is that perfect.

I can't hear them through the glass, but the scene speaks volumes — he's a natural with curious children. The kids lead him toward the school building, and I stand transfixed as they disappear from my narrow vantage point and reemerge through the main entrance visible from my classroom door.

"Should've brought my camera," I murmur. They're all smiles, blissfully unaware I'm watching. My heart swells with a mix of pride and something else—a fluttering warmth that has no business surfacing now, not when there's teaching to be done.

I scribble the last equation on the whiteboard, but then Chance is here.

"Okay, everyone," I call, turning to face my class, "let's put away our math materials."

The door creaks open, and in they come. Chance's presence fills the room, and he scans the sea of faces.

"Class, this is Dr. Chance Devereaux," I tell them as he shrugs off his leather coat.

For a moment, it's as though summer has returned, the air thickening around me. Chance's T-shirt clings to him like a second skin. His jeans, snug and worn in all the right places, sculpt him into a figure more fitting for a billboard than a fifth-grade classroom. I swallow hard, hoping the kids don't notice the flush on my cheeks.

"Bonjour," Chance says, his voice smooth and confident. "Est-ce qu'il y a quelqu'un qui parle français?" A few hands go up, hesitant at first, then steadier as their classmates turn to look.

"Zabān-e Fārsī baladid?" he continues, switching to Farsi. Another set of hands rise, accompanied by shy smiles and nods of recognition.

He moves on, speaking in a language that curls around the syllables with a rhythmic familiarity. It takes a half-second longer for me to catch up—Ukrainian. Half the class responds, hands waving like flags of pride in a sea of diversity.

"Shéi huì shuō Pǔtōnghuà?" A lone hand, belonging to little Ming, rises this time. His eyes gleam with the unique joy of being seen and addressed in his mother tongue.

"Who speaks English?" Chance's final question unites them all, every hand thrusting to the ceiling in a forest of eagerness.

"Speaking many languages is really important in my job," he explains. "And one of the great things about Canada is how we're a mix of people, all bringing something special to the table."

I watch, my heart echoing the sentiment, as the children absorb his words, their eyes reflecting a world far bigger than this classroom.

"Okay," Chance says, shifting gears with his easy charm. "I hear you've been learning about the heart."

The kids' eyes are fixed on him as if he's the most fascinating puzzle they've ever seen. He holds up a fist, muscles shifting under his skin. "This is about the size of your heart." Their eyes widen in amazement.

"Really?" someone breathes, and I recognize Ivan's voice, tinged with awe.

"Really," Chance confirms, and he delves into the leather bag he brought.

He brings out a large plastic heart. "And this is what it looks like inside of you, only it's the size of your hand."

From there he explains, at a ten-year-old level, the chambers of the heart and how it beats. Then he asks, "Who would like to listen to their heart?"

Every hand raises up high.

"This is the coolest part," Chance says as he hands out real stethoscopes, not the plastic playthings. He instructs them on how to place the earpieces and where to position the chest piece. "Now, everyone needs to be quiet so you can hear."

There's an initial fumble of fingers and giggles as they help each other, but soon enough, a hush falls over the room. And then, as directed, they gently press the cool metal to a neighbor's chest, listening intently through layers of cotton shirts.

"Sounds like horses," Anna whispers, and her partner, Artem, grins back at her, their ears filled by the black tubes of their stethoscopes.

As this unfolds, I feel a presence behind me. I turn

slightly to see the back of the classroom filling with curious onlookers. Teachers and aides weave between the desks, drawn by the novelty of the lesson—or perhaps by the man leading it.

"Is it getting hot in here, or is it just him?" Tiffany murmurs from the doorway, fluttering a hand near her neck.

I stifle a giggle. "Focus," I mouth to her, but there's no denying the warmth that's blooming in my cheeks or that it has little to do with the temperature in the room.

The room is abuzz with whispered excitement, the children locked on Chance as he moves among them. I lean against my desk, watching him engage with each eager student, their faces lit up with wonder and curiosity.

"Dr. Chance?" Remi's voice cuts through the murmurs, his hand raised. "Do you... Do you see a lot of dead people at the hospital?"

Chance kneels beside Remi's desk, his expression gentle. "Sometimes, unfortunately, it does happen," he admits. "But I—and all the doctors and nurses—work very hard to help people get better and avoid that happening."

Remi nods, processing with a solemn frown. The rest of the class is silent, hanging on Chance's every word. They're completely smitten, and I can't blame them, because so am I.

"Dr. Chance?" Kayla's voice pipes up next, and her question slices through the seriousness that had settled over the room. "Are you Miss Sheridan's boyfriend?"

Laughter bubbles up around us, but I'm too quick to let the teasing grow. "No, Kayla. Dr. Chance is someone I know who works at the hospital, so I invited him to help us with this lesson." But I can't contain the smile that spreads across my face.

"Miss Sheridan is a wonderful friend," Chance adds, winking at me.

From the corner of my eye, I catch Tiffany smirking. She's probably concocting some matchmaking scheme already. Thankfully, Chance and the kids don't seem to notice.

Several in my class sigh dreamily, no doubt imagining

themselves in fairy tale romances. I chuckle softly. Dr. Chance is breaking hearts left and right without even trying.

Our time is almost up. "Okay, everyone, let's return the stethoscopes," I call, gesturing toward the bag Chance brought.

"Actually," he interjects, holding up a hand, "you can keep them. The hospital just got new ones, and these were going to be destroyed anyway."

A collective cheer ripples through the room.

"Really?" one of the children asks, her voice tinged with disbelief.

"Yes, really." Chance holds up a roll of tape. "Since they all look the same, I thought you might want to put your name on them, just like doctors do."

Chance works his way around the room, giving each child a bit of tape, and after they've written their names on it, he shows them where to affix them to the stethoscope.

"Wow..." The word is barely audible, but it's mirrored in every child's awestruck expression. This isn't just a simple guest lecture anymore. It's something they'll remember for years.

"Class, what do we say to Dr. Chance for coming to speak with us today and for these amazing gifts?" I prompt.

"Thank you!" they chorus, loud and clear enough that it must reach every corner of the school.

I have them tuck their gifts away in their backpacks, creating a small stampede as they do.

I turn to Chance, about to thank him myself, when I notice the lineup that's formed at my door. Teachers, aides, even the librarian seem to have found reasons to wander near my classroom, each with that same hopeful look in their eyes.

"Dr. Chance, could you maybe come talk to my class next week?" one teacher asks, her eyelashes fluttering in a way that's probably supposed to be charming.

"Actually," I interject before he can respond, a protective edge to my voice I hadn't planned on, "Dr. Chance is very busy in the emergency department, and he's already done so much for us today. We don't want to ask too much."

Chance shoots me an appreciative glance, but it doesn't stop the others. They lean in closer, their laughter too high-pitched, their body language screaming flirtation. My stomach twists, and I press my lips together, trying to understand why this bothers me so much. It's not like he's mine, like we're anything more than friends. Hell, I've spent weeks willing him to disappear from my life. But the tightness in my chest won't ease, and I find myself wanting to steer him away, into the quiet sanctuary of an empty classroom.

I edge closer, tilting my head to offer a smile. My words are ready, a quiet thank you to ease him out of this unexpected spotlight, when Tiffany sidles up beside me. Her eyes flicker with mischief, and she leans in. "Girl, you better lock him down before someone else does," she stage whispers, nudging me.

Heat crawls up my neck as I shoot her a flustered glance. *Lock him down?* The absurdity of the idea sends a shockwave through me. Chance is just... Chance. Just a customer at the bar who rode his Harley into my world today and somehow made my classroom feel both too small and infinitely larger. Why would Tiffany say that? Is it so obvious that everyone but me understands what this flutter in my chest means?

Chance's laughter breaks through my thoughts, deep and genuine. Fortunately, it doesn't seem to be Tiffany's comment that's amused him. He's chatting with the librarian now. I watch as he handles the attention with an ease I envy. It's not fair, really, how he can just stand there, all casual charisma, and not see the effect he has on the rest of us.

"Sure, Tiff," I murmur without conviction, trying to shake off the weight of her words. "But I don't need to worry about Chance."

Do I?

CHAPTER 9

Chance

The bell rings, and the noise in the classroom goes from a gentle buzz to an all-out roar.

"Okay, Aleksander," Lucy says. "We're done for the day. Go on outside. Chase each other around and get rid of what's left of your energy."

He waves goodbye to me as he leaves. What a great day.

The kids were so excited and loud that other teachers and administrators from around the building were curious about the commotion. I pack up the plastic heart I brought and chuckle as another kid asks why we draw hearts that look like butts. I smother a laugh and play it safe. "I have no clue," I tell him.

Lucy shoos the rest of them—students and faculty alike—out of the class and turns to me. "Thank you so much. You were a natural with the kids."

I nod. "Lots of training in the emergency department.

But I enjoy this kind of outreach. Thank you for inviting me."

When I turn, I realize Farida remains. She approaches me with a quiet confidence that belies her years, the stethoscope I gifted her draped around her neck like a badge of honor. Her hand finds mine and tugs gently, guiding me toward the office with Lucy trailing behind us.

In the silence of the hallway, our footsteps are the only sound. As we reach the school's front door, I squat down to meet Farida's gaze.

"Farida," I tell her, "you're really smart, you know that? And if you want to be a doctor someday, I have no doubt you'll become one."

"Thank you," she says, her voice a whisper. She launches herself at me, her arms squeezing tight around my neck in a hug that carries the weight of dreams yet to be realized. Then, just as suddenly, she releases me and scampers away.

Turning back to Lucy, the shift in atmosphere is palpable. Her eyes, usually so full of fire and command, now glisten.

"Her parents..." Lucy begins, a tremor in her voice. "They were killed in the Middle East. She and her brother were sent here to live with an aunt who's doing her best, but it's hard. She's single and trying to keep it all together."

I nod. Farida's resilience, the quiet strength she must draw from some well within, makes sense now.

"Farida doesn't talk much, but she takes everything in. Today, with you, she opened up."

For a heartbeat, we stand there, each lost in our thoughts.

"Chance, I'd like to take you out," Lucy says. "Somewhere other than Barney's, as a thank you for today."

"Sure," I hear myself say, spurred by the warmth of her gaze. "How about tomorrow night—Saturday?"

"Tomorrow night it is," she confirms. Her smile seems a little forced now, though I can't fathom why.

"You're sure you're not working?" I ask.

"Checked this morning," she assures me, tucking a stray lock of hair behind her ear. "I'm not on the schedule."

"Okay, then." The words are light, but a heaviness settles in my chest as she says goodbye and walks back to her classroom.

Outside, I mount my motorcycle and navigate back toward the hospital, the wind whipping past me, offering a temporary reprieve from the swarm of thoughts buzzing in my head. The reality of our impending date slowly crystallizes. Lucy is attractive, of course, and she's quite accomplished in the classroom and has a fantastic laugh... A pang of regret jolts through me, sharp and unexpected. *What am I doing?* It's too soon. I've barely stepped out of my last relationship. *Have I fully stepped out of my last relationship?* And Lucy... Well, I've seen glimpses of how she could be if things don't go her way.

The beer issue. The way she tampered with the food. *Vindictive* might be too strong a word, but I'm smart to be cautious. I'm not worried about retaliation. I know how to handle myself. But the truth, raw and simple, is that I'm not ready to dive into anything new. I don't need the complication, whether I can manage it or not.

"Focus on the department," I tell myself, trying to suppress a muddle of emotions with the practicality of my day-off tasks. But even as the hospital looms ahead, a vision of Lucy, both fierce and tender, lingers stubbornly in my mind.

CHAPTER 10

Lucy

The following evening, I'm twisting my hair into a casual yet elegant knot, hoping it conveys the right message, appreciative but not overly eager. The speakerphone crackles with Janelle's laughter, filling the small space of my bathroom as I blend in a touch more concealer to hide the freckles on my cheeks.

"Seriously, you've got to admit that was smooth," she gushes through the phone, recounting the moment Chance walked into my classroom with a heart model and stethoscopes for every student. "And let's not forget that he could be on the cover of *Bad Boy Bikers* magazine."

Rolling my eyes at the mirror, I can't help the zing I feel with the memory of his leather jacket stretched over broad shoulders. "He's got charm; I'll give him that," I concede, dabbing on a neutral lipstick, steering clear of anything too bold. "And he had the kids eating out of his hand right away.

He may have missed his calling for teaching when he became a doctor."

"Charm and hotness! Plus, aren't you relieved he's not some enforcer for the Irish mob? After that weird suspicion we had?" Her voice bubbles with excitement.

"Janelle, you happily followed along when I cooked up that mob theory," I remind her, half-smiling at our wild imaginations. It was a ludicrous assumption based on nothing but his mysterious allure and leather jacket when he walked into Dad's bar.

A nervous breath escapes me as I glance at the reflection staring back. This isn't a date. It's just dinner — a thank-you-for-being-awesome-to-my-students dinner. Nothing more. I can't mix my personal life with Dad's business. If things went south, it'd be awkward at the bar, not just for me but for everyone involved. The guys from the hospital love Dad's place for unwinding after their shifts. Losing them because of a messy breakup is the last thing I want on my conscience.

"It's just dinner," I murmur to myself, practicing the carefree smile I'll offer Chance when he arrives. *A thank you. Nothing more.* "And if Beatrice calls out sick tonight, I'm going to demand a doctor's note," I tell Janelle.

"Lucy, you can't be your dad's crutch forever." Her concern manages to pierce my pre-date — or rather, pre-thank-you-dinner — jitters. "You've got more than enough on your plate with teaching."

I pause, a brush in mid-air as I contemplate her words, the soft bristles resting against my cheek. She's not wrong; between lesson plans and grading, my days are swamped.

"Maybe you're right," I admit, setting down the makeup brush. "Dad needs to sort through his staffing issues without me bailing him out."

"Exactly!" There's a victorious lilt in her tone. "And for tonight, just enjoy yourself. No overthinking, okay?"

"Okay," I murmur, though my stomach tightens at the thought of truly letting go.

The unmistakable rumble of a Harley cuts through the buzz of the city below, and I know it's Chance even before the sound comes to a stop outside my building. Mrs. Harrison, my elderly neighbor with an affinity for quiet evenings, will certainly have something to say about the noise. She complains about how loud the street is all the time, but that's a bridge I'll cross later.

"Janelle, I gotta go. He's here. Wish me luck," I say as I move toward the window, catching a glimpse of Chance dismounting his bike, helmet in hand. My heart skips a few beats. He is hotness personified. And those thighs. His hands. I shake my head and bring myself back to reality. *We're only friends.*

"Good luck! And please do everything I wouldn't do," she teases before I hit the end call button.

"Right," I whisper to myself. *It's definitely not a date. I should have met him somewhere. But he doesn't know where anything is.*

Checking my reflection one final time, I ensure my auburn hair is neatly pinned back, away from my face. My makeup is subtle yet effective at covering all the freckles, a balance I've mastered over the years.

Then the buzzer sounds, a sharp electronic chirp. I stride over to the intercom, pressing the talk button. "Hi, come on up. It's apartment two-oh-two, first door on the right when you walk up the stairs," I instruct.

With a click, I release the button. This is fine. It's just dinner. I can do this.

I swing the door open, and it's like the room exhales, shrinking a fraction as Chance steps inside. He fills the doorway, his smile easy and his leather jacket adding to his imposing figure. "Bonjour," he says, his voice deep and somehow even more resonant within the confines of my apartment.

"Hi, come in." I gesture awkwardly. As I slip on my jacket, I turn toward him, searching for some casual conversation to ease the intensity of his presence. "Do you eat sushi?" I ask.

He chuckles, a rich sound that stirs something in the pit of my stomach. "Yeah, I do."

"Great. There's this place, Manpuku. They have the best sushi in Vancouver, and we could get bento boxes to go. I thought we could sit by the waterfront if you're up for it?"

"Sounds perfect," he agrees, but then his brow furrows. "But I'm buying dinner."

Locking eyes with him, I'm determined to hold my ground. "This is a thank you for helping out with my class. That's non-negotiable."

"Lucy," he says, softer now, "you spend all your money on those kids. Save it for them."

His comment catches me off guard, and for a moment, I'm speechless. But the resolve Janelle instilled in me earlier flares up, and I manage a nod. "Fine. But next time, it's on me."

"Deal," he says, and we shut the door behind us. In that moment, I realize I've just extended our outings together past this evening's thank you, and that he's agreed. I celebrate silently inside my head.

As we slide into the rideshare, the shift from the quiet of my apartment to the hum of the city is palpable. Chance seems at ease, glancing out the window. I feel compelled to fill the silence, to share something of my world with him.

"Get used to the rain," I say. "It's pretty much non-stop from October to June. Do you have a car? It's going to be a wet ride to work every day if you don't."

He nods. "I still need to buy one. I'm renting a basement apartment up in West Van and taking public transit is tough. I don't mind getting wet, but backsplash from all the cars makes it pretty muddy. I end up taking an extra shower just to get it all off."

"One of the bar's regulars manages the local Ford dealership. He'll usually sell to me and my friends at cost. If you're interested, we can go check them out."

"You'd do that for me?"

"Um, you just let a bunch of ten-year-olds hang all over you. I think it's the least I can do."

We arrive at the restaurant and order our bento boxes. Chance chooses sea urchin, much more adventurous than my salmon and tuna. Once we have our dinners, I lead the way to the waterfront. Chance walks beside me, and it's not hard to miss the appreciative glances he gets from people—okay, mostly women—as they walk past.

We find a bench and settle down to unwrap our meals. The sushi is exquisite, each roll crafted with precision and care—a stark contrast to the hearty pub fare at Barney's. We enjoy our dinner as the float planes make their graceful descents, skimming the water before coming to a stop right in front of us here in Coal Harbor.

"Vancouver's beauty differs from Montreal's," Chance remarks, his eyes tracing the skyline where the city meets the mountains.

I nod. "It has its own charm. But you know, my favorite has to be Quebec City."

"Really?" He turns to look at me with genuine curiosity. "Why's that?"

"During grade eleven, I lived inside the old walled part of the city." We watch two seagulls fighting over some food. "I stayed with this retired couple who'd never had kids. They were like the grandparents I never had. I'd spend hours wandering the cobblestone streets. It felt like living in a piece of Europe."

Chance smiles, and there's a sparkle in his eye that tells me he gets it.

"What about you? What's your favorite city?"

He thinks for a moment, looking out over the waterfront. "Probably Vancouver," he admits. "The winters are milder, and there's something about the ocean... Plus, I always knew I wanted to come here."

"Is that why you moved here?"

The sun is beginning to set, and the water looks like glass. "I couldn't take another winter, and there's so much more opportunity here. I was ready for a change. My parents are in Montreal, and leaving them was hard, but they have my sister and her family to keep them occupied."

I nod. I've heard others say the same thing about the weather when they move here.

As we finish, Chance folds his empty bento box, his fingers deft and deliberate, and glances at me with a playful challenge in his eyes. "Lucy, what did I do to you when we first met?" he asks.

"Ah..." I chuckle, crumpling my napkin in my hand. "The burnt and dry burger and wilted salad. You missed out on the burned fish-and-chips special I had planned for you another night." My grin fades. "That was the night I found out who you really were."

"Guess I dodged a bullet," he says with a laugh, but his eyes search mine, seeking a glimpse beneath the surface.

I let my gaze wander back to the planes taking off, soaring into the possibility of clear skies ahead. I stand, and we begin to stroll along the waterfront. "My dad did some work for the Irish mob before we moved here. That's how he got the money to bring us over. And sometimes, I worry that past will come back to haunt us."

Chance's expression clouds over. "The mob? But why would they—"

"Once here, he bought Barney's," I continue, "and he's on good terms with the local leader. They grew up together in Dublin. That keeps them at bay, but if they ever decide to come back..." I trail off, not wanting to voice the rest of that thought.

"Your father doesn't handle confrontation well?" Chance fills in.

"He's a go-with-the-flow kind of guy." I nod, grateful for his understanding. A chill breeze from the ocean wraps around us, and I hug my jacket tighter.

"Wait," Chance says, scratching his stubbled chin. "How

could anyone think I'm involved with the Irish mob with my French accent?"

"The West End Gang in Montreal," I explain. "They're the Irish mob there."

Chance shakes his head. "Of course. I know them. They were regulars at my hospital. I didn't put that together."

"They mostly keep their distance because my dad ran with Frank 'The Weasel' Ryan back in Dublin. But every once in a while, someone shows up and tries to extort money."

"The Weasel?" Chance echoes, his brow furrowed. "Why call him that?"

"Beats me," I say with a laugh. "He has a nose that's been broken more times than he can count. Doesn't look like a weasel, though. Maybe it's because he weasels out of things?"

"Tell your father to be careful," Chance advises, the humor gone from his voice. "With the mob, once you're in, you're never really out."

"I know," I say softly. "I know."

"Look at that," he says after a moment, gesturing to a boat bobbing on the horizon, its sails a ghostly white against the darkening sky.

I smile, caught up in the simple beauty of it all, and for a moment, I let myself believe we're just two people enjoying an evening walk, untethered from the complicated tangles of our lives. I look over at him, the rugged line of his jaw, the soft curl of his hair. The urge to lean in, to brush my lips against his, swells within me, powerful and insistent.

Before the thought can become action, Chance turns to face me, his eyes searching mine. "Lucy, I wish… I wish I'd met you at another time," he murmurs.

My heart stutters, anticipating the words to come. "Why's that?" I manage, feigning nonchalance.

"Because right now, I'm trying to mend a broken heart." His gaze drifts toward the horizon. "Vancouver wasn't supposed to be a fresh start, but it's ended up that way. I'm still getting used to being without my partner."

The air between us shifts. Disappointment settles in my chest, but there's a sense of relief too. Now, I don't have to worry about whether starting something with Chance is a good idea. "Friends then?" I ask, keeping my voice light. "Is there room in your life for one more?"

A lopsided grin breaks across his face. "Yeah, friends. I think I can handle that."

"Good," I say, smiling in return. "Because everyone needs a friend, especially in a new city."

We resume our walk, and I find it's more comfortable now. We're stepping forward on common ground—no expectations, no pressure.

"Let me be your unofficial guide to the city," I offer, shrugging off my lingering disappointment. "Someone should show you the sights, and who better than a local?"

Chance's eyes light up. "I'd like that," he says, a smile warming his features. "This place... It's different from what I'm used to."

A little while later, we summon a rideshare on my phone, and the car pulls up smoothly. As we slide into the backseat, the driver nods through the rearview mirror, and we're off, the city lights blurring past us as we make small talk. When we arrive at my building, the car comes to a gentle stop.

"Just text me when you're free next weekend," I say as I step out onto the curb. "I'll plan something fun."

"Will do," he replies. "Thanks for spending the evening with me." With a final wave, he gets on his loud motorcycle and rides away.

Turning, I catch a glimpse of Mrs. Harrison's silhouette framed in her window. She's been watching, as she always does, protective in her own way. I lift my hand, waving lightly, and she responds with a slow nod before drawing the curtains closed.

The stairs creak under my feet as I ascend to the second floor. When I reach the hallway, Mrs. Harrison's door creaks open, and she steps out. "Be careful with that one," she warns, her voice low. "These bad boys, they draw you in like spiders weaving webs. Before you know it, you're caught up, and it's too late to escape."

"That sounds like the voice of experience," I reply. "But we're just friends, nothing more."

"This is experience talking. Friends today," she says with a pointed look, "but hearts aren't known for listening to reason. Just…be careful."

"Thank you," I tell her. But she has totally the wrong idea. Chance and I are only friends, and he's not nearly as bad a boy as he seems.

I turn from her worried gaze and unlock my apartment door, stepping inside. Tonight was a good night. I didn't worry about the lessons I need to mark or activities to plan for my students. I got out of my typical bubble of working two jobs and had fun…and I have a new friend.

I kick off my shoes and toss my jacket over the back of a chair. My phone vibrates.

Janelle: How was the date?? Details!

Me: Not a date. He's fresh out of a relationship. We're just friends, but I'm gonna show him around the city.

Janelle: Friends??? That man is hot for you. Don't be fooled.

Me: He didn't go into details, but I don't want to be his rebound.

Janelle: I get it. But this is a great opportunity to get out there. And don't stress about Beatrice. If she flakes, I've got your back. You focus on your friendship tour guide gig!

Me: Thank you. Goodnight. I'm beat, and I'm working at Barney's tomorrow.

I smile as I get ready for bed, grateful for Janelle's unwavering support.

Turning off the lights, I make my way to my bedroom and slide under the covers, the cool fabric soothing against my skin. I let my mind wander through the night's events. Chance's laughter, the warmth of his eyes, the way he listened. It would be so easy to tumble into something more, to ignore his honesty and open my heart. But this is better. I don't want to make things complicated when they don't need to be. My life is plenty busy, and I need to keep my work connections separate from anything personal anyway.

I sigh. I had fun with him, genuine and unburdened, but the lines are drawn. For now, I'll build this friendship, brick by careful brick. "Friends," I murmur once more before dreams take hold, hoping the word is strong enough to shield me from falling for him anyway.

CHAPTER 11

Chance

A week after my dinner with Lucy, the morning sun winks at me through the blinds on Saturday morning, promising a day free from the perpetual beeping and buzzing of emergency-department machinery. My first weekend off in what feels like an eternity, and Lucy's already got it mapped out — a road trip to Whistler.

When she arrives, I sling my duffel bag into the backseat of her car, glancing over at my motorcycle with a twinge of longing before shutting the door.

It's kind of her to offer to show me around Vancouver and spend the weekend in Whistler with me. Just the two of us. I know I was clear about my boundaries, but something within me remains unsettled. I enjoy her company, and I hope I'm being fair to her. This is uncharted territory for me.

"Ready for some spectacular views?" Lucy grins from behind the wheel, her excitement infectious.

I nod, settling into the passenger seat.

She drives us to the Sea-to-Sky Highway. The route is known for its beauty, but I've never actually driven it. There's something about being an ED doctor—always focused on the destination, the next critical case—that makes you forget to enjoy the journey.

"Check this out," Lucy says, pointing to the landscape unfurling outside the window. We're approaching Horseshoe Bay, and I press my forehead against the glass, taking in the beauty of my newly adopted home.

The quaint village strikes a contrast with the vastness of Howe Sound stretching beyond it. Lucy launches into an impromptu tour guide's speech. "Did you know this fjord is the farthest south in all of North America?"

I conjure images of ancient ice shaping the land, leaving behind deep waters hemmed by rugged cliffs. It's hard to imagine such a serene spot was born from violent geological upheavals.

"Too bad we aren't seeing any marine life today," Lucy muses.

Even without wildlife, the views are impressive. It's a reminder of how small the problems within the hospital walls are compared to the vast, enduring beauty of the world outside.

"Thanks for driving," I say. "I wouldn't have wanted to miss any of this."

"I love this drive," she replies with a knowing look.

For the first time in a long while, I allow myself to just watch the scenery unfold, no distractions, no responsibilities—just the open road and an unseen horizon waiting to be explored. Lucy and I are bound for Whistler, but for once, the destination seems secondary to the journey itself.

Lucy suddenly veers off the highway, the tires crunching over a gravel path. "Surprise detour," she announces with a mischievous glint in her eyes. The sign ahead reads *Shannon Falls Provincial Park*, and I have to wonder what we're in for.

"Thought you might enjoy stretching your legs by climbing to one of BC's highest waterfalls," she says.

We park, and within minutes, we're on the trail. It's more of a stroll than a hike, and the sound of cascading water grows louder with each step.

"Come on!" Lucy beckons, already ahead. She's got her phone out and waves it at me. "Selfie time!"

I have to laugh, joining her. Our faces, framed by the thunderous backdrop of Shannon Falls, fill her screen. We try out several poses — serious explorer faces, then wide grins that speak to the joy of this moment.

"Let's see who can do the most ridiculous face," Lucy challenges, and I accept without hesitation. We contort our expressions into exaggerated displays of shock, awe, and mock horror, the waterfall roaring its approval in the background.

The next leg of our journey takes us back to the Sea-to-Sky Highway. Lucy drives on, the landscape rushing by in a blur of greenery and rock. Then, something makes me sit up straighter, my eyes narrowing as I try to be sure.

"Stop the car," I say abruptly, pointing toward the sky. "I see a bald eagle."

Lucy pulls over, and we look out to the water's edge. A bald eagle is perched on a pier post, its white head regal against the blue sky above. Then we see a second one not too far away on another pier post. They're looking us over, even as we're looking at them. It makes me a little uneasy to see the sharp point of their beaks and their laser-focused eyes. They're massive — bigger than some three-year-olds I've seen in the emergency department.

"Wow," I breathe, stepping out of the car for a better look. These majestic creatures seem unfazed by our presence. I guess with talons as big as my hand, I wouldn't be too scared of much either. "Never thought wooden poles could serve as thrones," I muse, snapping pictures with my phone.

"Nature's royalty," Lucy agrees.

I watch, captivated, as one of the eagles spreads its

wings and takes flight, powerful and poised. For a few heartbeats, I follow its ascent, riding the current of wind.

"I don't think I'll ever get used to scenes like this," Lucy says, leaning against the car.

"Hope not," I reply, tracking the eagle until it becomes a speck in the distance. "Some things should always feel like the first time."

She smiles, and we climb back into the car.

The hum of Lucy's engine is a soothing background for the swirl of greenery and mountains that frame the Sea-to-Sky Highway. As we pull into Squamish, my stomach reminds me that it's been a while since breakfast.

"Ready for some food?" Lucy asks.

"Starving," I admit as she finds a parking spot near what looks like a hub of local eateries.

We settle on a small bistro with outdoor seating.

"Can you believe people do all those activities around here?" Lucy gestures with her menu toward the posters on the wall that showcase windsurfing, rock climbing, and mountain biking.

"We're definitely coming back for a hike," I say, already visualizing us navigating a steep trail, that sort of adrenaline rush a welcome change from what I experience in the emergency department. "Maybe even try climbing."

"Deal," she says. "But no cliff diving, okay? I don't want to end up bringing an ED doctor to an emergency room."

I laugh, the sound feeling foreign yet right, and then the server arrives to take our order—local fish for her, a burger for me. We continue to chat about everything and nothing until our meals arrive.

Fully sated once our plates are clean, we resume our journey, leaving Squamish behind as the road snakes farther north and inland toward Whistler. When we reach the village, there's a palpable shift in energy with the bustle of tourists and locals enjoying what's left of the afternoon.

Our rented condo is a cozy haven tucked away at the

northern edge of Whistler Village, surrounded by tall pines. We unload our bags, and I take a moment to appreciate the privacy and tranquility before we lock up and venture out again.

"Let's explore over here," Lucy suggests, leading the way down cobblestone paths lined with boutiques and galleries.

"Never took you for a window shopper," I tease, watching her survey all the handmade jewelry and local art.

"It's the best way to manage my budget," she retorts.

As we meander through the village, soaking up the vibrant culture and diverse culinary scents, I feel a sense of belonging. Here, without the constant reminder of life-and-death decisions, I can breathe a little easier. Lucy's presence, already a beacon of friendship and fun, now feels like something more—a connection. And I have to admit, if timing had been different, that connection might be more than what it is.

"Tomorrow's going to be epic," she says, her hand brushing mine as we walk.

"Today's not over yet," I remind her. I've planned the evening for us.

"I've set the bar pretty high," she taunts.

"I don't think you'll be disappointed." I pull a pair of tickets from my pocket. "Ever been on a gondola with a glass floor?" I ask.

"Can't say I have," she admits.

"Let's check it out. A doctor I work with said it's pretty spectacular."

We walk to the other end of the village, following the signs, and approach the sleek cabins suspended on a cable, like beads on an enormous necklace strung between the mountains. The doors open with a soft whoosh, and we step into one of the clear-bottomed gondolas. As the sun begins its descent, we climb higher on the mountain, and Whistler recedes beneath us. The vastness of Canada unfolds in every direction.

I look down between my feet on the transparent floor, a

thin barrier between me and the world below. It's exhilarating, witnessing the rugged landscapes from this vantage point — forests spreading like emerald quilts, lakes glinting like scattered jewels, and peaks that pierce the sky. I'm struck by the beauty and also the sheer scale of the land that surrounds us. "It's breathtaking," I murmur.

"I remember little of Ireland, but I know it is nothing like this," Lucy says, leaning close to the glass.

Hours later, we find ourselves at the summit and stepping into Christine's, a fine-dining oasis perched high above the world at the mountaintop. We're seated by a window, with a view that competes with the artistry on our plates.

We order a bottle of wine to share and enjoy the view as we sip in comfortable silence. "Thank you for organizing this weekend," I tell her.

"I did the easy part. This..." She looks around. "...is incredible."

The server arrives to take our order.

"Crab-stuffed salmon," I tell him. Lucy's choice of lamb chops seems just as enticing, and I make a mental note to steal a taste when she's sufficiently distracted by the scenery.

"Tell me about your class this week," I request once we're alone again.

Lucy becomes animated as she talks about her students — the disagreements she needs to mediate, the nonstop talkers, and the kids she's worried about. Even if I hadn't met her class, I'd know she's a wonderful teacher.

When the meal arrives, it surpasses expectations. Each bite is an echo of the landscape, wild and refined all at once. And the robust notes of our BC wine complement the delicate seafood and rich lamb perfectly. There's something about mountain air that sharpens the senses, making every flavor more vivid.

"Outstanding," I declare after savoring the last forkful, and Lucy nods in agreement.

"Any interesting cases this week?" she asks.

"Well, on a grand scale, I'm struggling with the chief medical officer."

She chuckles. "And that's Charles Johns, right? Kent's father."

"Yes. He's difficult."

She nods.

"We don't see eye to eye on safe-use clinics."

Her brow furrows.

"Several medical personnel on my team volunteer there, and he wants me to put a stop to it."

"Why does he care if they volunteer their time?"

"He's worried about the malpractice insurance, getting sued if something goes wrong there. But the clinics offer so much to us. In addition to helping the users, we see new drugs on the street before they hit the ED. And we save lives by keeping people out of the ED."

"Is he worried that they're not getting money for seeing the patients?"

I ponder a moment. I hadn't thought of that. Healthcare is no cost to us here in Canada, but the government pays the hospital for every patient we see. "That could be a factor, but it's not like we don't have lines of people twenty-four hours a day." I take a sip of my wine. "I think the hospital is doing fine, but maybe I can make that part of my proposal to him."

"What are you proposing?" she asks.

"A truce."

"Well, if anyone can do it, you can." She nods as if the matter is settled.

I'm moved by her words. She seems so confident in me. That feels good.

The conversation shifts to the drug trial. I give her all the background and explain my challenge in sorting it out.

She looks a bit concerned. "Are they experimenting on the unhoused?"

"When drug trials make it to this phase, human testing

is the final step. But from what I can tell, they've signed waivers."

"What is the drug?"

"I don't have the name. The contract would have that information, but we can't find a copy of it. I sent a sample to the lab, though. I don't want us giving them battery acid."

"How do you know they're paying you? Where is the money going?"

"They always pay, but so far I can't find records, so I don't know what the money's being used for." I shrug. "So far I don't even have anyone to call and ask."

Her brow furrows. "Are you compiling the data? Someone must show up to collect."

I raise my wine to her. "Excellent point. That's another avenue I can explore."

We linger over our glasses, the sun sinking behind the peaks, casting a warm glow. This dinner, this moment, it's more than a meal. It's a celebration of the day, of the unexpected turns that lead to unforgettable experiences.

The stars are out in full force by the time Lucy suggests we head back. The descent from the mountain top is quiet, reflective. We're both lost in the afterglow of dinner and the day's adventures. When our gondola touches down, though our weekend is just beginning, I feel a reluctance to leave the heights, where the world seems simpler. But I'm grateful all over again to have made this move, brought this change into my life.

CHAPTER 12

Lucy

After we woke up this morning, we decided to walk back to ride the gondolas so we could see the view in the morning light. We're currently on our way back up, and I love it here. Other than the village below, there isn't anything but trees and mountains as far as you can see. I press my hands against the cool glass, peering out as the world unfolds below us in an endless tapestry of evergreens and jagged peaks.

Beside me, Chance's eyes widen, a childlike wonder replacing his usual stoic expression. "Wow," he breathes, as if speaking louder might shatter the pristine beauty surrounding us.

"It's something, isn't it?" The top of Blackcomb Mountain greets us with a view that steals the breath from my lungs. When the gondola comes to a stop, Chance steps out onto the platform, his gaze sweeping across the horizon.

I fish my phone out of my pocket, snapping picture after

picture. "Do you have an account? Maybe I can tag you?" I suggest, scrolling through the photos and selecting the best ones.

He shrugs, a sheepish grin tugging at his lips. "Yeah, I've got one. I don't really use it much."

"Mind if I bring you into the twenty-first century?" I tease, already typing in his name, my fingers numb but nimble.

"Go ahead. It's Doctor Rebel." He chuckles, glancing over my shoulder at the screen.

I hit post, and suddenly our moment atop the world is part of the digital ether, tagged and shared. "How did you get that name?"

He looks away. "My ex gave it to me."

I wait for him to explain, but he doesn't. I suppose the Harley and leather jacket are the start of being a rebel. I heard Griffin once call a motorcycle a "donor cycle."

We wander the mountaintop and take a short hike down a ski trail. Suddenly, Chance grabs my arm and points to a large black blob much farther down the trail. Immediately, I recognize it as a black bear. We quickly retreat back to the bustle of the mountaintop and the gondola.

The ride down the mountain is no less exciting than the ride up. We watch mountain bikers race down the trails, jumping and spinning, protected only by a bike helmet.

Once we disembark the gondola, Chance looks around the village. "You up for some lunch?" he asks as he points to Molly McGee's Irish Pub.

I nod, and hunger gnaws at me as we step into the dimly lit Irish bar. I'm already critiquing the place in my mind, noting the mismatched furniture and peeling paint that tries and fails to add character. By the time we slide into a booth, I've mentally calculated the mark-up on their "authentic" Irish stew and am not surprised by the steep prices listed on the laminated menu.

"Bit pricey for pub grub, isn't it?" Chance observes, echoing my thoughts as he scans the menu.

I nod. "Feels like they're charging for the atmosphere

more than the actual meal," I murmur, trying not to let my disappointment show.

Our server approaches, her smile warm. "Hello there, I'm Mary. What can I get for ye today?" Her accent is thick, lyrical, a genuine slice of Ireland in this otherwise contrived setting.

"Your accent's lovely. Where in Ireland are you from?" I ask.

"Ah, thank ye! I'm from a suburb of Dublin. Stillorgan, if ye know it," she responds.

"Never been, but I bet it's beautiful," Chance says, and I nod along, charmed.

Mary laughs. "It's nothing compared to here when the snow starts falling. That's ski season and the whole village comes alive." She gestures around the bar with a flourish that almost makes me forgive the inflated prices. Almost.

"Must be exciting," I say. "Especially coming from Ireland."

"Sure is," she agrees, a wistful note creeping into her voice. "Plenty of us Commonwealth folks come over for a gap-year adventure. Canada's great for that, easy to work and live, ye know?"

"Sounds like the dream," Chance remarks, and I find myself smiling at his ability to find common ground with just about anyone.

"Anyway, what will it be for lunch?" Mary asks with a professional tilt of her head.

I glance at Chance, who seems unfazed by the prices now, and I decide to follow suit. After all, sometimes it's more about the company and the chance to meet people who carry pieces of the world with them.

"You choose," Chance says.

"Two stews, please," I say, handing back the menus. "And could we get two pints of Red Wagon?"

"Coming right up," Mary says, her smile never wavering as she retreats to the kitchen.

"Here's to new experiences." Chance lifts his water glass for a mock toast.

"Even overpriced ones," I add with a laugh, clinking my glass against his.

Later that evening, the soft glow of the television illuminates the room, casting shadows that dance across Chance's relaxed features. He's sprawled on the couch, utterly engrossed in the movie. I'm perched on the edge of the recliner, a safe distance away, nestled under a blanket that does little to ward off the chill of longing.

I want to close this space between us, to snuggle against him and feel the warmth of his body against mine. But I don't because he's made it clear. We're friends. Still, I wonder how long I can stay in this orbit without crashing into the burning atmosphere of my own desires.

He laughs at something onscreen, and I force a smile, but it feels as hollow as the room's echoing acoustics. When he starts to date again, no matter how amazing the woman might be, I know jealousy will color my perception of her. This thought presses against my chest, making it impossible to relax.

"Good movie?" Chance asks during a lull in the action, turning to gauge my thoughts.

"Yeah, it's hilarious," I lie smoothly, the words tasting like ash on my tongue.

"Next time, you pick," he says with an easy grin, seeming oblivious to the storm within me.

"Deal," I reply.

As the credits roll, I stand, stretching my limbs and carefully schooling my features into a mask of nonchalance. "I should probably get some sleep," I tell him.

"Sure, big day tomorrow. Thanks for watching this with me," he says.

"Anytime," I respond. *Why did I think going away for the whole weekend was a good idea? This is too much.* I retreat to my room, closing the door behind me.

Lying in bed, I stare at the ceiling. I love spending time with Chance, but it's already making me want more than he's willing or able to give, and that's not fair to him. Maybe we can't be friends. Though the thought of telling him why makes my stomach knot. I just need to get a handle on myself. Stop volunteering for days-long non-dates.

I move my pillow to cover my face, though I resist the urge to scream into it.

CHAPTER 13

Chance

I wake to the stillness of predawn, the hush of the world holding its breath before the day begins. Slipping out of the sheets, I dress quietly, mindful not to disturb Lucy. I peek into her room. She's sprawled across her bed, a peaceful expression softening her features. I pause for a moment, watching the gentle rise and fall of her chest and feeling the pull of something that could very well be more than friendship. But I can't ignore the fact that my heart is still torn over Céline. I'm surprised at how much I enjoy spending time with Lucy, and it makes me feel guilty for not being able to let go of my past. Still, I know deep down that I'm not ready for a new relationship. Lucy deserves someone who is truly available for her, and at least right now, that person isn't me. And anyway, regardless of what my heart might think it wants, now isn't the time for complicating things. I'm still getting my bearings here in Vancouver.

We agreed on an early start this morning, but I've planned a little surprise for Lucy. I continue down the hall to the kitchen.

"Morning," Lucy mumbles, rubbing the sleep from her eyes as she walks into the living area a few minutes later. She's dressed in yoga pants and a T-shirt. Her hair is tousled, and there's no trace of makeup—she's raw, real, and it's disarmingly attractive.

"Morning," I reply with a grin. "I ordered waffles with strawberries and cream for breakfast with a nice side of thick bacon. It will be delivered shortly."

She nods. "Thank you. That sounds amazing."

I walk over to the espresso machine and make her a cappuccino, and just as I hand it to her, the bell rings with our delivery. "Perfect timing."

We sit down at the table and dig into our waffles.

Lucy moans. "This is so good."

Suddenly, my pants feel a bit too tight. "I thought we could use a bit of pampering before we head home and back to reality," I say casually. "How about we spend some time at the Four Seasons' spa today?"

"Really?" Her eyes light up. "I mean, I suppose that would be okay." She gives me a sly smile.

"Thought you'd like it," I say, my heart doing a strange little flip at the joy in her voice.

Once we finish our breakfast, we head over to the spa. I remind myself yet again why this weekend is perfect as it is—simple and uncomplicated. This ease we have is rare, and the connection I feel with Lucy is something special. But that doesn't mean it has to be anything more than this. For now, I immerse myself in the laughter we share and in the quiet comfort of a friendship in bloom.

"Thanks for this," Lucy says a few hours later, her voice soft with relaxation as we lounge in the tranquility room after our treatments.

"Anytime," I reply. And I mean it. There's always time

for moments like these, for a friend like her.

When we've finished, we stroll through the bustling village one last time, and I soak in Whistler before we head back. The mountain air is warm but carries with it the crisp promise of evening. Shops flaunt their end-of-season sales while late-afternoon adventurers share tales over pints on patios. We're just another pair of contented souls in the crowd, making the most of our borrowed time.

"Hey." Lucy nudges me with her elbow, a mischievous glint in her eye. "Feeling a bit underdressed without your leather armor?"

I chuckle at her jab. It's true; my usual attire is conspicuously absent today. "Yeah, it's strange," I admit, rubbing my forearms. "But it's way too hot for that. I'm not about to pass out from heatstroke on a mini vacation."

"Good call," she laughs, bumping her shoulder against mine. "Besides, you look good without it. More...approachable. And the weather is going to change. We'll have rain in just a few weeks."

"Right. Like you said, I need to get a car. I don't want to take a shower when I get to work and again when I get home."

Our laughter lingers in the air as we continue to meander, and eventually, we make our way back to the condo, where the afternoon sunlight slants through the windows, casting long shadows across the floor. The silence feels heavy with our imminent return to normalcy.

I'm rolling up my shirts, methodically placing them in my duffel bag, when my phone buzzes on the nightstand. A familiar name flashes on the screen, *Céline*. My chest tightens. It's been months since we last spoke, since she made it clear she wasn't moving here. Still, old habits die hard, and some part of me wants to answer, even if it's just to fall back into the pattern of soothing her worries. But I let it go to voicemail.

The buzzing stops, only to be replaced by the ping of a new message. I pick up the phone, pressing play, and Céline's voice fills the room—strained, pleading. "Chance, please, come home. Why haven't you called? Just…please come back to me."

Her words hang in the air. *Good heavens, she hasn't moved on at all.* A twinge of guilt seizes me. But what do I have to be guilty for? I set the phone back down, closing my eyes for a moment to steady the storm of feelings within.

"Everything okay?" Lucy's voice drifts from the doorway.

"Fine," I reply, forcing a smile as I zip up my bag. "Just ready to hit the road."

She nods, though I can tell she's unconvinced. "Let's get going."

We load up the car, and the drive back is quiet at first. But as the miles unwind, so does the tension, and slowly, conversation resumes.

I'm grateful for that, and for Lucy's presence beside me, which has become a refuge in ways I hadn't expected.

"Home stretch," Lucy says as the traffic thickens and the Lions Gate Bridge comes into view in the distance.

"Looking forward to it," I reply.

I should be soaking it all in, the end of a perfect escape, but my thoughts are stuck on Céline's pleading words, the emotional echo of her voicemail on repeat in my head. It's absurd to think I'm betraying her. We're not together. She ended things. We made a plan, and she changed her mind. It's not my fault if she's changed it again. Yet guilt has a way of clouding judgment, of coloring moments that should be clear.

As North Vancouver creeps into view, I force myself to focus on the present. To be mindful of where I am. "Can you believe everything we did this weekend? And the stunning views," I marvel.

"Nature's way of showing off," Lucy quips, her grin wide. "Just like you."

"Like me? A showoff? I'll add that to my resume," I tease.

"Absolutely. You ride a big, loud motorcycle," she says. "And you can also add 'Expert in Surviving Road Trips with

Lucy.'"

"Surviving? Please, I could thrive on these trips." The words come easily, truth mingled with playful exaggeration. It's remarkable, really, how much I've enjoyed myself, how — for a time, at least — my worries melted away in her company.

"Thrive, huh?" She glances over, her eyes dancing. "Well, let's see if you can handle a real challenge next time. Maybe some rock climbing in Squamish?"

"Challenge accepted." There's a thrill in agreeing, a forward-looking excitement that's been absent in my life for too long.

We lapse into a comfortable silence as we near the end of our trip. There's something about Lucy, something undeniable and liberating, that makes me want to embrace the unknown, the very thing I once avoided at all costs.

For now, I push aside my conflict and returning worries and allow myself to be carried by the joy that seems to come so effortlessly when I'm with her.

Early the next morning, the shrill ring of my phone breaks through my dreams. I fumble for it, heart hammering. Usually, these calls are from the hospital and never good. My eyes aren't fully open, but I'm halfway out of bed when I press the device to my ear and mumble a groggy, "Dr. Devereaux."

"Chance? It's me."

It's Céline. Her voice is like a bolt of electricity through my sleepy haze, and suddenly, I'm wide awake, trying to concentrate on what she's saying in French since I even dream in English these days.

"Hey," I say, trying to sound casual. She's the last person

I'd expect to call at this hour. She's not a morning person, and I haven't called her back after the message she left.

"I saw your pictures online...with her." There's an edge to her words that sets off a fresh wave of alarms in my head.

I groan internally, feeling like some love-stricken teenager caught cheating. Except I haven't cheated. We're over. She made sure of that. "Céline, Lucy's just a friend," I assure her. "She's been showing me around the area, that's all."

The line crackles with silence for a moment; then I hear her sharp intake of breath. "It looks like more than that," she accuses.

I can almost see her brows knitting together, lips pursed as her jealousy flares.

"Come on, Céline." My fingers drum against my thigh, frustration simmering. "You decided to stay in Montreal."

There's a pause, and then a soft sob slips down the line. "I miss you. I want you to come back. Vancouver is so far from everyone — my friends, my family, you — I need you here."

Her plea tugs at something deep within me, a mixture of longing and bitterness. "Céline," I begin, but I'm not sure what to say. The room feels too small, the darkness pressing in from every corner.

"Please..." Her voice breaks, and for a second, I'm transported back to a time when her happiness was my priority. But that was before everything changed. Before I realized she didn't consider my happiness in remotely the same way.

"Montreal isn't my home anymore," I remind her, and there's a finality to the words. "You chose to stay there after we made plans and I signed a contract at the hospital."

"But I need you," she insists, her voice thick with tears.

The weight of the phone feels like an anchor in my hand. "I've signed a contract for three years, Céline," I say. "It's not as simple as just packing up and heading back."

"Your old hospital will take you. They always need good doctors," she counters.

I shake my head, though she can't see me. The hospital politics at my old job is a tango I have no desire to return to, and I left Montreal because I wanted something different. "I don't want to go back," I insist, pressing my free hand against my forehead. "If you miss me so much, come here."

"There?" Her voice rises in pitch, incredulous. "To Vancouver?"

"Yes. There are plenty of people from Quebec here. Many people here speak French. And you can find work easily here as a massage therapist. Just like we planned." My heart thumps in my chest, betraying the part of me that still yearns for her despite everything.

There's a protracted silence on the other end. Finally, she exhales. "It's so far from all of our friends and family," she murmurs.

"I know." It's all I can manage, and after that, it's not long before she disconnects the call.

I sit on the bed, the ghost of our conversation hanging heavy in the air. Why did I ask her again to come here? I know her patterns, the way she can waltz into my life and leave chaos in her wake. She's hurt me before, and logic dictates she'll do it again.

Yet there's that sliver of hope that wonders if this time might be different. If she could just summon the courage to give this a try… But deep down, I know better. I know that Céline walking through the door means inviting the storm back into my life.

I wrench myself from the tangle of sheets as dawn peeks through the blinds, then climb the stairs toward Ginny's part of the house to knock gently.

"Chance?" she calls through the barrier.

"Yes, it's me." She unlocks and opens the door between our two homes. She's wrapped in layers of cardigans, her face strained.

"Still no hot water?" I ask.

"Unfortunately not," she murmurs, managing a weak

smile.

"Let me take care of it." While the cold showers are a great wake-up call, it's been three weeks, and she doesn't have hot water either. I step back into my part of the house and dial the local plumber. The phone rings twice before a sleepy voice answers. I explain the situation, insist that they bill me for the work, and hang up with an assurance that help is on the way.

I return to Ginny. "The plumber should be here soon." I put my coat on and head for the door.

Her hands flutter to her mouth. "But Chance, I can't—"

"Hey," I cut her off gently. "Don't worry about it. We'll deduct five dollars from my rent each month until we're even, okay?"

After a moment, she nods. "You are too kind," she says.

"Take care, Ginny. I'll check in after work."

She waves and watches as I mount my bike. I need to make sure she's comfortable. She's been like a surrogate mother since I moved in. It doesn't sit right with me to see her in distress over something as basic as hot water.

And I feel better knowing this problem will be solved too. It will be nice to have hot water at home again, of course, but there's also something healing for me about helping someone else, a salve for the wounds I can't quite seem to mend within myself.

CHAPTER 14

Lucy

The final bell rings on Monday afternoon, unleashing a torrent of students into the sunlit corridors. As I weave through the crowd, my phone pings with a text.

Dad: Beatrice is out again. Can you cover?

Frustration rushes through me. He needs to do something about her. Her job is what allows her to stay in Canada. Without it, she's supposed to return to Ireland. Maybe I can move things around with Chance…

Me: Only till eight. I have dinner plans.

A feel a twinge of guilt for compromising what I already have in place and disrupting Chance's evening as well.

Dad: Thank you. I owe you one.

As I exit the school building, I grip my phone tighter, the edges digging into my palm. My disdain for Beatrice's lack of commitment to her job grows. If it was a serious problem, why wouldn't she just say so? Or ask to change her schedule? Near as I can tell, she just comes to work when she feels like it.

I pull out my phone and open the reservation app. A tap and a swipe, and our table for two at Zeffirelli's evaporates into the ether. With a heavy heart, I send Chance a message.

Me: Work emergency at the pub. Beatrice is out again, and I need to help my dad. I canceled dinner at Zeffirelli's.

I wait, watching the gray dots bubble up then vanish. Once. Twice. No response. Anxiety creeps up my neck as I imagine him disappointed or, worse, annoyed. But no, that's not Chance. He's understanding. He knows the crazy my life can be. And anyway, it's not like I owe him something. We're just friends.

Me: But I'm only covering until 8. Maybe we could meet later?

Chance: Okay. Thanks for letting me know.

I pocket my phone, stride toward my car, and drive to the pub.

A couple hours later, Barney's is in full swing, a blur of clinking dishes and chattering patrons, when Chance walks in a little before eight. He's the calm in the eye of the storm, dressed in dark jeans that fit just right and a T-shirt that outlines his physique, the kind of casual look that somehow seems put together on him.

"Hey." He greets me with that easygoing smile, which never fails to lift the corners of my mouth in response. "I was able to get a late reservation at Zeffirelli's. But after a long day at school and working here, are you up for going out?"

I exhale, feeling tension drain from my shoulders. "Yes, please." I tuck a stray lock of hair behind my ear. "Just give me a sec to finish up."

The ride over in the ride to Zeffirelli's is quiet, the city lights streaking by as we sink into the comfortable silence that has become our unspoken language.

When we arrive, the maître d' welcomes us. "Buona sera," he says.

"Buona sera," Chance replies.

What language does this man not speak?

The host leads us to a cozy table for two tucked away in a dimly lit corner.

The server immediately brings water, and we peruse the menu. Everything looks good, as it isn't Irish pub food. When the server returns, I still haven't made up my mind. "You first," I tell Chance. "I'll figure it out."

"Spaghetti and meatballs for me," he tells the server, handing back the menu with a confident nod.

I scan the options once more before settling on baked ziti, comfort food for a night that's taken an unexpected turn.

"House Chianti?" Chance suggests, raising an eyebrow.

"Sounds perfect."

Moments later, the server returns to pour ruby red wine into our glasses.

We raise them in a silent toast, the clink of glass echoing softly. Then Chance leans forward, the warm glow of the candle between us casting shadows across his face. And there it is— that scent. Woodsy, with a hint of cinnamon. It envelops me like autumn itself has decided to sit down at our table. I take a deep breath, trying to focus on the here and now, not the fluttering in my chest or the way my thoughts scatter.

Friends, I remind myself, hoping my hooha gets the message loud and clear. But it's hard, so much harder than it should be, with him sitting across from me, looking like every dream I've told myself not to have.

"How was school today?" Chance's voice brings me back, and I realize I've been staring.

"Sorry," I say, shaking the daze from my mind. "It was good. Everyone is a little frazzled on Mondays, but we made it."

"Can't argue with that."

"How about your day?" I ask.

"There's a full moon tonight, so I'm glad I'm off. But the pull of the moon is real."

He regales me with a story about an elderly woman who brought her cat in and a little boy who took a bad fall and broke his arm. I love hearing about his work. He has an exciting life.

Our dinner arrives, and we continue talking about everything and nothing. *Friends*. It's easy because we're friends. There's no sexual tension.

"Oh, I finally met the drug rep on the study."

My ears perk up. "Really? What did you learn?"

"The medication is a combination of psychotropic drugs for behavioral control and immune-system enhancers. And that matches what the lab told me."

"Do the test subjects know this when you give them the meds?"

"They give them a spiel, but they should be monitored if we're going to give them psychotropics."

I nod. That makes sense. "Are you going to stop doing the trial?"

He sighs. "I need the contract first. I need to know more. The rep is going to bring it in, and he'll also find out where the money is being deposited."

"You don't think your predecessor is taking that money, do you?"

He grimaces. "I don't know what to think yet."

My gaze traces his outline as Chance twirls spaghetti around his fork. Who am I fooling? Given the chance, I'd climb the man like a tree.

"So, are the kids still talking about my visit?" he asks.

"They haven't stopped talking about it," I report, feeling a bubble of pride. "Aleksander told everyone he wants to be a doctor now. Says he's going to go back to Ukraine one day to help those who are sick."

"Wow, I love that." Chance sets his fork down. "I didn't realize I made such an impression."

"You did," I assure him, and we share a smile.

A pause lingers between us, comfortable yet charged. "So," I ask, "you being a man of the world and all, how many languages can you speak?"

He chuckles. "Fluently? Just French and English." He takes a sip of Chianti, his gaze holding mine. "But, you know, being in medicine, you pick up bits and pieces. I can ask basic medical questions in about half a dozen languages. Helps patients feel at ease if you can speak to them in their own tongue, even if it's just a little."

"Half a dozen, huh?" I shake my head. "That's pretty incredible."

Chance shrugs modestly. It's clear he doesn't do it to show off. He cares about people and making a difference.

"Tell me more about you," he says. "I've learned a lot about Vancouver, but not so much about who you are."

I take a deep breath; something in his earnest gaze tells me it's okay to let down my walls. "My mother came with us when we moved from Ireland," I begin. "But she passed away several years ago. Most people think she died in a car accident or something mundane. But that's not true." My hands tremble, so I interlace them on the table. "She...she took her own life. Pills. I was the one who found her."

Chance's expression softens, and he reaches across the table, his hand hovering a moment before settling atop mine. "I can't even imagine how hard that must have been," he says softly.

I nod, looking down at our hands. "It's not something I tell people often. It feels like I'm burdening them."

"Thank you for trusting me," he responds.

I lift my gaze, meeting his once more, and the ache inside me eases just a fraction. "My mom was unhappy in Dublin. My dad did…some questionable things to get us out." My chest tightens at the memory. "But even after we moved to Vancouver, she couldn't find the happiness she was searching for."

"Lucy," Chance murmurs, his other hand now enclosing mine between his warm palms. "Your strength is remarkable."

"Strength?" I echo, almost scoffing at the word. But as I look into Chance's eyes, I see no pity, only admiration.

"Absolutely," he insists. "To go through that and still be here, sharing your story with me? That takes courage."

Suddenly, in this small Italian restaurant, with the scent of garlic and basil in the air, I feel a strange sense of release, a sliver of peace in acknowledging the scars of my past.

The warmth from the Chianti blushes through my cheeks, and the moment passes. Chance once again twirls his spaghetti around his fork. An impulsive thought races through my mind, igniting a reckless desire to leap over the table and press my body against his. But I squash the thought as I steady my breathing. "Chance," I ask, looking to ground myself in reality, "do you ever hear from Céline?"

He pauses mid-twirl, his blue eyes meeting mine. "She called the morning after we got back from Whistler," he says, setting down his fork. "Céline is… She's perpetually dissatisfied. I've decided she likes to be unhappy about something all the time. She was unhappy living in Quebec. It's cold for too long, the jobs are less than ideal, the government is crooked… So we came up with a solution. We'd move here and start over. I found a job, and we readied to move, but then she decided to stay."

As he speaks of her, it seems he's made peace with a situation beyond his control. He seems resigned, a stark contrast to the fire I feel simmering within me.

"At first, she was on board with coming to Vancouver?" I prod, swirling the wine in my glass.

"Yeah." Chance nods, a wry smile touching the corner of his mouth. "She thought it would be a new start. She was out of work and feeling stuck. But in the end, she couldn't make the leap. And some people carry their clouds with them, no matter where they go."

"Sometimes leaving isn't enough," I agree softly.

"Exactly," he says, reaching for his glass. "It's about finding happiness within, not just changing the scenery."

CHAPTER 15

Chance

The next morning, I blink into the soft light filtering through my bedroom curtains, noting a lightness in my chest. As I stretch, my muscles waking up with the day, it hits me — no dreams of Céline last night. That's a first since... I can't even remember. Always, she's been there, dancing at the edges of my sleep, but not this time. It's strange, unsettling almost, but there's a hint of freedom too, like fresh air after a long confinement.

I sit up, the sheet pooling around my waist, and my thoughts drift to Lucy. Our conversation from last night replays in my mind. I told her things about Céline that had never crossed my lips before. Why? What is it about Lucy that cracks open my vault of secrets?

The clock on my nightstand tells me it's still early, but my mind's already racing ahead to tonight — Lucy's date. She told me was going out with another teacher this evening, someone she met at a training session. She mentioned him in passing as we were heading home, her words breezy, but they left a mark on me, heavy as lead.

I swing my legs out of bed, feet finding the cold hardwood floor. I should be okay with Lucy dating someone. She's just a friend. Yet there's a gnawing feeling in my gut. It's not jealousy—I'm not that guy—but something stirs, something territorial. I told her I was still getting over Céline, but what if I might be ready for more with her?

Would she want that? How do I navigate this? Maybe it's not even real. But something in me wonders what it would be like if Lucy looked at me and saw more than just a friend.

Right now, I need to get into the hospital. And the pitter-patter of rain against the window yet again reminds me that I need to find a vehicle. But today, I need to get paperwork done and dig deeper into the Prometheus Health drug trial.

I arrive at the ED to find that one of the doctors scheduled today had a last-minute emergency. So rather than order a locum—a doctor temp—I step in to help. I'm determined to get to the bottom of the drug-trial situation, but locums cost me almost twice as much as my docs cost, and the one who's out today is still getting paid. I'd rather put money toward the nursing staff.

The shift passes with its usual assortment of illness and injury, and hours later, after a long day in the emergency department, I stop off in my office briefly. But I don't have the mental strength left to make progress on this drug-trial mystery. Instead, I head across the street and push open the door to Barney's.

It's an attempt at normalcy, but I find that being here just sends my thoughts toward Lucy and her date. Janelle, with her perpetual smirk and a notepad ready in hand, glides over to my spot at the counter.

"Hey, Chance." She pushes a menu across the polished surface. "What brings you here? Didn't Lucy tell you she had a date tonight?"

"She did," I confess, rubbing the back of my neck. "I'm trying not to think about that."

Janelle raises an eyebrow, pouring me a glass of water. "Oh yeah? Well, I've heard about him." She leans in conspiratorially, her voice dropping to a whisper. "He canceled on her last week, then sent some picture that made Lucy go red as a tomato — not in a good way if you catch my drift."

My grip tightens around the glass, a surge of protectiveness flaring within me. The thought of someone disrespecting Lucy like that... "Seriously?"

"Yep," Janelle confirms, polishing a glass with more vigor than necessary. "And from what I hear, he's the type who thinks a fancy dinner means he's entitled to...more."

Something stirs within me, dark and unpleasant in my chest. Even if Lucy and I are just friends — *only friends* — this sounds like bad news for her.

"Chance, you've got that look," Janelle observes, snapping me out of my storm of emotions.

"What look?" I ask, feigning ignorance.

"The I'm-going-to-do-something-stupid look," she replies.

"Maybe I should check on her after," I muse, the words spilling out before I can stop them.

"Isn't that a bit...more than friend-like?" Janelle probes.

"I think it's exactly what a friend should do," I counter. But she appears to see right through me. "Maybe," I concede. "Either way, I can't shake this feeling. Something's off."

"Off enough to lose sleep before your early hospital shift tomorrow?" she asks, perhaps making one last attempt to tether me to reason.

"Apparently," I reply with a shrug. I need to make sure Lucy is okay.

Concern for a friend — that's all this is. At least, that's what I tell myself as I decline to order anything and, instead, take my bike over to Lucy's apartment. It's still pretty early. She may not be home. *Will I wait around until she gets there?*

In no time, I stand at the entrance of Lucy's building, my finger hovering over her buzzer. The night air is cool against my skin, a contrast to the heat in my chest. I press the button before doubt can change my mind.

"Hello?" Her voice crackles through the speaker, steadying my racing heart.

"Hey, it's Chance. Can I come up?"

"Sure, I'll buzz you in."

The door clicks open, and I step inside to climb the stairs two at a time. *What am I doing here?* Janelle's words echo in my head, but they're drowned out by the louder drum of my own concern — or is it jealousy?

When I reach her door and knock, it swings open almost immediately, revealing Lucy in yoga pants and a T-shirt, her eyes wide. "What are you doing here?"

"Janelle and I were worried about you," I admit, my throat tight.

She steps aside, allowing me entry. I cross the threshold, suddenly aware of how intimate this unexpected visit feels.

"Really? Why?" There's warmth in her smile, but confusion lingers in her furrowed brow.

"Your date… We just wanted to make sure everything went okay." My hands slip into my pockets.

Lucy lets out a soft chuckle as she closes the door behind me. "We had dinner, and I came home. That's pretty much the whole story. No chemistry there."

Relief filters through me. Yet, as I watch her, I'm unable to fully grasp why I'm so rattled.

"I was going to make myself a cup of tea. Would you like one?" Lucy offers.

My thoughts bounce every which way. I don't know what to do, now that I'm here and she's okay. "Sure."

Lucy moves about making tea. The kettle whistles a soft tune, and she pours the steaming water into two mugs, a faint aroma of chamomile lifting into the space between us.

"Want to tell me about your evening?" I finally get out.

We settle onto her couch, and she starts in on the details. She wraps her fingers around her mug, and her voice carries a tiredness that wasn't there yesterday. "And then, when I told him about an incident with a student who wouldn't focus..." She pauses and takes a sip. "He started lecturing me on classroom management, as if I haven't been doing this for years."

I lean back, my own mug cradled in my hands, and listen. There's an earnestness in her venting, a need to be heard and not advised. And so, I offer silence, a nod, a small smile where it fits, but mostly, I just take her in.

The slope of her neck draws my gaze as she tilts her head back, laughing at the absurdity of her date's arrogance. It's an elegant line that runs down to her shoulders, disappearing under the fabric of her shirt. Strands of her auburn hair escape her bun, curling rebelliously against her skin.

My eyes trace the contours of her face, lingering on the soft curve of her lips as she talks, the way she bites the lower one when she's in deep thought. It's easy to get lost in the details of her, the ones I've memorized unknowingly, unintentionally.

"Lucy..." I find myself interrupting, my curiosity piqued by something that's nagged at me for a while now. "Why do you always wear your hair up?"

She blinks, seeming surprised by the question, and reaches up to touch the twisted knot at the back of her head. "Oh." A small laugh escapes her. "Silly reason, really. When I was a kid, children used to tease me about being a 'carrot top'. So, I guess I just got used to hiding it away."

"Hide it? But it's beautiful," I say before I can stop myself, my words more than a compliment. They're an admission, a revelation of sorts.

Her cheeks flush a shade that rivals the fiery strands, and she looks away with a bashful smile. "Thank you," she murmurs.

The air shifts slightly, charged with something new. I

clear my throat, hoping to steer us back to safer waters.

But I don't know what to say. I look around, and the ping of fat raindrops begins its tune on her patio. "Is it early for this much rain?"

Lucy laughs. "Nope. It's a little late actually. How's the Harley these days?"

"Ready for the garage. I really need to go shopping for that car. Are you still okay with getting your friend to offer me that discount? I've checked out the Explorer, and I think that would be a good vehicle for me."

"I'll call him tomorrow and see if he can meet us. Do you have a color in mind?"

"No. Whatever is fine, unless it's some strange pink or something. White or black would be perfect."

She picks up her phone and sends a text. It immediately pings back. "Looks like he has a new shipment coming in later this week, and he can see us this weekend."

"Great. Thank you."

"No problem. We can go Saturday afternoon, maybe?"

"Great." I look out at the rain. "Anyway, tell me more about this guy. He sounds like a real piece of work."

She begins to speak again, and I'm perched on the edge of her couch. She's so close that if I shifted just a bit, our knees would touch. A part of me aches to bridge that gap, to lean in and confirm whether her lips are as soft as they look. But then I'd cross a line that can't be uncrossed, wouldn't I? And I'd go against everything I've told her about where I am right now. I exhale slowly, watching the steam curl from my tea and vanish into the air.

"Chance?" Her voice is gentle, tinged with concern, and it pulls me back from the precipice of reckless decisions.

"Yeah?" I manage.

"Is everything okay? You seem...distant."

I offer her a lopsided smile, a shield against the truth of how close I am to shattering our comfortable camaraderie. "Just tired, I guess." It's not a lie, not entirely. The weight of

CHAPTER 17

Chance

My new car keys jingle in my pocket. I'm really glad Lucy got me the deal on the SUV. I don't miss being soaked after every ride home, and even though driving a car puts me in the awful traffic longer, all the bells and whistles make it worth it.

This week has started out better without all the extra time showering and drying off from the rain, but today's still ending with a visit to Dr. Johns. Nothing's perfect, and this needs to be done. I stop when I reach the door marked *Chief Medical Officer*. The brass plaque glints under the harsh fluorescent lights, and I take a deep breath to steady my resolve.

I smile at Dr. Johns's admin. "Good afternoon, Catherine. I think he's expecting me."

She smiles wide. "Go ahead and knock on the door."

I give it three hard raps and wait.

"Come in," calls a voice from within.

images of him instead of Jamie.

"Lucy," Tiffany says softly, her eyes gentle, "it's okay to feel things. We're human."

I nod, sucking in a breath. "I know," I murmur, "but feelings just complicate everything." I focus on the rich, dark swirls of coffee in my mug. *Just friends*, I remind myself fiercely. *That's all we are. That's all we'll ever be.*

I look up at Tiffany and Janelle. "Chance is just... He's uncomplicated," I say, forcing a laugh. "You know? He never oversteps, never assumes too much."

Janelle sips her latte, eyebrow quirked. "Sounds perfect to me."

"Too perfect," I admit, the admission pricking at my pride. "We go out, we have a blast, and then nothing. He drops me off, gives me this brotherly hug, and that's it." My fingers tighten around my mug. "He has this way of making me feel so...safe and yet so off-limits."

Tiffany rests her chin on her hand. "And that's what's making you crazy, isn't it?"

"Yes," I confess. "Because I'm angry at myself for having these feelings. For wanting more than what we have." I shake my head. "It's like he's drawn this line, and I'm the one who keeps looking over it, wondering what if?"

"Lucy, honey, frustration is love's annoying cousin," Tiffany says, her eyes sympathetic.

"Annoying is right," I mutter, taking another sip of my coffee. "And the worst part? I think the reason he felt the need to friend-zone me in the first place is because our chemistry is obvious. We get along great, and I suspect both of us feel things, but we may never actually act on them."

Tiffany nods. "Sam will take good care of him. Chance is lucky you're doing that for him."

Janelle hesitates and then meets my eyes with a sheepish tilt of her head. "Lucy, I need to confess something. I...told Chance about your experiences with Jamie before your date."

I shake my head. "He showed up at my place that night. I'd told him I had a date. He said you both had been worried, so he was checking to make sure I got home okay."

"I know that man is dealing with his ex, but he is into you," Janelle counters. "I can see it with my own eyes."

I look pointedly at her. "What did you tell him about Jamie?"

She shrugs. "Just that he sent you a dick pic and I was sure you were going to land in bed together."

My eyes grow wide. "Janelle! I can't believe you! You knew there was no way I would sleep with him, especially after that picture."

Janelle narrows her eyes. "I knew nothing of the sort. I didn't know he'd mansplain teaching to you. But regardless, telling Chance about it had exactly the effect I thought it would. He went straight to you."

My thoughts swirl, and Janelle gives Tiffany an I-told-you-so look before she turns back to me.

"Chance wouldn't let anyone bulldoze you," Tiffany says.

"Exactly," I reply, feeling a reluctant smile tugging at my lips. "With him, it's easy. No expectations, no mansplaining, just...fun."

"Sounds like someone prefers the company of our dear Dr. Friend Zone," Janelle teases, nudging my arm.

I feel my cheeks heat, and I press my lips together, trying to steer my runaway thoughts back on track. "I don't— It's not like that," I stammer, though the flutter in my stomach tells a different story. After Chance left my place that night, I lay awake, restless and wound tight with unwanted yearning. And then I managed the issue, my mind shamelessly painting vivid half the menu. And I mean just for himself. It was like watching a nature documentary on feeding frenzies."

"Are you serious?" Tiffany's eyes widen.

"Dead serious. He barely came up for air between bites. It was like dinner theater, minus the entertainment." I pause to sip my coffee, which does little to wash down the embarrassment. "And then, as if his culinary performance wasn't enough, he had the audacity to split the bill. Fifty-fifty, as though he was doing me a favor by having me pay for food I barely touched."

"Ugh, that's the worst," Janelle says, shaking her head.

"Wait, it gets better," I add. "During the meal, we talked about some of the issues we face in our classrooms. You both know a lot of mine are about the economic challenges my kids face. He works in West Van, and all his school does is ask for money and it comes pouring in. So he spent all this time talking about how we're not asking our parents for money *the right way*, and then he segued to how I could be a better teacher. You know, because apparently my years of experience amount to nothing compared to his infinite wisdom."

"Did you remind him you teach different grades in different cities?" Tiffany asks, seeming puzzled.

"Of course. But according to him, teaching is teaching." I roll my eyes, feeling the frustration bubble up again. "I swear, I would've paid for his entire gluttonous feast if it meant I could have escaped earlier."

"Sounds like Jamie needs a lesson in manners more than anything else," Janelle comments.

My friends' sympathetic looks are a comfort, but they do little to erase the sting of humiliation. *Why do I do this to myself?* I take another gulp of my latte, wishing it were strong enough to erase the memory.

"Anyway, onward and upward. I've got other things to do. I'm meeting Chance later today and taking him over to see Sam. He's ready to store the motorcycle and buy a car. He's looking at an Explorer."

CHAPTER 16

Lucy

Thank goodness I was able to vent to Chase on Tuesday night because I wouldn't have made it until I could talk to Tiffany and Janelle again. It's Saturday morning before we're able to get together. But now, the sun filters through the café windows, casting a warm glow over the small table where we cradle our coffee cups. My head throbs with the memory of last week's disaster.

"Okay, spill it," Tiffany urges. "I've been waiting until we're not at school."

I take a deep breath. "So, I went out with Jamie on Tuesday," I begin, the words leaving a bitter taste not even my caramel latte can mask.

"Right. The one from the district learning event," Janelle confirms.

"Yep, the very same," I reply. "We hit this Indian restaurant he picked. Decent place, but he proceeded to order unspoken words is exhausting.

She nods, accepting my excuse without question, and I'm grateful. I value what we have—this easy friendship, her laughter, the way she trusts me enough to share the raw edges of her day and her life. Would I risk losing all that for a moment of selfish indulgence? Because that's what it would be—selfish. Lucy deserves more than a clumsy advance borne of jealousy and a moment of weakness.

"Lucy," I start, my voice firmer now, the decision made, "we haven't known each other long, but you've been such a wonderful friend to me. I'm here for you, always. And I want you to value yourself. Make sure your dates are worthy of your time." I manage a smile, but my words are a vow, an anchor grounding me to the role I've chosen.

Her eyes soften, gratitude and something deeper gleaming within their depths. "Thank you. That means a lot."

I take a sip of my tea, letting the heat move over my tongue, washing away the remnants of temptation. Tonight isn't about what I want or don't want. It's about being here for her.

"Anytime," I say, and I mean it. We're friends, and that's enough. It has to be.

I enter to find Dr. Johns hunched over his desk, glasses perched precariously on the bridge of his nose, peering at a mountain of paperwork. He looks up, the lines in his forehead deepening. "Chance, what can I do for you?"

"I wanted to speak with you about Prometheus Health Solutions." I'm direct, no time for pleasantries as I take a seat. "Do you know anything about a drug trial they're running through our ED?"

His brows knit together. "Prometheus Health Solutions?" He shakes his head, pushing back his chair with a muted screech. "I don't know what you're talking about."

I can't tell if he's playing dumb or genuinely clueless. Either way, I need to press on. Reaching into the satchel slung across my chest, I retrieve some of the paperwork Eleanor left behind. It's a lot of data points and annotations but not much synthesis that makes sense. Without a word, I set it before him, the papers sprawling across his orderly desk.

Dr. Johns leans forward, adjusting his glasses and begins to sift through the documents. The initial skepticism on his face dissolves into concern as he turns the pages. He's silent, and I watch his eyes track back and forth, consuming the information that I hope will spur him to action.

"Where did you get this?" he finally asks, not looking up from the report.

"Eleanor left it. It's an ongoing drug trial, but William Long in legal doesn't have a contract. I don't know who to speak with or even where to submit our findings. I have reports that go back over a year," I explain, keeping my tone even. "It seems Eleanore had been compiling the data for them."

He doesn't respond immediately, his focus still tethered to the pages beneath his fingertips. I wait.

"Prometheus Health Solutions," Dr. Johns mutters again, finally looking up from the report with furrowed brows. "I remember a drug rep came by, dropped off some…gifts." He waves a hand dismissively as if the thought of such perks is trivial, but I can see the discomfort in his eyes.

"Gifts?" I probe, leaning forward in my chair.

He sighs. "iPads for all the staff, a couple of lunches to 'thank us for our time.' It's not unusual in this business, but…" He trails off and glances at the documents again, a silent admission that the swag might be more than just corporate generosity.

"Look into it," I press. "Please. There's something off about this trial."

He nods, his expression hardening. "I will. Give me some time."

"Thanks," I say, standing. "I appreciate that."

As I return to the ground floor, the conversation with Dr. Johns lingers in my mind. He didn't have a clue what my predecessor was doing. Why is that? I push my concerns aside for now. There are other things, lighter things, waiting for me beyond this hospital.

Exiting the building, the cool evening air is welcome against my tired face. I pull out my phone, the light from the screen cutting through the dusk. There's a message from Lucy. A picture loads, and I'm staring at a child's painting—vibrant colors, bold strokes, and there, unmistakably, is a figure in a white coat, stethoscope around the neck, a benevolent smile painted on its face.

Aleksander's artwork. I feel myself grinning. It's humbling, touching even, how a simple visit could mean so much to a kid.

Me: Tell Aleksander he's got a fan in me.

Stowing the phone in my pocket, I head to my new Explorer and make my way home, smiling all the way. Small victories like this remind me why I do what I do, both inside the hospital and out.

Back home, I lean against my kitchen counter and fire off another text to Lucy.

Me: Had a Houdini on our hands today. A patient with an enlarged prostate tried to make a break for it. Security caught him hiding behind the vending machines!

Almost immediately, my phone buzzes with her reply, a string of emojis that convey raucous laughter. The corners of my mouth tug upward. I take a sip from my lukewarm coffee, considering the ease between us, how conversations with Lucy never need a roadmap. They just...flow. The thought is comforting—and unexpectedly thrilling.

Later, as I'm sprawled on the couch, flipping through channels, the familiar ping sounds again from my phone. My pulse quickens, hoping it's Lucy with tales from Barney's, maybe even inviting me over.

But the name on the screen isn't Lucy's. It's Céline. My heart doesn't just drop. It plummets. And a knot tightens in my stomach. There's no escaping the past when it clings to your present with the persistence of a shadow.

Céline: Comment ça va? I miss you.

The words hover in the air, even as I put the phone face down on the coffee table, leaving the message marked unread. Every time I try to forget her, it's like she senses this and reaches out. With a deep breath, I try to shake off the unwelcome intrusion and refocus on the here and now, where thoughts of Lucy offer me comfort.

The television drones on, a low murmur in the solitude of my apartment. Another ping, and my gaze flits back to the phone.

Céline: I've been thinking about you. How are you?

My thumb hovers over the screen, feeling an instinctive twitch to reply, to fall into old patterns. But no, not this time. I let out a sigh and press the power button until the display dims and quiets.

I lean back, pressing my head against the couch, willing Céline to move on so I can too. It's time to cut these threads that bind me to a past that chose to stay behind in Montreal. And that more and more seems like it wasn't right for me anyway.

Lucy. Her laughter surfaces in my memory. It's her face, bright with humor and sincerity, that fills my thoughts more often than not these days. Keeping it friendly with her is becoming more and more difficult. Despite what I told her I wanted, every text, every glance, seems laden with something deeper. It's getting harder to ignore the current pulling us closer, harder still to ignore what I want to happen.

"Keep it simple," I mutter to myself, pushing off the couch. Simple is safe. Simple is uncomplicated. But with every laugh we share, every inside joke, I'm realizing all the things I didn't have with Céline.

CHAPTER 18

Chance

It's been a long day, and I need to see Lucy. Though we text most days, it's been nearly a week since I've actually seen her. Last weekend, I helped out covering extra shifts, and she worked at Barney's. I'm hoping that's where I'll find her tonight. Pushing open the door, I survey the scene in what has become my favorite hangout. Janelle saunters over and places a pint in front of me, her voice a casual lilt. "So, Lucy's got another date tonight."

"Oh?" I keep my voice level, feigning disinterest. *A date? Again?* And not a word about it from Lucy herself. That gnaws at me, this omission. But it shouldn't. We're just friends. She's got lots of others to confide in as well.

"Yep, saw her swipe right on some dude with a six-pack and a puppy. Typical." Janelle smirks.

"Good for her," I manage, putting my glass down harder than I intended. The clang echoes, much like the dull thud in my chest.

"Sure you don't want to know more? I could play spy…" She waggles her eyebrows.

I shake my head. "No need. She can handle herself."

Yet the thought festers as the night drags on—Lucy laughing at someone else's jokes, leaning into another man's touch.

I order dinner and eat alone.

Why didn't she tell me she had a date?

If I'm this upset that she's on a date, what will it be like when she's serious with someone?

What if she falls for this guy?

What if he won't let us be friends anymore?

Okay, that last one is a little ridiculous, but I don't have good answers for any of the questions rattling around in my head. I should head home and let sleep erase these pointless musings. Instead, when I leave the pub, I find myself steering my Explorer toward Lucy's neighborhood.

Through the raindrops on my windshield, I can see her place has a light on. And as I watch, she walks past the window dressed in pajamas—and not spend-the-night kind of pajamas. I feel a moment of absurd relief, until I see her nosy neighbor at the window, looking out at me. I shouldn't linger. Lucy's safe, and I'm confident she's alone.

"You're pathetic," I mutter, chastising myself for this detour into stalker territory.

I drive away, taking comfort in the image of her walking past the window. *I was just checking in on a friend*, I tell myself, but my heart thrums a different truth, one I'm not ready to confront.

Back at home, I wave to Ginny as I park and walk around to my basement apartment. The sudden glow of my phone cuts through the dimness as I step inside, a message notification pulling me out of my daze. It's Lucy. My pulse quickens.

Lucy: Found the Barbenheimer films we talked about! Popcorn and Hot Tamales are on me. Your place or mine for movie night on Friday?

I text back before I can stop myself, a smirk playing at the corner of my mouth.

Me: A Barbie movie? I'm good with Oppenheimer.

Lucy: Ha-ha. You're going to love Barbie. Promise.

Me: Okay, I'll come to your place. But only if I buy dinner. Maybe sushi.

Lucy: Deal. See you Friday at my place! Prepare to enjoy!

At the end of the week, I walk up to her door, tray of sushi in hand. It took all my willpower not to dig in. I'm starved.

Lucy buzzes me up and meets me at the top of the stairs, her eyes bright. "Perfect timing!" she says, ushering me inside.

We fill our plates and sit next to each other on the couch. I shut my eyes a moment, pushing back the desire to pull her close.

We settle in, and she starts the first movie, *Barbie*. I chuckle at the over-the-top scenes but the movie does grab me. I soon find I'm liking it more than I thought I would.

When we've finished dinner, Lucy pauses the movie and disappears into the kitchen. She returns with a large bowl of popcorn, and I watch, fascinated, as she tears open a bag of Hot Tamales and sprinkles them among the buttery kernels. "Trust me," she insists, seeing my skeptical look.

"Never doubted you for a second," I lie smoothly, taking a handful of the concoction. The sweet cinnamon heat of the candy meshes well with the saltiness of the popcorn, and I find myself reaching for more.

"Good, right?" she asks, smug satisfaction in her voice.

"Better than expected," I concede, and she laughs.

She returns to the couch beside me, close enough now that I can feel the warmth of her shoulder against mine. Her presence is comforting, familiar yet charged with an undercurrent of something exciting. I don't know how I'm going to navigate this. I don't know if I want to. I shift my position and relax into the cushions, into the moment.

When *Barbie* ends, Lucy turns to me. "What did you think?"

I cross my arms grumpily. "I liked it." But then I smile. "There's a patriarchy in medicine that has always amazed me, given that there are more women in the field than men. It's a good reminder for me to be more aware. What did you think?"

"I think education is similar to medicine in that regard. There are more women in the field, but there always seem to be men in the highest roles. I really liked it, though. I like to see women who fight for themselves. It inspires me."

I smirk. "I can't imagine you need a lot of inspiration in that area. You're assertive and strong. You speak your mind."

"Is that a bad thing? Usually when someone calls a woman assertive and strong, it means she's a bitch on wheels."

I laugh. "Nope. In my book, it's a compliment."

She smiles. "Thank you. And now, on to our next feature." She pushes the button for *Oppenheimer* to begin.

Everything is going great until the sex scene. My mind races, caught in a war between longing and logic. I've been on the edge of a semi all evening with Lucy just sitting next to me, and now, I'm watching a woman bounce on some guy's lap. I shut my eyes and try to think of something else, otherwise she's going to see the tent in my pants.

Even with my eyes closed, the moans are getting to me. I haven't been with anyone since before Céline told me she wasn't coming to Vancouver. It's getting harder and harder not to tear Lucy's clothes off and move her so far out of the friend zone, she'll forget she was ever there.

Finally, the movie moves on. I look over at Lucy, her face illuminated by the screen's glow, and something tugs at my heart. She looks content, happy even, and I realize I really like having her this close. It reminds me again what's at stake if the nature of our relationship were to change. The risk may be too great, no matter what my dick thinks.

Oppenheimer is intense, but it's no match for how hard Lucy works. Her breaths grow deeper, more rhythmic, and I know she's slipped away into sleep before the credits roll. I watch her for a moment. There's a tenderness in the way her chest rises and falls, a peace I don't want to disturb. And this is likely the excuse I need to escape before my self-control unravels and I reach out to touch the soft fabric of her sweater, just a hair's breadth away from my fingers.

"Time to go," I mutter to myself.

Careful not to wake her, I rise from the couch. In the kitchen, I find a scrap of paper and pen to scribble a note.

Thanks for the movie night. You conked out, but Oppenheimer would approve of your dedication to rest. – Chance

It's light-hearted, it's friendly—everything I need to maintain between us.

I drape a blanket over Lucy's sleeping form, tucking it gently around her shoulders. Then I force my feet toward the door, let myself out, and start the drive home. The streetlights streak by in a blur, reflecting the turmoil I feel. Lucy, with her easy smiles and Hot Tamales-infused popcorn, has crept into corners of my heart I thought were reserved for someone else.

Céline. Her name echoes through my thoughts, an

unwelcome reminder of what I've lost or perhaps what's been holding on to me. She's a ghost lingering in the background, a past that's had its time. But there's still work to be done if I'm to truly leave her behind.

"Get it together," I chide, gripping the steering wheel a little tighter.

Lucy deserves better than half-hearted affection shadowed by doubt and hesitation. And I deserve to explore this new potential with a clear conscience. That means Céline's hold on me, her desire to keep me close, despite there being no common path forward for us, needs to be released.

Tonight was close — too close — and as much as I yearn for the warmth I left behind on that couch, I know I made the right call. For my sake and Lucy's, I need to figure out where my heart truly lies. Only then can I offer Lucy everything she deserves.

CHAPTER 19

Lucy

Tiffany knocks on the table to grab my attention. "Hello? Anyone home?"

On Saturday morning, Tiffany, Janelle, and I are enjoying our periodic breakfast at our favorite hole in the wall, and my mind is on Chance. He and I are spending the day together—again—and I don't know what to do.

"What's on your mind?" Janelle presses.

I fidget with the hem of my shirt, the fabric twisting as I finally spill the words that have been blooming in my chest. "I think—no, I know I'm falling for Chance."

Janelle's eyes light up. She claps her hands together in delight. "I knew it!" she exclaims. "Lucy, this is fantastic! I'm telling you, he's got it bad for you too. He absolutely detests it when you're out on dates."

The warmth from Janelle's excitement should spread through me, but it's dampened by a lingering cloud of doubt. "But he's still hung up on Céline," I remind her, my voice dropping to a murmur. "It's not as simple as you make it sound."

"Lucy, honey, you've got to talk to him about it," Tiffany chimes in. "It might be exactly what you need to break out of this friend-zone purgatory."

"I tried and fell asleep during *Barbenheimer* last night," I counter with a humorless laugh. "I also acted like an idiot once he told me I was strong and assertive. One little compliment, and I was ready to jump him."

Janelle reaches out, her hand warm on my arm. "Everyone stumbles, Luce. It doesn't mean you stop walking the path. You just need to find the right moment, and when you do, everything will fall into place."

"I think you *should* jump him," Tiffany adds. "Attach your face to his and climb that man like a tree."

I hear the rumble of a motorcycle, and my heart races. Today, there's no rain in the forecast, and Chance and I are exploring more of Vancouver, so we're taking the bike. He's convinced I'm going to love the exhilaration of the wind in my face and the bike between my legs. I had to bite back my comment about what I'd prefer between my legs when he told me that.

Rising, I prepare to leave Janelle and Tiffany behind at the diner. They're going shopping downtown at the boutiques on Robson Street. "Have fun. I'll talk to you later." I wave.

They wave to Chance through the window.

"You two have fun, and do everything I would do," Tiffany says.

I can feel my face heat.

Chance grins at me and hands me a helmet as I step outside. "I take it Tiffany is up for anything?"

"What? You read lips too?" I'm mortified, and we haven't even started our day together.

"You could say that." Chance helps me with the chin strap and looks me over. "Don't look so worried. You're going to do great." He reaches into a saddlebag and pulls out a black leather jacket. "I thought you might like this."

I grin. "Thank you!" I shrug into the jacket, and it fits perfectly. "Were you worried I was going to embarrass you in my fleece?"

Chance laughs. "Not at all. This is just a little safer, and it will block the wind."

I nod.

"Ready?" he asks.

"Let's do this. Show me the power between my legs." *Oh gawd, did I just say that?*

Chase looks down at the ground, and his shoulders bounce with laughter. He straddles his bike and holds out his hand. "Put your feet there and climb up right behind me." Once I've done that, he adds, "Hold on to my waist and lean into the curves. And try to enjoy it."

I reach around him, and every nerve in my body goes on high alert.

He pushes off, and we ride down the street. It feels like everyone we pass looks at us. I usually feel awkward and clumsy, but right now, I'm at the cool kids' table.

After a bit, we pick up speed, and the world blurs past in a rush of exhilaration as I cling to Chance's back. The motorcycle purrs beneath us, a steel beast on the open road that leads to Capilano Suspension Bridge Park. It was Chance's idea to come here, and his suggestion seems like serendipity. Maybe I'll even weave Tiffany's advice into our Saturday plans.

"Here we are," he calls over the rumble of the engine as we pull into the parking lot. The bridge looms ahead, a thread of adventure strung across the rushing water below. My heart skips with anticipation, not just for the hike, but for the conversation that hangs between us. Will I be brave enough to have it?

"Ready for this?" I ask, slipping off the bike and pulling

off my helmet.

"Always," he replies with his easy smile, yet there's a tightness around his eyes I haven't noticed before.

We buy our tickets and join the throng of people at the bridge's entrance, the structure swaying gently with the collective movement of footsteps. I steal a glance at Chance, trying to read his expression as the bridge begins to wobble more noticeably under the weight of the crowd. The river, far below, runs loud and gushing.

"Whoa," he murmurs, a hint of vulnerability in his eyes. "Didn't expect it to be this...lively."

"Are you okay?" I probe, noticing his knuckles turning white as he grips the railing.

He chuckles. "I'm not exactly a fan of heights," he admits.

Without thinking, my hand finds his, fingers lacing with a comfort that feels as natural as breathing. The contact seems to ground him, and together, we step forward, joining the slow procession across the bouncing bridge. Each bump and sway tests our balance, but Chance's grip on my hand never falters.

"Look at us," I tease, hoping to ease his tension. "Braving the heights together."

"Couldn't do it without you," he says.

By the time we reach the other side, my pulse isn't just racing from the precarious crossing. It's this new closeness with Chance, one that might just shift the balance between us.

Solid ground on the other side is a welcome relief, but my heart feels suspended in mid-air. Still, I can't help but feel victorious. We made it.

"My heart's going a mile a minute here," he confesses, his voice shaky but laced with laughter as we move away from the bridge.

I study him, the way the sunlight filters through the trees and plays upon his face, casting it in warmth and soft shadows. "You did great," I assure him, stepping closer. I rise on my tiptoes, aiming for his cheek. But as I lean in, Chance turns his head ever so slightly, and my lips brush against his instead. It's a spark catching flame—unexpected yet impossible to pull away from. The world falls silent except for the sound of our synchronized breaths.

The kiss deepens, lengthens, and time loses meaning. Our break is abrupt, a mutual retreat driven by surprise more than intent.

"Sorry," he stammers, his eyes wide. "I didn't mean—"

"Chance," I interrupt, my own surprise melting into a smile. "I think I kissed you first."

His laugh is a release valve, and the tension that had built up dissipates into the forest around us.

"I'm sorry if that's not respecting your wishes," I tell him. "I don't usually kiss my friends, but…"

To my relief, he nods. "It's a bit embarrassing how in line with my wishes that was." He looks down a moment. "Being your friend is wonderful, but I'm pretty sure it's not enough."

"Okay, then. I guess we open ourselves to other possibilities?" I don't want to push, and I'd really like him to meet me halfway on this.

He opens his mouth as if to say something, but then he just nods. "I think that's perfect," he says.

We spend the rest of the afternoon hiking the trails, conversation flowing as easily as the river below us. Laughter comes naturally, and there's an undercurrent of excitement, a buzz that neither of us names but both of us seem to feel.

Hours later, back at my place, I fumble with my keys with one hand, the other still clasped in his. As I finally push open the door to my building, I turn to him with a smile. "Starving?" I ask.

"Definitely," he agrees, following me inside and up the stairs.

"Let's order something," I suggest as we repeat the key struggle at my apartment door. I kick off my shoes and pad into the living room. "What are you in the mood for?"

"Anything," he replies, but his attention doesn't seem to

be on food. His gaze lingers on mine.

We decide on Thai, and as we wait for the takeout to arrive, the space between us diminishes until there's none. No room left for anything but the magnetic pull drawing us together. This time, when our lips meet, there's no hesitation — just the insistent, growing need to be closer. His hands find my waist, mine wrap around his neck, and the world fades away.

The buzzer sounds, a distant, almost inconsequential noise, and we part with reluctance, breathless and flushed. The evening stretches out before us, filled with promise, and I can't help but think we've crossed more than just a bridge today.

Chance's forehead meets mine. "I've got this."

I nod, and he disappears down the stairs.

He's back within moments. He sets the delivery bags on the countertop, the scent of spicy noodles hanging in the air, but our meal is promptly forgotten. Chance's fingers are on my spine, tracing fire down the length of me, and I arch into his touch, a gasp slipping from my lips.

"Lucy," he murmurs, voice hoarse, his breath hot against my earlobe.

"Chance," I whisper, tugging him closer, eager for the rough stubble of his jawline against my skin. There's an urgency between us, one that's been simmering since our eyes locked over the trembling bridge, since our lips crashed together in an unintended confession.

I spin around within his grasp, and we're chest to chest, heartbeat to heartbeat. Electricity jolts through me as I press myself against him, capturing his lips once more. His hands roam with purpose, mapping the terrain of my body with a possessiveness that sends shivers to my toes. He's everywhere all at once, and it's overwhelming, intoxicating.

"Bedroom," I manage to pant, though the distance feels like miles when every nerve ending begs for more. We stumble through the doorway, a tangle of limbs. Clothes are shed in a trail of reckless abandon, a testament to the fevered need taking hold of us.

Rid of our jeans and T-shirts, I lie on the bed, my heart racing at the sight of Chance's bare chest. I run my fingers over his defined abs. The bulge in his boxer briefs makes me shiver with desire.

Chance's dark eyes meet mine, filled with a hunger that mirrors my own. With a low growl, he closes the distance between us, his hands tangling in my hair. I gasp as his lips crash against mine, igniting a fire that has been smoldering between us for far too long.

He breaks the kiss. "Are you okay with this? Tell me now because I might not be able to stop once we start."

I nod my consent. "I want you."

Chance's eyes glint with lust. With a smirk on his lips, he leans forward again, this time trailing kisses down my neck, leaving fire in his wake.

My breath hitches as his lips brush my collarbone, and my hands find their way to his shoulders. I hold on to him tightly, desperate for the contact. He continues to kiss his way down my body, and as his lips reach my chest, I feel a tremor of excitement coursing through me.

With a deft move, he hooks his thumbs into the waistband of my panties, but then he pulls back slightly. "You're sure about this?" he asks again.

"Yes," I whisper, my voice shaking but determined. "I want this. I want you."

A wicked grin spreads across his face. "If it becomes too much, just tell me."

His mouth attaches to my breast, and I arch my back. He pushes his thick fingers into me, and I groan with pleasure. My nails dig into his shoulders as he explores my body, every touch sending shockwaves coursing through me.

His fingers are magic, twisting and stroking, touching the deepest parts of me, bringing me to ecstasy. As I rise to meet him, our bodies meld in a desperate dance of need. The air grows heavy with the scent of sweat and desire.

He moves lower, his lips grazing my stomach, and I feel

a jolt of heat spreading through my body. His fingers tease my core, and I cling to the sheets as he begins to lick and explore me. I'm lost in the intensity of our connection.

Our eyes meet.

"You taste so good."

As his fingers delve deeper, I cry out, my hips bucking against him. His mouth finds my clit, and he sucks it deep. I moan loudly as his tongue dances over me. I'm lost in the sensations, the only sound in the room my breathy whimpers of delight.

And then, just as I'm on the brink of shattering, Chance withdraws his touch, leaving me yearning for more.

"Don't stop," I plead, but he simply smiles.

He rips a foil wrapper and rolls on a condom, and I feel like I could combust as I wait. But then his eyes lock onto mine as he crawls up my body. I feel the head of his erection pressing against me, and I arch my back to meet him.

With a low growl, he enters me, and I cry out in pleasure. Our bodies sync into a rhythm, hands gripping and pulling.

"You feel so good," he whispers.

I tug him closer, our breaths mingling as we lose ourselves in each other. Sensation builds within me, growing stronger with each thrust. Time seems to slow, and our movements become more intentional, more focused.

Then the release hits, my body shaking as I nearly scream in pleasure. Chance groans, his own orgasm taking over. After, we lie spent, our bodies still joined. Our breathing slowly returns to normal, and I smile. This may have been worth the wait.

We pull apart, and he rests his head on my chest. "That was incredible," he whispers.

"I agree."

We're a mess of sweat and tangled limbs, and in the dimming light, I can see the glint of something new, something terrifying and wonderful, in Chance's eyes. We've crossed a line we can't uncross, and that's just fine, as I don't ever want to go back.

CHAPTER 20

Lucy

The moment Chance walks through my door, midway through the following week, I can tell he's been caged too long. His eyes scan the room, darting from one corner to the next. It's clear he's agitated.

"Rough day?" I ask, though the answer is written all over him.

He exhales, a gust of relief, and I'm acutely aware of how much I've missed him, though it's only been hours and I had a full day of school to keep me occupied. We've spent every night together since our relationship changed. "You could say that," he replies as he wraps his arms around me.

As we press together in the living room, I can feel his erection against my hip. I reach down and gently run my hand along its length. "Is there anything I can do to make you feel better?"

Our kiss deepens, his lips leaving a trail of heat on my

skin. I slide my hand under his shirt, feeling the warmth of his skin as I explore the muscles of his abdomen. I trace the lines of his belly, teasing the hair that dusts his lower stomach. As his kiss becomes more urgent, he thrusts his hips forward.

I lower to my knees and unbuckle his pants. His cock almost leaps into my face. "Anxious, aren't we?" I tease.

"You have no idea. I need this."

I cradle his ass in my hands, pulling him closer as I take him into my mouth. He groans, a low, hungry sound that vibrates against my lips, urging me on. I swirl my tongue around the tip, then sink down, taking him deeper. His flavor fills my senses, and I suck hard, teasing the sensitive skin on the underside of his shaft. He thrusts against me, his hips bucking in time with my movements.

Before he can finish, he pulls me up, and his lips again find mine.

Our mouths lock together, tongues twisting and dancing in a matrix of passion. He presses me against the wall, hands roving over my body, his touch making every nerve ending come alive. Soon, all that exists is this moment, this connection.

His hand slips under my sweater, and he rolls my nipple between his fingers.

"Yessss," I hiss. I rock back and forth, looking for friction. Any kind I can find. This man lights my body on fire. "Pleeeeeasssse," I moan.

In moments, he's pulling my jeans away as I lie on the couch.

He stares at my naked body. "You're fucking perfect."

I gasp as his fingers explore, sending waves of pleasure through my body. I cling to his shoulders, nails digging in as the intensity overwhelms me.

He pulls his fingers away, leaving me panting and desperate for more. His gaze locks with mine a moment before he looks around. "Where did my pants end up? I need a condom."

"No, you don't— I mean, if you don't want to. I'm clean,

and I've had the shot."

His head drops back toward the ceiling, and he smiles. "Damn."

In that moment, I know that whatever comes next will be unforgettable.

With a low groan, he pushes himself inside, filling me completely. I arch my back, crying out in a mix of pain and pleasure. He pauses, allowing me to adjust to his size.

He thrusts again, his hips grinding into me. The rhythm is powerful, and I can feel it growing stronger with each passing second. I cling to his back as I try to anchor myself.

His fingers find their way back to my core, and he strums my clit as he pivots in and out. I gasp. He gives me everything I need and then some. This man, this connection, is all I want right now. I fall apart, and just as I'm regaining control, he gives one final thrust and then stills, his body shuddering against mine. His warm release fills me.

His eyes never leave mine as he moves closer. His hands cradle my face, his thumbs brushing away the tears that have formed in the corners of my eyes as he kisses me.

"Are you okay?" he asks.

I nod. "I'm more than okay," I whisper. "Let me know when you're ready to go again."

He throws his head back and laughs.

I want to hold myself back, keep my heart shielded. I'm not naïve enough to miss the signs of my own spiraling emotions. But when he looks at me with that warm intensity that seems reserved just for me, my defenses disappear and something else starts to bloom.

"Let's go out tonight," he suggests, his voice vibrant with pent-up energy. "Do something spontaneous."

The proposition is tempting, thrilling even, but a part of me hesitates. Chance is like a comet streaking across my night sky – brilliant and possibly fleeting. I'm drawn to his light, but comets are notorious for their brief visits. I'm probably just a stop on his orbit, a rebound from the celestial body he left behind.

"Spontaneous sounds perfect," I find myself saying anyway, because despite the warning sirens in my head, I'm already tumbling, helpless, into my feelings for him.

We shower and dress, and as we step outside a little while later, I can feel the electric buzz of his restlessness. It's contagious.

"Thanks for coming out with me," he says, tossing an arm around my shoulders, carefree as we move through the cooling twilight. "This is the perfect counterpoint to what I endured earlier. I think I would have gone crazy if I'd to sit through one more budget forecast today."

I laugh, leaning into him. The thought that I might be just a distraction doesn't fully vanish, but right now, with Chance's laughter mixing with mine, I let myself fall a little harder. Maybe being the rebound isn't so bad if it means I get to be caught in his whirlwind, even if it's just for now.

The cool breeze whispers between us as we stroll down the sidewalk, our steps in sync. Chance's hand finds mine, our fingers intertwining.

"Where are we going for dinner?" I ask.

"Surprise." He winks, the mischievous glint in his eyes stirring butterflies in my stomach.

My phone vibrates against my hip. One glance at the caller ID and my chest tightens—Dad.

"Sorry, hold on," I murmur, releasing Chance's hand to take the call. "Hey, Dad. What's up? Chance and I were just heading out to dinner."

"I'm so sorry to do this to you. Beatrice isn't showing up again. I need you to cover her shift tonight." Dad's voice is apologetic but firm, a tone I've come to recognize all too well.

"Did you try anyone else?"

"Janelle is behind because she covered last week. If you do this tonight, I promise I won't call you next time."

I sigh. "Okay, I'll be there soon," I reply, masking my disappointment.

"Thanks, love. You're a lifesaver."

Ending the call, I look up at Chance, expecting frustration. Instead, his brow furrows with concern. "Everything okay?"

"Beatrice bailed. Again." I shrug, trying to keep the mood light, but heaviness settles in my chest. "I have to go into Barney's. Raincheck on dinner?"

"Mind if I tag along?" he asks. "I'm not letting you get away that easily."

"Are you sure?" I hesitate, torn between wanting him by my side and fearing the strain it might put on this fragile thing between us.

"Absolutely." He smiles, reaching for my hand once more as we change direction.

"Thank you," I whisper, grateful yet guilty for pulling him into my messy world.

We drive over in my car, and as we enter Barney's, Chance nods at Griffin and Kent, who raise their glasses in greeting before returning to their conversation.

"Grab a seat with them," I suggest, heading behind the bar to tie on an apron. "I'll be right here."

Chance hesitates, then nods, making his way to their table. As I start pouring drinks, I can feel his gaze on me, protective and unwavering. I steal a glance and catch him scowling at a patron who looks a second too long in my direction. My heart swells with a complex of emotions—appreciation for his presence, sorrow for the night interrupted, and a deep-seated ache as I think about why I can never say no to Dad.

Dad is behind the bar, and I give him a look that I hope tells him I'm not happy to be here.

"Thank you for coming in" he says. "Evidently Beatrice is sick."

He really needs to remind her that her work visa is dependent on, you know, actually working. But right now, I'm too angry to have that conversation.

The night wears on, filled with clinking glasses and laughter, but through it all, Chance stays. With every protective glare and easy grin, he shows me that maybe I'm not just a rebound to him. Or that's what he thinks. But I'm not sure he can truly know at this point.

I slide a pint across the polished mahogany to a waiting hand, but my eyes stray again to the corner where Chance sits, his laughter mingling with Griffin's booming voice.

"Can you believe it?" Griffin slaps his knee, his face alight with excitement. "Tori and I are heading up to St. John for the entire summer. Fresh air, fishing—it'll be like being a kid again."

"Sounds amazing," Chance replies, and for a split second, our gazes lock.

"Amelia and I will be missing out on all your fish tales, I'm afraid," Kent chimes in, his British lilt cutting through the din. "We're off to London next week. Mum's not been well, and she could use the company."

"Family first." Griffin nods, clapping him on the back. "Always."

I tuck a stray lock of hair behind my ear, watching as a group of women saunter up to the bar. They're all fluttering lashes and coy smiles as they order a round of cocktails, their attention fixed on the table where the doctors sit. I pour their drinks carefully, steeling myself against the unwelcome twist in my gut.

"Thanks," one of them purrs, brushing her fingertips against mine as she takes her drink. Her gaze drifts to Chance, lingering in obvious invitation.

Hockey players have puck bunnies, doctors seem to have on-call girls—the women who work at the hospital and are looking to snag a doctor. These seem more like call-room coochies, skanks that come to the pub looking for doctor sugar daddies.

But Chance, thankfully, doesn't bite. He remains engrossed in his conversation with Griffin and Kent, who are both happily married. The women huff in disappointment before flouncing away.

As the last stragglers from Barney's filter out into the night, I hang up my apron, and Chance and I head to his place. It's the first time he's invited me there. The air between us is charged with unspoken words and lingering glances, but we both pretend it's just another casual evening as we traverse across the bridge to North Van.

When we arrive, it's late, but an older woman steps out onto the porch.

"Lucy, this is Ginny," Chance introduces me to her. She has a kind face and a warm smile.

"Hi there!" Ginny greets me with enthusiasm. "You must be the girl who's got Chance acting like a teenager again. It's about time."

Her comment makes me blush, and I feel the weight of her gaze—friendly yet piercing.

"Chance just had this new tankless water heater installed for us, and let me tell you, it's a game-changer," she exclaims.

"Never-ending hot showers," Chance chimes in, grinning.

"Sounds heavenly," I respond, sharing a laugh with them and marveling at how domestic this feels.

As if on cue, Ginny leans closer. "Between you and me, he's quite the catch," she says. "Not just because of the fancy water heater."

"Okay, okay, that's enough," Chance cuts in, though there's no heat to his words, only a bashful sort of charm that makes him look boyish for a moment.

We bid Ginny goodbye not long after, with Chance walking me to the door of his apartment. He takes me in and shows me around the space. "Thanks for giving me a ride home."

"Anytime."

He runs his hand up my arm. "Are you sure you can't

stay the night?"

"I have school in the morning, and already the night will be short. How about Friday night?"

He nods and kisses me softly. It's so hard to pull away, but we've spent so many nights together lately, and I need to protect my heart. I can't fool myself much longer, though. Chance already has my heart.

CHAPTER 21

Lucy

The bell rings, and the kids are out the door within seconds, typical for a Friday afternoon. I'm excited because Chance and I are staying at his place all weekend, and our plan is to be in bed. Maybe we'll even get some sleep. But then, as I'm gathering my things, my cell phone pings.

Dad: Can you come by the bar after school today?

My stomach sinks. Beatrice must be flaking again. I understand the allure of being young and free, but this is bordering on ridiculous. And Dad is ridiculous too. When she ruined my date with Chance on Wednesday, he promised I wouldn't be the one he called the next time.

Me: Sure, I'm on my way.

By the time I push through the front doors of Barney's, my frustration is simmering just below a calm exterior. I'm ready to confront my father about Beatrice's unreliability when I spot him behind the bar, a serious look on his face.

"Beatrice, take over for a bit, will you?" he calls over to her without breaking eye contact with me. "Lucy and I need to have a chat."

My mouth opens and then closes. My entire premise for being here has just dissolved.

"Sure thing," Beatrice responds, sliding behind the bar.

"Let's step into my office," Dad says, and there's a gravity in his tone that sets my nerves on edge.

"Is everything okay?" I ask as I follow, trying to decipher the unreadable expression on his face. He hasn't been to a doctor recently. Do we have a giant tax bill? What could have him so serious?

"Let's talk in private," is all he says.

Inside his office, I sink into the worn leather chair across from Dad's cluttered desk. He doesn't sit but instead leans his hip against the edge of the desk, his fingers gripping an envelope that looks too formal for this place of spilled beer and laughter.

"Lucy," he says, voice heavy, "this came for you." He hands me the envelope.

My name is written on the front in a script that is unfamiliar, the postmark a smudge from Ireland. I tear it open, extracting the thick fold of paper with fumbling urgency. A letter penned on legal stationery unfolds in my trembling hands.

My gaze lifts to my father, seeking some kind of anchor in the storm.

Dear Ms. Sheridan,

Re: Estate of James O'Connor

I trust this letter finds you well. My name is Jack Murphy, and I am an estate attorney based in Dublin, Ireland. I am writing to inform you that you have been named as a beneficiary in the estate of the late James O'Connor.

As per the terms outlined in James O'Connor's last will and testament, you are entitled to receive the following:

- A sum of £1,000,000 (One Million Pounds Sterling), to be transferred to your designated bank account
- An apartment building in Dublin; this property includes 115 (one hundred and fifteen) units and is currently fully occupied.

Verification of Identity and Documentation
To proceed with the transfer of your inheritance, please provide a copy of your identification (e.g., passport or driver's license) and proof of address. You may submit these documents via email or by post to our office.

Bank Account Information
Kindly provide your bank account details for the transfer of the monetary inheritance. All information will be handled with strict confidentiality.

Property Transfer Process
For the transfer of the apartment building, you will need to appoint a solicitor to handle the conveyancing process. Our firm can assist with this, or you may choose to appoint your own solicitor.

The letter goes on about estate tax considerations and how to contact them, but I'm confused. Why would this man I've never met be giving me so much money and an apartment building in another country?

"Who is James…" But when I look up at Dad, the rest of the sentence dies on my lips.

"Your biological father," he supplies, his voice almost swallowed by the hum of refrigerators behind us.

"Biological father?" I parrot, my mind refusing to process. The walls seem to tilt, and I grip the arms of the chair, fighting the surge of panic.

"Lucy, listen. I… Jimmy—James—he and your mam were…involved before she was with me. I was in love with her from the moment I met her, and I didn't care. I wanted you both."

The air in the room feels too thick, cloying. I blink at Dad, the man who raised me, who bandaged scraped knees and cheered at graduations. His face is a map of sorrow and resignation.

"Jimmy left her," he continues. "He is the head of an organized crime syndicate, and he didn't want that for your mam and you. It broke her heart. She always loved him, not me. But I—I loved her, regardless."

A twisted part of me wants to laugh; it sounds like a tragic play, not my life. "Then why are we here?" I ask. "Why Vancouver?"

He pushes off from the desk and begins to pace, each step measured and heavy. "We needed a fresh start. I did one last job, and we had enough to get away, start anew here."

"Here," I whisper, the word echoing hollowly. I think of Ginny, her praise of Chance, and suddenly, I'm not just grappling with my mother's past love, but my own precarious heart.

Dad stops pacing and looks at me. "I'll understand if you need time—to think, to…to find out about James."

"Time," I repeat, the concept alien. A million pounds. Is my last name Sheridan or is it O'Connor? A legacy of crime and lost love. It's too much, yet somehow, I'm still here, rooted to the spot by a sense of duty that seems to have been woven into my very DNA.

"Lucy?" Dad prompts gently.

But all I can do is nod, clutching the letter as I try to make sense of a world that's shifted beneath my feet. Tears, hot and unbidden, stream down my cheeks.

"Your mother," he says, voice thick with emotion, "she loved you fiercely. There wasn't a day she didn't shower you with affection, trying to compensate for the absence of...of Jimmy."

I blink through the tears, seeing not the office around me but the past, the countless moments of joy my mother crafted from the simplest things. Yet beneath her laughter, there'd always been an undercurrent of sorrow. A sorrow born of rejection, a ghostly presence at every birthday, every holiday. Jimmy's shadow had loomed, though I'd never known its name until now.

"Lucy." Dad's voice is closer, and I feel his hand on my shoulder. "He came back once."

My breath catches. Another piece of the puzzle slots into place.

"Jimmy couldn't stay away. He wanted to take your mam back with him to Ireland. But he was too deep in it all, too entangled with organized crime and the IRA. It was no life for a family—for you."

The sobs come harder now, each one wracking my body with the force of revelations that reshape my childhood. My mother's eyes, always tinged with sadness, mourned not just a lost love but a life that could have been.

"He made sure they never touched us, though," Dad continues, his grip tightening. "The Irish mob stayed away because of him. But it wasn't enough to keep your mam happy, not really. She missed Ireland, her friends, her family. This city… It was beautiful, but it was never home for her."

And as I cry, I understand the true price of our fresh start. The high cost of safety and the void left by a love denied. My mother's heart had remained across the ocean, even as she built a life here with Dad and me.

I clutch the crumpled tissue in my fist, my tears soaking into its fragile fibers.

"Lucy, I did everything I could," he says, his voice like gravel. "Tried to fill the house with laughter, to make her feel loved. But there was always something missing for her. A piece of her heart stayed in Ireland." He pauses, his eyes distant. "I love her still, you know. Always will."

The thought that this man, who has been the bedrock of my existence, might somehow fade from my life now that the truth is out… It terrifies me. My chest constricts, a knot of panic lodging in my throat.

"Why didn't you tell me?" I rasp.

He looks up at the ceiling, his eyes avoiding mine. "Every time I tried, something made me stop. I talked to Jimmy about it after your mam passed, and he was worried for your safety. I swear, I was going to tell you."

"Dad…" My voice is barely a whisper, and I have to clear my throat before I can speak again. "What…what does this mean for us?"

He reaches out, his calloused hand cupping my cheek. "Lucy girl," he says with such tenderness, "you are my daughter. You've always been my daughter. And nothing—not blood, not history—can change that."

His blue eyes, so like my own, meet mine, and they're filled with an ocean of love and reassurance. "If you need to go to Ireland to find out more about Jimmy, I'll understand. Take all the time you need. I love you, and I always will. I'll be here, waiting, no matter what."

CHAPTER 22

Chance

The heart monitor goes flat. I work quickly to stabilize another overdose victim—our third today. "Another Narcan, stat!" The command leaves my lips without thought, instinct taking over where training ends. The nurses spring to action, a well-oiled machine amidst the bedlam.

As I glance at the clock, I realize Lucy and I have dinner planned tonight. A small smile breaks through the gravity of the moment. She's become the unexpected center in my life. With her, it's easy. Simple. Everything I do, I want to share with her. Even the thoughts of Céline have faded.

"Dr. Devereaux," a nurse calls, snapping me back to the present, "we need you in bay three."

I nod and wash up, ready to dive back into the fray. As I push through the double doors, a pang of guilt nibbles at me. There's a new heroin on the streets, and volunteering at the safe-use sites feels more than ever like an extension of the care we provide here. But our chief medical officer would disagree. We've yet to come to an agreement on this, so I've kept mum about the nights when I know members of our staff volunteer. Maybe it's my own rebellion, one last stand against the system, but even that urge has dulled. Being a rebel is standing up to him.

"Easy, buddy," I murmur to the young man convulsing on the gurney before me, his eyes rolling as we fight to bring him back from the brink. Encouraging rehab for those we save becomes a mantra, and for those who refuse, safe-use sites are all we can offer.

But even so, the sense of accomplishment is undeniable. We're not just treating symptoms; we're trying to mend broken lives. It's a battle worth fighting, even on days like this when our resources are stretched thin and the tide of desperation crashes against us relentlessly.

"Good job, everyone," I say once the young man's breathing steadies and his seizure subsides. Weariness clings to me, yet it's tinged with the satisfaction of knowing I've made a difference. I glance at the clock again, eager to scrub off the day and meet Lucy, to immerse myself in the normalcy she brings to my life.

"Dr. Devereaux," someone calls.

I turn, ready for the next crisis, the next person in need. Because no matter how good life gets outside these hospital walls, this is where I'm needed most. This is where I make a stand, however quiet or unseen. Lucy understands that. She's doing the same thing from a different angle. It's part of how we connect.

I'm threading a catheter when Griffin sidles up to the sterile field, his eyes shadowed with the toll of the day. "I just heard from the safe-use on Hastings. They've had four deaths and are worried that after dark it's going to get worse," he murmurs, just loud enough for me to catch over the beep of monitors and activity around us.

I glance up, my hands steady despite the surprise that

jolts through me. "Yeah?" I respond.

"I'm going. But Kent said his father was watching the clinic for hospital staff."

I nod, sliding the catheter home and taping it down. "I don't know what I can do to protect you."

"I'll be fine. If he wants to fire me, I'll land somewhere else. But I need to do something. This is bad." He sighs. "I just wanted you to know."

I nod. "I'll let you know if I hear from him."

"Dr. Devereaux…" The intercom crackles, and I know before the next words come that it's Dr. Charles Johns summoning me, as if he's somehow heard our conversation. I peel off my gloves and give Griffin a tight smile. "Hold down the fort."

"Always do," he replies.

I stride through the bustling emergency department and up to the administrative wing, my mind a whir of potential scenarios. At Dr. Johns's office. Catherine isn't at her desk. I take in a deep breath, bracing myself, and knock on his door.

"Come in." His voice is terse, clipped with impatience or maybe disappointment. I can't tell which.

"Dr. Johns." I greet him as I enter, noting the steeple of his fingers and the stern set of his jaw. "You wanted to see me?"

"Sit down," he instructs, and I comply, the leather of the chair cool against my scrubs. "I've been hearing things," he begins.

"About?" I prompt, though I suspect where this is leading.

"Your fit here. Your…philosophies." His gaze holds mine, searching, probing. "I'm beginning to question whether you're right for this hospital."

My heart rate picks up, a drumbeat of concern that matches the distant wail of sirens. I've only been here three months, but the staff seems happy. We're getting on well together, as near as I can tell. Of course, I've had conversations with Dr. Johns before, debates over policy and practice, but this feels different. This feels personal.

"Because?" I ask, though it's more of a statement than a question. I'm aware of the unspoken rules, the lines we walk as doctors, as healers. I've never been one to stay neatly within those lines.

"I told you how I felt about your staff moonlighting at the safe-use clinics, and I understand they're still there every night. Among other things…" he concedes, and there's a flicker of something—regret, perhaps—in his eyes. "We need a certain…conformity here. A predictability."

And there it is, the crux of it. Predictability has never been my strong suit, not in love, not in life, and certainly, not in medicine. I think of Lucy, of the calm she brings to my world, and I realize how much I crave that balance now.

"I do understand your feelings. But I believe you also understand my perspective. The staff make their own decisions about their off-work hours. I am hopeful we can come to some consensus about this, but it seems we're not there yet," I say, keeping my voice even. It's a chess game, and I'm now unsure of my next move. Dr. Johns doesn't dismiss me, but the silence stretches between us. "I assure you, it is not my intention to undermine you. But I feel a responsibility to my staff as well."

"Thank you," he finally says, a dismissal if ever I heard one.

I stand, the office feeling smaller somehow, constrictive. I need air, space, the controlled mayhem of the ED over this quiet judgment. My jaw clenches so tight I fear it might snap. The words Dr. Johns has laid before me feel like a slap. He's questioning my fit for the hospital over something as human as empathy? We've been improving lives, cutting wait times, and now, we're seeing more patients than ever. I want to argue, to fight for every decision that's led us here, but insubordination isn't a card I can afford to play. So I'll have to do it diplomatically.

"Dr. Johns," I begin, my tone carefully neutral. "The morale in the ED is the best it's been in years. We're not just meeting targets; we're surpassing them." I pause, searching his face for any sign of concession, but it remains an unreadable mask.

"That may be, but rules are rules," he says, showing me what matters to him, above anything else. "If you can't manage your team within the parameters set by this hospital," he adds, voice cold as steel, "perhaps it's time to reassess your place here."

A fire ignites in my chest, but I tamp it down, refusing to let it consume what little ground I have left to stand on. Instead, I pivot, steering us away from the precipice. "Of course." I nod, though it sticks in my throat. I exit his office, the door clicking shut behind me.

How does Kent do it? How does he stay so damn normal in a world where every decision feels like walking a tightrope? I shake my head, pushing the thought aside as I navigate the maze-like corridors toward Legal.

William Long, Dr. Johns's son-in-law and one of the hospital lawyers, looks up from a stack of papers as I approach. His office is immaculate, everything in its place, a stark contrast to the emergency department.

"William, got a minute?" I ask, leaning against the door frame.

He motions me inside. "Sure. What's up? Any news on the Prometheus Health?"

"I gave that project to Dr. Johns—Charles. I actually have a legal question for you." I fold my arms across my chest. "What's the difference, malpractice-wise, between volunteering at a government-sanctioned safe-use clinic versus running into an accident and helping someone on the road?"

"Interesting comparison," William muses, resting his temple against his fist. "There are nuances, immunity provisions... I'll need to look into the specifics. It can get complicated."

"Great," I say with a smile. "Please let me know when you have something."

"Will do." He nods.

I thank him and start my return to the ED. My steps are heavy, tension in my shoulders. The weight of leadership, of decisions made and yet to come, bears down on me. But there's no time to dwell; the ED won't manage itself, regardless of the politics playing out behind closed doors.

I burst through the swinging doors into the emergency department. My head is still swirling with legalities and looming decisions, but I shove it all aside. My focus narrows to the care I want to provide.

"Dr. Devereaux!" Jennifer, the nurse in charge, calls.

I zero in on a woman curled on her side, clutching her abdomen, her face a tapestry of pain. "Talk to me," I say, slipping on gloves as I kneel beside her. Her breaths are shallow, punctuated by sharp gasps.

"Severe abdominal pain, onset a few hours ago, no known allergies or pre-existing conditions." Jennifer rattles off the stats, a dance we've done a hundred times over.

"Possible ectopic pregnancy," I murmur as I palpate her abdomen gently, watching for signs, cues that might guide us. We need confirmation, a clear image of what's happening inside. "Get an ultrasound here, stat."

"Already on it."

A figure in blue scrubs strides toward us, the OB/GYN attending, Dr. Andrews. "I'll take over from here," he says, his voice leaving no room for argument.

"Keep me updated," I reply, rising and stepping back as the team moves in.

"Dr. Devereaux!" Jennifer calls again as I'm about to turn away. She holds out a hospital phone, her expression apologetic. "It's your landlord, Ginny. Says it's urgent."

My heart skips a beat, sensing a different kind of emergency. "Thanks," I mutter, taking the receiver and pressing it to my ear.

"Chance, dear," Ginny's voice comes through, tinged with a note of concern. "You've got a visitor from Montreal. A tall, thin, dark-haired woman. She's waiting here at the house."

The edges of my vision narrow, the world outside my spiraling thoughts dimming. *Céline*. It can only be her. My pulse quickens. "Did she say what she wanted?" I ask, trying to keep my voice steady despite the adrenaline.

"She just kept repeating your name. I'm sorry. My French isn't very good," Ginny replies.

"Thanks, Ginny. I'll be home as soon as I can," I assure her.

"Be careful," she adds before hanging up.

Careful. Of course. With Céline, caution is always warranted.

I replace the receiver slowly, feeling the weight of the past pressing in around me. I stand caught between the life I've built here and the ghost of another that's just reappeared.

I get back to work, and the clock ticks closer to the end of my shift. But after a while, I can't focus on the charts anymore, as Ginny's words echo in my head. I sign off on the last patient file and find myself stripping off my white coat before I've fully registered the decision to leave early.

I wish Griffin luck, head down to my car, and drive home. *Why is Céline here? What does she want? What will I do if she wants to stay? What about Lucy?*

I pull into the driveway. Before I even reach the door, it swings open, and there she is — Céline, from a life I thought I'd left behind. Her eyes lock on mine, emotions swirling in their depths.

"Chance!" The word slips from her lips.

My hands rise as she rushes toward me, catching her shoulders and holding her at bay. The touch is electric, familiar yet unwelcome.

"I want us back," she breathes in rapid French. "We're meant to be together."

I shake my head. "Céline, why are you here?"

Her dark eyes well up, tears spilling over. "How could you cut me off like that?" she chokes out. "I thought you'd come back. For me, for us."

My chest tightens at her distress. I hate seeing her in pain, yet the mere thought of giving up my life for her—living without Lucy—sears through me, threatening to cleave my heart in two. I can see now that Céline's not interested in what I want or need, and maybe she never has been. I've wasted too much time not seeing her for what she is.

"Montreal was another time, Céline," I whisper. "Things...they change." When she still seems unconvinced, I force myself to continue. "Lucy," I add, the name falling heavily into the space between us. "She's the one you were asking about."

A look of confusion flits across Céline's face, quickly replaced by a stubborn resolve. "Chance, seeing you again—don't you feel it? It's still there between us," she insists, her voice a sultry whisper that once might have unraveled me. She steps closer. But I'm not the man I was in Montreal. Lucy, the new work I'm doing here in Vancouver—it has reshaped my world.

I manage a half-smile, tinged with regret. "Céline, I won't lie. It's good to see you. But things are different now. You should've called." My words are gentle but firm.

Her eyes darken. "We just need to be together—make love—and everything will fall back into place. You'll remember us." She moves in, arms reaching for an embrace I can't return.

Instinctively, I step back, hands raised in a weak barrier. "No, Céline—we can't." The boundary is set.

"But you're mine," she accuses sharply, a raw edge of betrayal sharpening her voice. "You're cheating on me!"

I close my eyes. This isn't how today was supposed to unfold. Everyone wants answers I don't yet have. I need space, time to think, to sort out who I am and how best to be that person—at work and at home. But first, I must navigate the storm in front of me, where every move feels like a potential disaster.

CHAPTER 23

Lucy

I pause outside Ginny's house, my heart hammering against my ribs. Chance is silhouetted in the upstairs window on the gauzy curtains. I need him now more than ever, to unravel the knots of my inheritance and the truth about my father — or rather, the man who isn't biologically my father.

Taking a deep breath to steady myself, I slip into Chance's apartment downstairs. The back stairs creak under my weight as I ascend into Ginny's abode and knock.

"Lucy?" Ginny's voice is soft through the tension that crackles in the air as I emerge from the stairway. She reaches for my hand, her touch grounding, but my eyes are already drawn past her, to where Chance stands, jaw set, hands gesturing with contained vehemence.

"Chance —" I begin, but the words stall in my throat when I see her. A tall woman, dark hair cascading around her like midnight waves, locks horns with Chance in a rapid-fire exchange of French. Their words dart too quickly for my language skills to capture every word.

My grip tightens around Ginny's hand. Even without full understanding, I know. This is his past come to stake its claim. Her posture, the tilt of her head, the way she invades his space; it's all a dance of possession, and I'm an unwanted spectator.

"Merde, Céline!" Chance throws his hands up in exasperation. Her name registers, a bitter pill dissolving on my tongue. *Céline.* The one I hoped he'd never hear from again.

As their argument crescendos, I stand overwhelmed, a silent plea caught in my throat. I came here to expose my vulnerability, to seek solace in Chance's embrace. Instead, suddenly, even more things feel unstable. Chance has his own battle to fight at the moment, and I have nowhere to turn. Plus, what if I'm looking at the possibility of my heart being shredded into a million tiny pieces?

Céline's gaze cuts across the room to me. Her eyes narrow, darkening with contempt. "Why is she here?" She spits the words, her English clipped and venomous. "What is she doing here?"

"Lucy—she's—" Chance starts, but Céline barrels over him, her voice rising to a crescendo.

"Ah, the little home wrecker!" she exclaims. She continues in French, and I'm lost. The sting of her words feels like a slap.

"Enough, Céline!" Chance's command booms as he steps between us. He fixes her with a steel-edged stare. "Stop right now," he growls. "This is not about her. It's about us."

His defense should offer comfort, but it serves as a stark reminder of the complexities of our relationship. A knot tightens in my chest, constricting breath and heart all at once. I can't bear another second. Nothing in my life is what I thought it was.

Chance hasn't fully let Céline go. It's not just her who isn't finished fighting this battle. I see it in the way his body leans toward her even as he wards her off. It's in the tension that lines his jaw, the fire behind his eyes.

"Excuse me," I murmur. I turn, retreating down the back stairs.

With each step, the weight of the truth grows heavier. Nothing feels solid right now. The secrets I carry with me will remain locked within. I'm halfway down the stairs when Chance's footsteps thunder after me. I don't stop, don't turn, but his voice, strained with urgency, slices through the air.

"Lucy, wait!" he calls from the top of the staircase. "She showed up uninvited, I swear to you."

I pause, one foot hovering over the next step.

"She won't be staying long," he insists, his voice descending as he takes the steps two at a time, trying to bridge the distance my hurt has carved out.

But before I can muster a response, Céline's voice cuts through the tension. "Je ne vais nulle part!" Her declaration rings with challenge, each syllable sharp and clear. *"I'm not going anywhere."*

That much I understand perfectly.

The tears press behind my eyelids, a dam strained to its limit. I can't manage this right now. With a blink, I force them back, unwilling to show the cracks in my armor. "I understand," I whisper, the words catching in my throat.

Chance is before me now, his eyes searching mine for something—understanding, perhaps, or maybe just a sign that I won't disappear from his life as quickly as I entered it. But all I see is the storm of emotions warring within him, and through my own turmoil, I don't know what I can offer him.

"You said you were still getting over her. I see that now. You have nothing to apologize for. Do what you need to do."

His jaw clenches, and he doesn't answer immediately. In that silence, I feel the chasm widen.

"Lucy, I—" He starts but falters, the right words eluding him.

He doesn't know what to do with this situation either.

And I'm only a distraction, adding fuel to her fire. I need to go. He's not available to me right now. And I don't have any way to help him.

I turn away, walking out Chance's front door to my car.

"You can do this," I say over my shoulder, trying for a smile. And I'm sure he can. I just don't know what he's going to decide to do.

The drive over Lion's Gate Bridge is a blur of city lights and tears. Vancouver sprawls before me, indifferent to the heartache unfolding in individual lives. I feel completely untethered, as if all the things I knew about myself and my life have been called into question at once.

By the time I reach my place, the tears have dried into salty tracks on my face. The quiet of my apartment amplifies the hollow feeling inside me.

I text Janelle and Tiffany.

Me: Today is a lousy day that went to hell in a handbasket. I'm eating ice cream. Please come save me.

Janelle responds immediately.

Janelle: Walk away from the ice cream. You can do it! I'm at the pub until 2 a.m. I'll call you when I get home. ((Hugs!))

It takes time for Tiffany to respond.

Tiffany: We're at dinner. I'll call when I get home. And Janelle's right. Back carefully away from the ice cream.

But I'm not as strong as they seem to think, and there's no one available for me to talk to, so I do find solace in the cold comfort of ice cream—three pints, to be exact. They form a trio of frosty consolers as I sink onto the couch, the *Barbie* movie playing mindlessly before me. It's just noise in the background while I wait for Janelle to get home from Barney's and Tiffany to finish her date so we can talk.

"Get it together," I mutter to myself. But the tears return anyway, unbidden, spilling over as I spoon mouthfuls of sweet, creamy escape. The laughter and chatter from the screen seem so distant, so disconnected from the heaviness in my chest.

Sometime later, I press the spoon against the rim of the pint, scraping up the last of the mint chocolate chip. The Barbie characters dance across the screen, their solutions wrapped in a neat bow by the time the credits roll. If only life were scripted like a movie. "You're strong. You can handle this," I tell myself. I just need time to sort through all of this, to let it play out. But I fear where I'll end up after all is revealed.

I'm upset with myself for being upset, though it should be understandable. As of today, my father is not my father, and the relationship I'd convinced myself I was building with Chance now looks shaky all over again. What if he chooses Céline? I take a deep breath. I just need my friends, need a reminder that here are some things that remain solid in my life.

CHAPTER 24

Chance

Anger coils in my stomach, a living thing, as Céline's accusations and theatrics fill the room. I can feel tension radiating up to my temples. Ginny's eyes are wide with disbelief, her lips pressed into a thin line of disapproval.

"This yelling needs to stop!" she finally yells, her voice mirroring my feelings. She shakes her head, muttering something about drama queens under her breath, but it's lost in Céline's outburst.

I close my eyes for a moment, summoning an image of Lucy. The hardest thing I ever did was watch her leave. I can still see the hurt on her face, the confusion. It's haunting me. I should have jumped in that car with her, escaped the mess that is Céline.

"Enough, Céline," I say, my voice harsh. I'm done being passive. "You need to stop."

Her tirade pauses for a heartbeat, surprise flickering

across her features before she regains her composure. "Chance, how can you be so cold?" she asks, her voice rising again.

"I'm not being cold. I'm being realistic," I reply, steeling myself against the onslaught of guilt that always accompanies Céline.

Everything I value threatens to slip through my fingers. Céline will wreck it all if she gets her way. She doesn't care about me as a person or give any thought to what I might want. She wasn't the only one who had reasons to leave Montreal. She is an endless chasm of need, paralyzed by her own fears and unable to see beyond herself. She wasn't truly happy when we were together. I'm not sure she can be. But I know for sure I can't do it for her. She's only clinging to us because it's familiar, and I'm done being that for her. I won't let her take my relationship with Lucy, the life we could potentially have, my new career here. Céline has come here expecting…what? That I'll acquiesce and fall back into old habits? Not anymore.

"Céline, listen to me," I start, trying to keep the tremor out of my voice. "I'm going to book you a hotel room. You'll stay there tonight."

Her mouth opens, then closes, and for a brief second, I see something other than anger in her eyes. Disappointment? Maybe even fear?

"Chance, I—" she begins, but I cut her off.

"No, I need space to figure things out," I insist. Though my heart is pounding, I know this is the only way forward. "Please, Céline."

She doesn't argue further, perhaps sensing the finality in my tone, or perhaps thinking she still has a chance to convince me. She nods stiffly, arms crossed over her chest, and turns away. After a moment, she storms out of the room.

Ginny gives me a sympathetic look, but I know what she's thinking. I should have done this long ago. And she's right.

I punch the number for the Delta Hotel into my phone. "I need a room for tonight," I inform them, spelling out Céline's name. Credit card details are exchanged, and it's done. The reservation is set.

"Your room is booked," I tell her, walking into the next room as I call a taxi from the app. Her jaw tightens, the only clue to her frustration. I scrawl the Delta's address on a piece of paper and hold it out to her. She snatches it and strides past me, her heels clicking on the hardwood floor.

Outside, the taxi arrives, and Céline pauses at the door, her silhouette framed against the fading day. For a fleeting second, I expect to see her shoulders shake with sobs, but she's unyielding, and not a tear stains her cheek.

"Goodnight, Céline," I call, but she doesn't turn back.

The door slams shut behind her, and the cab pulls away, offering me at least a short reprieve, though I know this battle is far from over. I reach again for my phone, finding Lucy's number. We were supposed to go to dinner this evening. My thumb hovers over the call button, hesitating. What will I even say? Sorry won't cut it. But I have to reach out. She deserves that. And I need to hear her voice.

The line rings, once, twice, thrice…voicemail. There's been a lot of drama today, but still, that feels like an omen.

"Lucy," I begin after the beep, "I'm so very sorry. I hate that you had to witness that, and I'm so sorry she's here. I guess dinner is off the table this evening… I hope you're doing okay. Please get in touch when you have a chance. I… Okay, thanks. Bye."

I pocket the phone, it's weight heavy against my thigh.

I lean against the railing of the porch, staring out at the street. I think about the life I've started to build here — my job, the camaraderie with my team, the satisfaction when our efforts bear fruit. A twenty-three-minute reduction in wait times is truly a victory. Then Dr. Johns looms in my mind, the one blemish on my professional landscape. Yet even that struggle seems minor compared to this mess I have to navigate with Céline. While I once thought she would realize she belonged with me in Vancouver, I know now she doesn't. She never did.

I am a means to an end for her, not a partner. She belongs back in Montreal, close to what's familiar to her, where she can get what she needs. Vancouver is my city, my life now. My future. I think again of Lucy. I desperately hope she will understand all this, that she'll give me a chance to sort through it and explain my newfound clarity.

A cool breeze whispers through the trees, and I tug my collar up against the chill. Time to go inside, to face an evening alone with my thoughts. Lucy's absence is a void, Céline's presence a ghost. And here I am, caught between what was and what could have been.

Ginny appears as I come in, her arms crossed, an eyebrow raised.

"Sorry," I murmur, the word feeble against the drama that has unfolded tonight.

"Chance," she says "you're tearing these women apart. And that's not you. It's not the man I know you to be." She steps closer, her gaze unwavering. "You need to figure out what you want and go after it. Stop this…this juggling act. It's not fair to anyone."

I nod, taking in her words like a splash of cold water. She's right. This isn't who I am, — or at least, it's not who I want to be.

"Thanks, Ginny. I'll… I'll sort it out."

She gives me a pat on the shoulder before slipping off to her room. I turn and go down to my bedroom, each step heavy with thoughts of Céline's angry departure and Lucy's withdrawal. My bed is neatly made, a stark contrast to everything within me.

Slipping between the cool sheets, I close my eyes and let the darkness envelop me. But sleep is elusive; images of Céline flicker behind my eyelids, days when love seemed unshakable, nights wrapped in passion and promises. Yet there's an emptiness to those memories now, a realization that our connection might have been shallower than we believed.

And then there's Lucy. The thought of her sends a flutter

through my stomach. Her laughter rings in my mind, a sound that lights up even the dreariest days. With Lucy, everything seems brighter, lighter. I crave the way she tilts her head back when she laughs, the spark in her eyes when she's excited about something, the warmth of her hand in mine.

Céline was once my everything, but somewhere along the line, we lost the tune we used to dance to. Now, with Lucy, it feels like music has returned to my life, but the song is different, richer somehow.

I roll to my side, burying my face in the pillow. The way forward is bound to be tangled, but one thing is crystal clear. I want to be here in Vancouver, and I want to be with Lucy.

I reach for my phone, the weight of Ginny's words still heavy on my shoulders. I dial Lucy's number again, my heart hammering against my chest. When she answers, her voice instantly sooths the turmoil of my thoughts. "Lucy, I'm so sorry about Céline," I start.

"It's okay. You told me at the beginning you were trying to get over her. That process is not quite finished, I guess?"

I sigh. "I didn't ask her to come here. I didn't know she was coming. I've told her we're finished, but she's not listening. I need you to know, though, that she and I are finished. She is my past, and my future is here in Vancouver. I know that. It just may take a little time to convince her and get her to leave."

"She's still here?" Lucy's voice sounds a little shrill.

"She's staying at a hotel," I assure her. "I couldn't just kick her out on the streets."

"Okay," she says after a long silence. "Do what you need to do. I want you to have the space and time you need. And I... I think I need some space too."

Her voice cracks, then the line goes dead before I can protest. I stare at the ceiling, the dull ache behind my ribs sharpening. I need to fix things—and quickly. That's the only way I'm going to get back to moving forward.

With shaky fingers, I compose a text to Céline.

Me: Can we meet for breakfast tomorrow downtown?

She needs to understand, and I need closure. After a moment, my phone vibrates with her response.

Céline: Oui.

Me: DeDutch is across the street from your hotel. Does 9 work?

Céline: 8 is better.

Me: See you then.

I close my eyes, trying to picture what tomorrow will bring, how I'll manage to convince Céline of the truth. That we're finished, and that's what's best for both of us. It's a tangle of emotions and history, one I'd rather not delve into, but there's really no choice. My future depends on it.

Tomorrow, I decide, will be a day of hard truths and, hopefully, the first step toward a future where the only knots are the ones I tie myself, deliberately and with purpose.

I slide into the booth at the breakfast place, my gaze fixed on the door. The scent of freshly brewed coffee fills the air. I check my watch for the third time. It's eight o'clock on the dot, eleven to Céline's body clock.

Eight twenty rolls around before she finally sweeps into the diner. Céline's entrance never changes, always grand, always late. My jaw clenches as she slides into the seat across from me, not a word of apology crossing her lips. It's typical behavior, the kind that used to be endearing but now grates on my nerves like sandpaper.

I nod, pressing my lips together to keep from saying what's on my mind. Instead, I flag down the server, eager to get this meeting underway.

"Morning, folks. What can I get ya?" the server asks with a chipper tone that does not at all match the tension at our table.

"I'll have two eggs, scrambled, with bacon and toast," I say.

Céline gives a delicate sniff, as if the very idea of food offends her. "Just black coffee for me, thank you," she tells the server with a dismissive wave.

The server scribbles on her notepad and disappears.

"Black coffee? That's it?" I catch myself. Arguing over her choice of breakfast isn't why I'm here. She is free to do as she wants. Always has been. There are bigger fish to fry.

"I never have breakfast. You know that," she says, her eyes avoiding mine as she pulls out her phone and fiddles with it.

I lean back against the vinyl seat, tapping an impatient rhythm against the Formica table. We're here to talk, yet silence has enveloped us. And as much as I crave clarity, I find myself fearing the conversation, the mess it's going to create.

"Chance?" She finally looks up at me, her expression unreadable.

"Yeah?" I reply.

"Never mind," she murmurs, turning her attention back to the phone.

Eventually, Céline fills me in on what's going on with her family and her best friend, Marie. Nothing different from when I left months ago.

The server returns with my plate of eggs and Céline's coffee. I mumble a thanks and watch as Céline wraps her hands around the steaming mug, her fingers tracing the rim.

"Is it good?" she asks, nodding toward my plate as I take a bite.

"It's fine," I respond. But the food doesn't matter.

"Fine," she echoes, a ghost of a smile playing on her lips.

"Yes," I affirm. I clear my throat, bracing for the questions I must ask. "What made you come out here, Céline?" My voice is calm, but it takes effort to keep it so.

She hesitates, fidgeting. "I've been waiting for you to come home," she says.

"Home..." The term feels foreign now. "Céline, I took this job because we wanted to move here together." I feel the weight of that, the choice I made to please her, not fully considering how it would impact me. Fortunately, I've been happy with the outcome. Most of it, at least. "Now, my work's here, and I'm locked in a contract for three years. But more than that, this is where I want to be. This is what's right for *me*."

Frustration tightens her features, a response I'm not accustomed to invoking. Usually, I fold under her displeasure, but something's changed within me. "What does your mother say?" I prod gently, knowing the influence her family holds over her decisions.

"She thinks I should just move here," Céline admits, her gaze dropping to the table. It's a surprising revelation.

"But that's not what you want, right? It's not what you've ever wanted."

"I thought I could do it, but my friends, family..." Her voice trails off, a mixture of defiance and doubt coloring her confession.

It's clear to me that our lives are diverging, our needs anchoring us to different shores. From this vantage point, I find it amazing that we managed common ground for as long as we did. I am not that person anymore. Inadvertently, she is the one who showed me that when she left me to do this on my own.

Céline's eyes lock with mine as she reaches across the table. "Chance, please," she pleads. "Come back to Montreal with me. We can start over."

I feel my jaw tighten, a familiar ache setting in at the base of my skull. I want to be anywhere but here, caught in this tug-of-war. Why can't she just let go? "Céline, my life is here now," I say, forcing the words out past the lump in my throat. "This is where I want to be. We want different things, so it makes sense that we're in different places."

"If you loved me, you'd come back," she insists. It stings, that suggestion that love should be measured by sacrifice alone. I realize this is truly what she believes. That love is a matter of meeting her needs, without regard of what it costs anyone else.

"I will always care for you, Céline. You have been an important part of my life. But that part is over now. I need you to let go, to see that's what's best for both of us." A wash of clarity flows over me, and I can't believe this ever felt confusing to me, though I know it did. I was tangled in this just as deeply as she still is. The moment the words leave my mouth, I know it's futile. We are at an impasse, rooted in our separate ways of seeing the world.

She stands abruptly, chair scraping against the floor. Without a word, she strides away, her figure disappearing into the sea of people outside the restaurant window on the sidewalk.

I stay put, resisting the urge that tugs at me to chase after her, to comfort her. But even if it's painful, I need her to see this truth. Perhaps it has to be painful for her to truly acknowledge it. So much of her life is about avoiding pain and discomfort… Deep down, I think I've always known Céline would never leave Montreal. I came to Vancouver, perhaps subconsciously, to let distance help with the work of untangling our lives. I certainly couldn't see how to do it—or even fully realize it needed to be done—in Montreal.

It's time to move on, to embrace the possibilities ahead. Lucy is the one who fits into my life. She's the partner I want—a true partner who considers my wellbeing as well as her own. I've confused her and hurt her, I know. With one battle fought, and, hopefully, finished today, now, it's time to make things right with her.

CHAPTER 25

Chance

After breakfast this morning with Céline, I was ready to head straight over to Lucy's, but I stopped by the hospital for what was supposed to be a brief check-in, not wanting to bother Lucy too early, but then an emergency kept me there for hours. I'm only now headed to see Lucy.

I'm thrilled to find a parking spot outside her apartment building, and I carefully wedge the Explorer in. I'm taking this as a good sign. I scan the windows, searching for any indication of her presence, but the blinds are drawn tight, no light or the flicker of her TV. With a sigh, I step out into the cool afternoon air.

"Lucy?" I call up to her window as I approach the door, knowing it's a long shot. No response comes. I buzz and then wait. She doesn't answer. She's not here; I can feel the absence like a weight in my chest.

I retreat back to my car and drive back the way I came,

to Barney's this time. Maybe she's been called in to work at the pub.

Barney's is buzzing when I arrive, as it is most Saturdays. But as I survey the room, there's no trace of Lucy.

"Hey!" Janelle calls from behind the bar, her smile warm. Her hair is pulled back in a neat ponytail, a few strands framing her face.

I sit down across from her. "Hi, Janelle." I manage a smile. "How are your nursing classes going?"

"They're great. Thanks for asking. I have one more semester, and then I'll be begging you for a job." She wipes her hands on her apron, her brow lifting. "You seem off. What's going on?"

I sigh. "I'm looking for Lucy. Is she working today?"

Janelle's brow furrows. "No. She's not. What happened?"

I hesitate, rubbing the back of my neck. I know she and Lucy are tight, so I open up. "It's...complicated. My ex, Céline, showed up out of nowhere and made a big scene last night. It ruined my plans with Lucy. I talked with Céline again this morning, though, and now, I need to talk to Lucy about it, let her know everything's okay."

"Are *you* okay?" she asks.

"Been better," I admit, avoiding her gaze as I fiddle with a coaster.

After a moment, Janelle comes around the bar with a glass of amber liquid. She directs me to a booth, sets it in front of me, and slides into the booth on the other side.

"Spill."

"Céline and I — we were together for nearly ten years."

"Wow, that's..." Janelle trails off, her eyes searching mine.

"Complicated?" I offer, managing a wry chuckle.

"Something like that." She leans back.

"Everything happened so fast. We were living together by our second date," I continue.

"Sounds intense," she observes.

"Intense," I echo, the word tasting sour. "It was. Céline is. But then...things changed." I hesitate, hating how vulnerable these admissions make me feel, but the truth claws its way out, regardless. "She stopped being the person who lifted me up. We just seemed to coexist. She wasn't working, and she was consistently unhappy. We talked about moving here, and I thought the change would be good for her and for us."

"She wanted to move?" Janelle asks.

"She said she did. Neither of us was where we wanted to be back in Montreal." I run my finger around the tiles on the tabletop.

Céline's pervasive discontent had seeped into every corner of our life together, leaving little room for joy or growth. I'd convinced myself this was a real chance for us to make things better. And I thought she'd believed that too, that it wasn't me pushing for this and dragging her along.

I stare into the half-empty glass of amber liquid. "Moving was supposed to be a fresh start," I murmur. "I thought if we changed the scenery, the rest would follow."

"New city, new beginnings?" Janelle prompts.

"Exactly." I force a smile, but it feels as hollow as the hope I'd harbored. "She supported me when I came out for the interview. And we celebrated when I got the job. Together, we found the apartment in North Van. Then we packed up most of our stuff, but three days before we were going to leave, she told me she was staying."

Janelle's eyes widen. "That must have been quite the surprise."

"I was shocked, and it was terribly difficult, but I'd already committed to the job, so I went anyway. At the time, I kept telling her I hoped she'd join me eventually. But I'm able to admit now that a part of me was relieved." I sigh. "Now, I'm definitely relieved. Last night was a stark reminder of why we aren't right for one another." My hands clench at the memory, the sharpness of Céline's words still ringing in my ears.

"Are you wondering if you made a mistake moving to Vancouver?"

"No." I shake my head. "I love it here. But everything is just a mess. Céline makes me feel guilty for leaving her, but I know that's just her fear. If she truly cared about me, she'd see that this is where I need to be." I let out a ragged sigh.

Janelle's head tilts, and she gives me a sympathetic smile. "You're braver than you think. Starting over takes courage. And it sounds like that's really what you want to do."

I take another sip from my glass.

Janelle leans back in her seat, her gaze steady on mine. "And how do you feel about Lucy? Where does she fit into all of this?"

"She's wonderful. I want her to be part of my future, but I—" I force myself to take a steadying breath. "She's nothing like Céline, and spending time with her has helped me see all the things that were missing from my previous relationship." A lump forms in my throat. "But I have to convince her of that. I've been dealing with the confusion of this mess from the beginning, and I haven't been entirely fair to her. And then she came over right in the middle of Céline's tantrum yesterday..." I scrub my hands over my face. "I've made it as clear as I can to Céline that I am done with our relationship, but I can't guarantee she's heard me. Lucy may not want all this mess. I'm not exactly a catch right now."

"Nobody's perfect," Janelle replies, a smile touching the corners of her lips. "We've all got our baggage. What matters is finding someone who helps you unpack it, not someone who adds to the load."

I nod. That's it exactly. Her words are comforting, offering a glimpse of hope in the dark tangle of my thoughts. "Do you know where Lucy might be today?"

The door jingles, and Janelle turns toward a group of newcomers, laughter heralding their arrival. She stands. "Sorry, I don't. And I have to get back to work. Let me know if you need anything."

I thank her, and my gaze drifts across the room, finding a few faces from the hospital. They're a comforting sight, reminders of routine and normalcy. We exchange pleasantries, and their words are kind, but I find no solace in the banalities of work schedules and weather predictions.

Restlessness gnaws at me, urging me to move, to escape. Leaving cash on the table, I wave to Janelle as I walk out the door. I'll just do one more pass by Lucy's place. Maybe she's home now. I'd feel so much better if I could just talk to her.

The result is the same for my second visit to Lucy's place today. It remains dark, and she does not answer, so I drive home. As I push open the door to my place, I hear Ginny knocking on our adjoining door. I climb the stairs and open it, greeted by the scent of chamomile. She motions me to a backgammon board laid out between mugs of steaming tea.

"Hey," she says. "How are you doing?"

"I feel a bit like I'm caught in a riptide," I admit, dropping onto the couch. "I need to talk to Lucy, but I can't find her."

"Let's play," she suggests, her hand hovering over the stones and dice. "It'll help take your mind off things."

Nodding, I join her at the table, and we fall into the rhythm of the game. The clack of ivory stones against the wooden board punctuates our conversation. Each roll of the dice, each strategic maneuver, feels like a metaphor for the choices I've been grappling with. Sometimes, it's not just about the move you make, but how you adapt to the roll you're given.

Ginny doesn't press, doesn't prod; she simply listens,

letting me unfold my tale all over again. How I realize Céline and I are not good for each other, and I need to get her to go home. How Lucy is part of my new life here, and she's shown me so much about how another person can be a true support. We have so much fun together, but I worry Céline's reappearance and my confusion have wrecked it all. I feel like a broken record after my conversation with Janelle earlier, but perhaps, if I do this enough times, the way forward will finally become clear.

I roll a four and a two, advancing my stones with a distracted flick of my wrist.

"Chance," she says. "Be honest with yourself."

I look away, unable to meet her knowing eyes.

The click-clack of the backgammon pieces seems to mock me as Ginny scoops them up after yet another victory. "Chance, you need to think carefully about what you want and what you're doing with Lucy," she says, her fingers pausing over the board. "You and Lucy... That's not just fun, and deep down, you know it."

I want to argue, to tell her she's wrong, but the words catch in my throat, strangled by the truth I'm not ready to face. Instead, I muster a feeble smile, stand, and shuffle toward the door. "Thanks for the game, Gin. I'll see you later." But the weight of her gaze follows me out.

Down in my apartment, the silence is deafening. I collapse on my bed, the springs creaking. The ceiling stares back at me, blank and indifferent to the turmoil inside my head. Lucy's laughter echoes through my memory, her smile flickers behind my closed eyelids.

I let out a sigh and roll to my side, pulling a pillow under my head. It should be simple, shouldn't it? Move on, start fresh, heal. Yet here I am, more tangled than ever. The thought of Lucy sends a surge of warmth through me, and that scares me a little. This isn't just fun. It's not. I've fallen — hard — and I don't know how to get back on firm footing.

My phone rings, and I flinch to find Céline's name

flashing across the screen. A surge of anger wells up within me. I've said everything I need to say, and she got up and left, rather than respond. She always expects that I'll be waiting whenever she's ready. But not now. I can't deal with this now. I press the ignore button, but the damage is done. The fragile reprieve I'd found, the hope that she'd actually heard me this time, shatters.

After a minute, I push the play button on the voicemail, and her voice, thick with tears, invades the room. "Chance, I love you. If you want to stay, I'll stay too. We can make it work." The words are a plea, a last-ditch attempt to get what she wants, what she thinks she needs.

But it's too late. I see things so differently now. She's not the partner I want, no matter where we are. She'll never be happy until she finds that within herself. I can't give it to her. I deserve more than what she can offer me. There's a better way forward. Yet I can't erase our history. I listen to her sobs, each one a painful reminder of what used to be. A decade of my life is now reduced to a voicemail full of empty promises. I turn away, pressing my face into the pillow to muffle the sound, but it's no use. I hear every word.

"Too late," I whisper to the emptiness around me. Too late for us, Céline. My heart is elsewhere, entangled in a mess of feelings for someone who's shown me what it means to truly live. Lucy has claimed the parts of me I thought were beyond repair. And there's no turning back now.

I sit up, the edges of my vision blurry with a cocktail of anger and revelation. I press my hands to my eyes, as if I could physically wipe away Céline's words, wipe away the years entwined with regret.

Ginny's right; she's always been right. Lucy and I—there's a depth to us, something real and profound that's grown in the spaces between our laughter and shared experiences.

Love. That's what this gnawing, insistent ache must be. Not the comfortable, worn-in love I thought I had with Céline, but something raw and fierce that threatens to consume me whole. With Céline, it was about enduring, surviving another day of cold words and colder silences. But with Lucy? It's about thriving, about the rush of blood through veins and the hunger for another smile, another touch.

"Lucy." Her name is a whisper, a prayer, a curse all at once. What I've built with her offers a chance at something real, something vital. But I have to convince her it's real, that Céline's not a factor, even if she refuses to disappear.

I lean my forehead against the cool glass of my window, feeling my heart beat against my chest. It's not about Céline anymore; it never really was. It's about what comes next, about the terrifying, exhilarating possibility of letting go and falling into something new, side by side.

I just need to explain all this to her. If only I could find her. I feel the evening stretching out before me, and it makes me a little panicky.

I thumb out a text message to Lucy.

Me: I tried stopping by, but you weren't home. Can we talk?

CHAPTER 26

Lucy

The intercom buzzes, and I know it's Janelle even before she announces herself. I buzz her in and open my door to the scent of tomato sauce and fresh basil wafting up from the hallway. When she appears at my threshold, she's holding two Gusto's pizza boxes, a house salad balanced precariously on top.

"Got our faves," she says. She steps inside, kicking the door closed behind her.

"Smells amazing." My mouth waters, despite the turmoil churning in my stomach.

"Caprese for the cheese fiend…" She points to me. "And fungi for the earthy mushroom lover." Janelle smiles proudly as she sets our dinner on the coffee table.

"Perfect." We sit cross-legged on the floor, divvying up the pizzas so we each get half of both.

She watches me over a forkful of salad, her eyes soft with

concern. "So...how are you holding up after the whole Jimmy O'Connor bombshell?" she asks.

"Conflicted," I admit, picking at a slice of caprese. "I kept myself busy running errands all day, but I can't stop thinking about it no matter what I do. I mean, he's practically a stranger, yet..." My voice trails off, and I gesture toward an old photo album on the coffee table.

Janelle scoots closer, and together, we flip through the pages. "Was he always..." Her question fades as we come across a picture of my baptism in Dublin. There's Jimmy, lurking in the background.

"Right there, and I never noticed." The words taste like ash on my tongue. "I always thought his presence was just...coincidental. He was a friend of my dad's visiting or here for his work."

"Lucy, look at this one." Janelle points to another photo, taken not long after we'd arrived in Vancouver. A younger me sits on Jimmy's lap amidst a crowd of patrons and friends at my parents' bar. "It's like he's been hiding in plain sight."

"Exactly." I feel the pieces clicking into place, a puzzle I never asked to solve but can't ignore. Jimmy O'Connor, a name that now carries weight beyond any crime headline or family scandal. He's part of me, whether I like it or not.

I reach for the next page, my fingers brushing against glossy memories, and there it is—a strand of truth in a sea of questions. "You know," I murmur, tracing the outline of a woman with hair like spun gold, "I always assumed my red hair was a gift from my father's mother. But she was more strawberry than anything."

Janelle leans over, her gaze following mine to the photo of my grandmother holding me as an infant. "She's beautiful," she says. "But yeah, I see what you mean. Her hair's lighter, not quite the same as yours."

I nod, flipping back a few pages to a candid shot of Jimmy O'Connor. The setting sun casts a fiery glow on his hair, mirroring the color that cascades in waves down my own shoulders. "But look at him," I say, the realization tightening around my heart like a vise. "I got his auburn."

Janelle reaches out, her hand warm and steady on mine. "It's a lot to process, Luce. But it's also just hair, you know? It doesn't define who you are."

"Maybe," I concede, though the thought offers little comfort.

We sit in silence for a moment, and then Janelle shifts, her practicality surfacing as she tucks a strand of hair behind her ear. "So, are you planning to go see the apartment building in Ireland?" she asks.

I sigh, feeling the pressure of decisions yet to be made. "Eventually, yes. But I can't just put my life on hold. It will have to wait for the end of the school year at least. And right now, everything's being managed by a lawyer. It's complicated enough without adding travel into the mix." I give a rueful laugh.

Janelle nods, her expression sympathetic. "Well, when you do decide to go, you won't be alone. I'll come with you if you'd like. We can face whatever's waiting together."

"Thanks," I whisper. In a world filled with unexpected shadows, her friendship is a constant light. I'm grateful. I take another bite of pizza.

"Have you talked to your dad about all this?" she asks. "Have you talked to him since he gave you the letter yesterday?"

I set down my half-eaten slice. My chest feels tight. "We haven't really spoken," I admit. "He's... he's hurting. This whole situation is tearing him apart, and I know he loves me. I mean, he raised me as his own." The words escape in a whisper, and then the tears come, betraying the pain I've been trying to keep at bay.

Janelle scoots closer, her arms wrapping around me. She doesn't say anything, just lets me cry. After a while, when my sobs subside to sniffles, she speaks again.

"What about Chance? Have you spoken to him?" When

I shake my head, she continues. "He was at your dad's bar today looking for you. Sat there for over two hours, waiting."

"Chance?" His name is a splinter under my skin. "Why would he look for me?"

"From what he said, he needed to talk to you about Céline, what happened and how it ended between them."

I shudder at the mention of her name. "He's not over her. I saw his face. He was mortified when I showed up while she was there."

"Maybe," Janelle counters, "the look on his face wasn't because of Céline. Maybe he was embarrassed that you had to witness that debacle."

"I don't know," I say without conviction. "That's what he said when I spoke to him after, but I was overwhelmed. He needs to deal with this in the way that works for him. This is all just terrible timing. I don't have the bandwidth to help, and my presence there was only making it worse."

I twist a strand of auburn hair around my finger, the color a painful reminder of truths I'd rather forget. I sigh. "I don't know how this is going to sort out, and it's my fault for getting so involved, believing he could open his heart to me."

Janelle leans forward, her brown eyes earnest. "He was very clear about what he needed to say to you," she insists. "That has to mean something, especially after all these months without Céline."

"Means he's as lost as I am," I murmur, hugging my knees to my chest. "He's not cruel. He wants to let me down easy. He's not over her. I'm just the girl he uses to try to forget."

"Lucy…" Janelle's voice is soft, but there's steel behind it. "You know pain too well. Don't let it cloud everything. Your mom…what happened with her was tragic, but you're not her. You can't live fearing love because of the past."

Tears sting my eyes. "But history has a way of repeating itself, doesn't it?"

"Only if you let it." Janelle settles her warm hand on mine. "Don't give up on Chance just yet. There's something amazing there, waiting for you both. Just have a little faith."

Faith. A fragile thing, easily broken. Yet I want to cling to it, to believe in the possibility of a different ending.

Night falls, and we shift from the living room to my bedroom, neither of us ready to be alone with our thoughts. We talk about everything and nothing, and eventually, our conversation dwindles into silence.

"Lucy," Janelle murmurs just before dreams overtake her, "it will get better. I promise."

In the dark, with my best friend by my side, I allow myself a small, tentative hope. She's proven I'm not as alone as I felt there for a while. So maybe she's right about this too.

CHAPTER 27

Chance

The following Monday afternoon, I push open the heavy door to Joe Forte's, a popular restaurant and bar known for television and movie star sightings and a decent steak menu. Céline selected it for us. She's already at the bar. We've been going back and forth for days now, and I've mostly avoided seeing her. But something in her voice when she called this meeting made me feel like I should show up. I have to be at work a little later, so that will keep things from spiraling out of control.

I just want this done so I can face Lucy with a clear conscience, my past left firmly behind me. She and I have exchanged a few messages and spoken briefly, but she's made it clear I need to handle this on my own. So that's what I'm going to do.

"Hey," I say as I slide onto a stool beside Céline, offering a smile that feels stiff around the edges.

"Chance," she says with a nod.

She orders something pink and frothy in a martini glass, and I ask for glass of water because I have to work later. It's become a taste of home or what's starting to feel like it. I take a pull from the cool glass when it arrives.

We attempt small talk, batting trivialities back and forth. "How do you stand all the rain?" she asks, swirling the stem of her glass between slender fingers.

I shrug, watching the droplets race down the windowpane. "Better than shoveling snow," I reply, thinking of Quebec winters. "There's something about the rain, the way it cleanses everything. Makes the world feel…renewed."

She doesn't seem convinced, peering into her drink as if it holds answers or perhaps an escape route. She finally sighs, a sound that seems heavier than the atmosphere in the room. "I'm leaving," she says. Her voice is soft but steady, like she's practiced this.

"Back to Quebec?"

She nods, and I notice a slight tremor of her hand. "I can't leave my sister, my family… I thought I could, but…" She trails off, looking away. "I may not have a job right now, but they're my everything."

My mind shifts to all the arguments we had when we were together. All the cajoling and talking about how great it would be here, but Montreal is where she belongs; I see that now. I just hope she really means this.

"Family's important," I concede. "You need to be where your heart feels at home."

She searches my face for something—resistance, maybe, or a plea to reconsider—but she finds none. Because even though saying goodbye carries a sting, it's not the sharp, unbearable pain it might once have been. It's an ache, a pang of what was, and perhaps also a silent acknowledgment of what will never be.

"Will you be okay?" she asks after a moment, concern knitting her brows.

"Yeah," I assure her, and I mean it. "Yeah, I'll be okay."

Céline's eyes shimmer with unshed tears. "Chance, I was lying to myself," she admits. "The idea of moving here, it was all so…romantic in my head. But when it became real, I panicked."

I lean back, taking in her confession. It's been some time since I felt she was truly being honest. Sadness sparks in my heart. I remember the connection we once had, and I wonder what changed. I wonder if somewhere beneath all her discontent, she's still that woman I once loved. But then…

"Come back with me," she begs. "Let's go back to what we had, to Quebec, to us."

A sigh escapes me. Nothing has changed. She's still ruled by fear, by a desire to control me and my choices. My hand wraps more tightly around the cold water. "Céline, I can't," I say firmly. "I won't. I love my life here in Vancouver."

Her head snaps up, eyes searching mine for an explanation. Maybe the truth will help this become real to her.

"I'm doing important work at my job, and there's Lucy," I confess. I've told her these things all week. I don't know why we have to go through it again. "She's important to me."

"Is it serious?"

"Could be," I murmur, thinking of Lucy's fiery hair.

"You will always be my biggest regret," Céline says, each word laced with pain. "I thought if I came here, you'd fight for us."

She hasn't heard a word I've said for months. Or maybe I wasn't saying it clearly, unsure what I truly wanted as well. I close my eyes briefly, wrestling with guilt and relief in equal measure. I want to comfort her, to reach across the gulf that has opened between us, but it wouldn't be fair. "I'm sorry," I finally say, and mean it.

She doesn't cry, doesn't make a scene. She simply nods, seeming to accept the finality of my words. "Then I guess this is goodbye," she whispers, standing.

"Goodbye, Céline." My voice is steady as I watch her

walk away, her shoulders squared.

I look down at my watch; it's time to prepare for my night shift. As I stand and button my coat, my mind drifts to Lucy, to all the things I need to tell her. I think I might finally be ready. Once this shift is behind me, I'll put everything I have into making things right with her. Showing her I'm ready for us to move forward. I hope that's what she wants too. I hope the damage can be repaired.

I pay the tab and step out into the Vancouver drizzle, the rain a fitting backdrop to the end of one chapter and the uncertain beginning of another.

A few hours later, the fluorescent lights of the emergency department flicker above me as I lean over the chart, my mind churning a constant pattern of worry in the background. The more I think about Lucy, the more I worry about the chasm that's opened between us over the last week. What if it's too late? What if it took too much time to resolve things with Céline? What if she doesn't believe me that the past is done?

The patient before me, a middle-aged man with deep-set lines in his face, is contorted in agony, his breaths shuddering through clenched teeth.

"One hundred milligrams of morphine," I order.

Melissa, the nurse standing across the bed with syringe already in hand, freezes. "I can't do that."

Frustration flares. "He's in pain, Melissa. We need to manage it now."

She doesn't back down, her eyes shifting to something behind me. "Look at the chart," she says.

I spin to grab it, the patient's moans a dissonant soundtrack to my own racing heart. In bright red, almost screaming off the page, I read, *Severe allergy to opioids.*

"Damn it." A rookie mistake, one that could have been catastrophic. I'm not this careless. But then again, I've never been this distracted. What is happening to me? *Do better, Chance.*

"Chance?" Griffin's voice cuts through the fog of self-reproach. He's got that look, the one that says he's not asking so much as telling. "Dinner break. You're coming with me and Kent."

"Griffin, I—"

"Nope." He's suddenly right up in my face, his expression unyielding. "You're making time."

The urgency in his voice pulls me away from the precipice of guilt. There's no arguing with that tone; besides, maybe stepping away is exactly what I need to reset. I nod, leaving instructions for an alternate pain-management plan, and follow Griffin out of the ED.

We walk in silence, the rhythmic sound of our steps on the wet pavement grounding me in reality. Kent joins us, jogging to catch up. The sandwich shop a few blocks away feels like a world apart from the life-and-death decisions of the hospital. Maybe here I can clear my head enough to figure out how to fix the mess I've made of things—with Lucy, with my job, with myself.

I pull open the door and step inside, flanked by Kent and Griffin. The smell of fresh bread and grilled meat does little to ease the tightness in my chest, but we order sandwiches and find a corner booth, away from the other patrons.

"All right, spill," Kent says. "What's got you so twisted up that you're almost dosing patients with their allergens?"

I run my fingers through my hair and exhale deeply. "It's my ex, Céline… She showed up out of nowhere and made a big scene. Took me days to get rid of her, and I think I may have alienated Lucy in the process."

Griffin leans forward, elbows on the table. "I thought the Céline chapter was closed."

"It was," I agree, tracing the grain of the wood on the table with my fingertip. "Or at least, I'd told myself it was. But I don't think Céline had been hearing me, or maybe I wasn't clear. I was twisted up in a mess with her for a long time. Threw me off balance." I look up at them. "I think she understands that we're finished for good now, though."

"And what about Lucy?" Kent asks. "How does she fit into this?"

I hesitate, my mouth dry. "She's helped me see what a relationship can truly be. What it means to be in partnership with someone, but she walked in at a really bad moment with Céline, and I realized I haven't been fair to her from the beginning... She's not really talking to me," I confess. "She wanted me to take the space and time I needed to sort this out. I think I have, but now, I don't know if she's going to want to hear it."

"Look, man," Griffin says with a wry smile, "sometimes all it takes is getting between the sheets to clear your head, make things right."

I manage a weak chuckle, knowing he means well. "Maybe for some people, but I don't think Lucy wants that kind of fix—if she wants any part of me at all."

Kent nods. "You'll sort this out. I know it. And remember, we've got your back, no matter what."

Griffin claps me on the shoulder, and we turn our attention to the menus. The comfort of their solidarity settles over me. Their friendships are another thing new for me since moving to Vancouver. So many things are better here, so surely, I can navigate through this storm, get Lucy to understand how clear things are to me now, even as I'm still realizing the depth of my feelings for her.

Back in the ED, buoyed by the support of my friends, my mind feels a bit clearer. The shift is a slog, with one minor emergency after another, but I am grateful to avoid any further mistakes. I treat a child's infected ear canal, swollen and weepy, and then a twisted ankle, skin stretched taut over swelling, the owner looking embarrassed at his own clumsiness. I open another curtain to the sharp distress of a kidney stone, sweat beading the patient's brow.

This isn't the adrenaline-fueled pace of critical care that fuels my passion, but there's still satisfaction in easing these quieter urgencies. In the grand tapestry of life, every thread has its place, and I remind myself that each bit of relief I provide weaves strength back into someone's world. Things come together one piece at a time. That's how problems are solved. I should remember that in my own life as well.

I emerge from the hospital early the next morning, and the rain lashes down, relentlessly. Lucy was right about losing the bike and buying the SUV. I can almost hear her voice, that light I-told-you-so lilt, and for a moment, the memory of her smile calms me.

It's Tuesday, and Lucy's school day is just starting, so I know going to her now wouldn't do me any good. I navigate the slick streets, wipers working overtime and every turn a cautious negotiation with the elements. When I finally pull into my driveway, the house looks welcoming, with a lamplight beacon through the downpour. I check on Ginny before anything else.

"Hey, you okay here?" I ask, stepping inside, feeling the chill of her space through my scrubs.

"Yeah, just saving on heat." Ginny's voice floats from the living room, a touch too nonchalant.

"Come down to my place for dinner later? I'll order in Chinese, and we can play some backgammon. But first a nap for me."

"Sounds lovely," she replies, and I catch the relief in her tone, hidden beneath layers of independence.

"I'll see you about five?"

She agrees, and I disappear down the stairs. My eyelids are leaden as I collapse onto the bed. The constant churning of my brain from earlier has given way to total exhaustion. I have to recharge before I'll be any good to anyone. The hum of the rain against the window is a lullaby, coaxing me into sleep's embrace. In the quiet space between consciousness and dreams, Lucy's image flutters behind my eyes. Part of me wants to drive to her school, make a scene, and lay out all my cards.

But I don't. I need to do this carefully, respect her wishes. For now, I let the exhaustion claim me, and I fall into a deep sleep, where Lucy still exists in softer hues, untethered by reality. She laughs, unrestrained, in my dream, and for a moment, everything feels like it could be okay. But even in sleep, there's a weight that presses down on me, the need to face what's been left undone, to right the course of a ship that's veered too far from its path.

When I wake up, the afternoon light filters through the blinds, casting thin stripes across the room. The dream clings to me but recedes as reality sets in. It's not yet time to order dinner, and Lucy's still at work, so I'm at a bit of a loss as to what to do with myself. I grab my phone and walk out to the kitchen, dialing home to check in with my mother.

After a moment, her voice fills my ear, warm and inviting. "Chance, mon cher," she says.

"Hey, Mom. What are you up to?" I ask.

"Making tourtière, your favorite. With minced venison this time." Her voice holds a smile I can practically see.

"Venison? Sounds perfect." My stomach rumbles. "Save me a piece?"

"Of course, my boy. When are you coming to get it?" Her laugh tinkles through the air.

"Hopefully soon, Mom. Hopefully soon." I lean against the kitchen counter, phone pressed to my ear. "I've been working on reducing the ED's wait times," I tell her, feeling a mix of pride and exhaustion as I explain.

"Ah, you can do better than that," she replies, her tone both challenging and supportive. Her belief in me is a beacon, always urging me to push harder, reach farther.

I hesitate before delving into more personal matters, my gaze drifting across the room. "Céline came out and tried to convince me to return to Montreal," I confess, the words bitter on my tongue.

There's a pause, and then, "Mmm…" That single hum of contemplation tells me all I need to know about my mother's feelings for Céline She's never one to hide her opinions, especially not from me. "I'd love to have you back, but Céline was always more interested in the latest fashion than anything substantial," she notes. I can't deny the truth in that observation.

The conversation shifts, lighter now as she tells me about her planned visit. "We're coming out there this summer, and your sister too. Make sure you can take some time off."

"Will do, Mom," I promise.

After we say goodbye, I hang up and look out at the yard. Vancouver might not get buried in snow like we do back home, but winter here demands its own rituals of readiness. And I still have a little time before dinner. Lucy's done with school, but is this the right time to drop all this on her? I'm not sure. As much as I want things to be good between us again, I'm having trouble mustering the courage to face her.

Instead, I pull on a jacket and step out into the chilly air. Ginny's bushes need protection from the frost, so I start with them, wrapping each one carefully in burlap. My fingers work deftly, memories of past winters guiding my movements.

Next, I tackle the garden, raking out the dead leaves and spent perennials that Ginny had planted with such hope in the spring. The physical labor is grounding, pulling me away from tangled thoughts of repairing things with Lucy and into the simple reality of earth and debris.

"Chance, you're an angel," Ginny calls from her window. Her gratitude warms me against the biting air.

"Just doing what needs to be done," I reply with a smile. The work might be mundane, but it feels good to be useful, to make things a little better for someone else. It's the same drive that propels me in the emergency department, though the stakes are undeniably higher there.

As darkness begins to settle and the last leaf is bagged, I straighten, muscles protesting pleasantly. I make a call as I head inside, and in no time, the aroma of garlic and soy sauce wafts through the air. I set the white plastic bag of Chinese takeout on the counter as Ginny makes her way down the stairs. My stomach growls in anticipation. Ginny's favorites are also my guilty pleasures. I extract the containers of egg foo young and beef and broccoli, arranging them on plates as Ginny arranges the backgammon board on the dining table.

"Thanks for dinner," she says. "I've been craving this all week."

"Least I can do," I reply, trying to keep my tone light despite the heaviness in my chest. We settle into our respective seats, the familiar pattern of the game unfolding between us, a welcome distraction from the restless thoughts that refuse to give me peace.

Several dice rolls later, as I contemplate yet another losing position, Ginny finally breaks the silence, her words sharp and direct. "So when are you going to get off your butt and go fix things with that beautiful redhead?"

I flinch and put down the dice. "Céline left yesterday, and I think she's gone for good. Lucy made it clear that she wanted me to sort out that situation before I approached her again. So I think that means I'm ready now, but I don't know how to reconnect with her. I want to talk, but I don't know how hard to push. I don't want to make things worse," I mutter, a defensive edge creeping into my voice.

Ginny *tsks*, shaking her head as she captures another one of my stones. "Chance, Lucy wouldn't be so torn up if she didn't have feelings for you. You need to see that. And if something's bothering her, she needs a friend. I can't think of much that gets better in a vacuum."

Her words shine a light inside my head. Could Lucy have deeper feelings for me? Not just be annoyed? Is that why she's been pushing me away? A jolt of hope surges through me, but it's quickly doused by uncertainty. I still don't know quite how to approach her. "Damn," I whisper, losing all interest in the game.

Ginny's gaze softens. I'm grateful for her insight, even if it leaves me more confused than ever. "Think about it," she advises.

"Thanks, Ginny," I tell her. "I have to get ready for work, but I definitely will."

CHAPTER 28

Lucy

I muddled through school today, as has been my pattern since my life went crazy last week, and now, the final bell has rung, releasing me. Though, immediately, I feel a pull toward the bar. I need to talk to my dad, but since this bomb dropped, Beatrice has become the bastion of responsibility. She hasn't called out once, and Dad took me off the schedule. Rationally, I know that's likely because he's giving me time to deal with all that letter revealed, but it's also left me feeling adrift at the worst possible time and left me without an excuse to go to the pub.

So I guess I'll just have to go on my own. It's not like I need a reason to see Dad. I toss my backpack onto the passenger seat of my beat-up sedan and drive over to Barney's. A warm gush of air greets me as I push open the heavy wooden door. The bar is its usual hive of activity, but I don't see Dad.

"If you're looking for your pa, he's in the back." Mick,

the current bartender, nods toward the office without looking up from polishing glasses.

"Thanks, Mick," I tell him, slipping past the regulars and down the narrow hallway that leads to Dad's sanctuary.

The door is slightly ajar, and I knock softly before pushing it open. There he is, my father, hunched over a mountain of papers strewn across his desk. The sight of him stills me—eyes bloodshot and ringed with shadows deep enough to drown in, his hair unkempt and wild. He looks as though he's been wrestling with more than just inventory and payroll.

"Hey, Dad?" My voice is tentative, unsure. He doesn't respond, and I step closer, concern squeezing my chest. "Is everything okay?"

He finally lifts his gaze, and there's a vulnerability there I've never seen before, a raw edge to the man who has always been my rock. I swallow hard. Whatever is happening, whatever is tearing at him, I need to know. I want to help.

"Talk to me, Dad." I reach out, laying a gentle hand on his shoulder. "Please."

He tries to muster a smile and waves away my concern with a shaky hand. "Lucy, I'm fine," he says, but his voice is as crumpled as the papers before him.

"Fine?" The word fractures in my throat. "We've been each other's constants, the steady hands in the storm of life. And now, he's retreating into this shell, this husk I barely recognize. "You're not fine, Dad. Look at you!"

The frustration and fear claw up from my gut, and I can't stop the words that burst forth. "Why did you marry her? Why did you take me on—another man's child? What were you thinking?"

He recoils as if I've struck him. His shoulders slump, and his defenses crumble. "Lucy, I…" His voice trails off. Then, gathering the shards of his composure, he starts again. "I was so worried about you. I still am." His eyes, red and weary, brim with a sorrow so deep it threatens to engulf us both. "I loved your mam more than life itself. She was everything to me. And when she brought you into this world... You were hers, which meant you were mine too."

I reach out, pull him into an embrace, and hold on tightly.

"Jimmy O'Connor," he scoffs. "He took her from me. And now, he's going to take you too."

"Me?"

"I'm sorry I didn't tell you. Your mam and I talked about telling you, but then she left us."

Tears blur my vision as I pull back to look at him. "Dad," I choke out. "Jimmy O'Connor... He's just a man. A name. He wasn't there to hold my hand when I took my first steps or to patch up my skinned knees."

My father looks up at me, and I take a deep breath, steadying myself before I continue. "He didn't stand beside me at Mam's funeral, holding me together while everything else fell apart." My voice cracks, but I push on, needing him to understand. "You did. You've always been there. You're my dad, in every way that counts."

The dam breaks. His arms encircle me, pulling me into a bear hug that smells of old cologne and the faintest hint of whiskey, the scents of my childhood. We're both shaking, our tears mingling as we cling to each other.

"Lucy," he whispers, his voice thick with emotion. "My girl. My only girl."

I nod against his chest. This is where I belong, safe in the knowledge that nothing can sever this bond.

After a moment, Dad pulls back slightly, wiping his eyes with the back of his hand. A sheepish smile plays on his lips as he switches gears.

"By the way," he says, his voice hoarse but lighter now, "I had to lay down the law with Beatrice. She's not calling out anymore, and she's been covering for Janelle while she's off studying for finals."

I raise an eyebrow, fighting back a smile. "So, you

figured out how to be the tough boss, huh?"

He gives me a reluctant grin, scratching his head. "Had to be done. Can't let the place fall apart, now, can I?"

"Of course not," I reply, my heart swelling with pride. This man, this beautifully flawed and resilient soul, is mine. No blood tie could ever compete with the love and history we share.

"Come on," I say, squeezing his hand. "The others can handle it. Let's go home."

I navigate through the dimly lit pub, feeling the curious glances of the staff as I take my father's arm. "I'm taking Dad home for the night," I announce, steel in my voice leaving no room for questioning. "He'll be back tomorrow."

"Sure thing." Beatrice nods as we pass.

The chill of the evening air hits us as we step outside and begin the familiar journey to my childhood home. Dad's steps are unsteady, but his grip on me is firm.

We reach the house, its facade bathed in the soft glow of the porch light. I usher him inside, steering him toward the bathroom. "Go shower, Dad. You'll feel better."

I'm determined to have us remember the good times, so the first thing I do is locate our home movies. I think the last time we watched these was when Mam died, but they always bring a smile. We need that right now. While the sound of water running fills the silence, I set about restoring order to the crazy that has crept into our lives. The phone feels heavy in my hand as I dial Zeffirelli's. Their spaghetti and meatballs have been a comfort food on countless nights before.

"Two orders, please. Yes, delivery. Thank you," I say as I hang up.

With dinner on its way, I turn my attention to the living room where empty takeout containers from the pub have colonized the coffee table. As I collect them, my gaze falls upon a shattered frame, a jagged fracture obscuring the smiling face of my mother. My breath catches.

"Lucy..." Dad's voice quivers from behind me. He's

fresh from the shower, his hair damp and sticking up at odd angles. "I—I did that. In a moment of anger... I thought I was losing you too."

I see the vulnerability written on his careworn face, the haunted look in his eyes that speaks of fears and regrets. Without hesitation, I close the distance between us. "There's no way you could lose me, Dad," I whisper fiercely, holding him tight. "Never. I'm right here. And I always will be."

The doorbell rings, and I peel away reluctantly, brushing a stray tear from my cheek as I go to answer it. The air carries the rich scent of tomato sauce and garlic, and a warmth that has little to do with the food wafts over me as I take the bags from the delivery person. "Thank you," I murmur, offering a small smile before closing the door.

"Smells like Zeffirelli's," Dad says eagerly.

"Only the best for tonight," I reply. We settle on the couch, plates balanced on our laps, the comfort of spaghetti and meatballs a cure to our frayed nerves. I load up one of the video tapes I found earlier, press play on the remote, and the screen flickers to life with scenes of my youth. The joy we shared, just him and me, plays out in every scene. Birthday parties, Christmas mornings, school plays—he was always there, front and center.

"Look at us," Dad says, his voice cracking. "We were quite the team, weren't we?"

"Are," I correct, reaching for his hand. "We are a team, Dad."

He squeezes my hand, his eyes glistening. And in that simple gesture, all doubts evaporate. Jimmy O'Connor may share my DNA, but Declan Sheridan is—and always has been...my dad.

CHAPTER 29

Lucy

The rain is a constant companion in Vancouver, a persistent reminder of the city's moody temperament. I shepherd my grade-five class outside, the droplets forming rhythmic patterns on our hoods and boots. We are a parade of colorful rain gear — slick yellow jackets and polka-dotted galoshes — the kids' laughter piercing through the gray drizzle.

"Kids, stay in line! Watch your step," I call, my voice barely cutting through their excited chatter.

Tiffany, teaching the adjacent class, falls into step beside me. "How's it going?" she asks.

"Every day's a little better," I reply, squeezing water from the hem of my coat. "But it's hard, you know?"

She gives me a side hug. "You're strong. This is a lot, but I know you're going to come out on top of all of this."

I manage a smile, grateful for her steadfast optimism. It buoys me, even when my heart feels like it's dragging along the ocean floor. "Thanks, Tiff. That means a lot."

We reach the covered playground, and the kids burst forth like corks from champagne bottles, scurrying across the wet concrete, swinging from bars, and chasing each other around the play structures.

"Be careful!" Tiffany and I chorus.

After half an hour, we have to believe their energy is back at a manageable level, so we traipse back inside to make another run at the day's lessons.

When we reach the classroom, the kids shed their rain-soaked layers with all the grace of molting birds. Puddles form under chairs, and the air fills with the earthy scent of wet soil-tracked indoors.

"All right, everyone, let's calm down," I tell them.

"Can we play games?" someone shouts, and a chorus of agreement rises.

"Games it is," I concede, pulling the boxes from the cupboard. There's checkers, Monopoly, Jenga, Ticket to Ride... "Remember to share and take turns," I remind them as they divide into groups, some making a beeline for the tablets on the charging cart.

"Spelling and math games are available too," I add.

I watch them find joy in simple pleasures and settle at my desk, occasionally glancing up to monitor their progress, ready to mediate any disputes or answer questions about rules. For now, though, they are content, and so am I.

A little while later, though, the checkerboard becomes a battlefield under Ivan and Ziar's intense stares as they each strategize their next move. I hover nearby, sensing tension. Their fingers twitch over the smooth disks, the air thick with silent accusations.

"Hey, guys?" I intervene just as a black checker is about to make a contentious leap over a red one. "Remember, it's just a game."

Behind me, Artem seems to be amassing an empire in Monopoly with all the focus of a seasoned mogul. It brings a smile to my face, seeing them so engaged, their earlier energy redirected into tabletop challenges.

I've just returned to my desk when a knock on the door sharpens my senses.

"Miss Sheridan," our principal says as she enters, her eyes twinkling above a large basket cradled in her arms. "This came for you."

"For me?" My brow furrows as I take the unexpected offering, the colorful array of apples peeking out like jewels in a treasure chest. Curiosity blooms inside me as I return to my desk and fish for the card nestled among the fruit. The familiar scrawl greets me, and my heart stutters before I steady my breathing.

> *Lucy,*
>
> *It's been far too long since I last saw your lovely smile and held you in my arms. I've missed you every day. I'm sorry I hurt you, and I'd very much like to explain, to talk things through with you. Céline has returned to Montreal, and we both understand that our time together is finished for good. Thank you for encouraging me to handle that situation. Your support and patience means everything, and I am looking forward to all the future holds — for both of us.*
>
> *They say an apple a day keeps the doctor away, but giving an apple to a teacher dates back to when apples were a form of payment, symbolizing knowledge and appreciation. I owe you so much more than apples, and I appreciate and*

miss you. Would you please have dinner with me?

Yours,
Chance

I tuck the card into my pocket and look up at the room full of expectant eyes.

Forcing a smile, I take a knife and a stack of paper towels from my drawer and slice through the shiny skin of a crimson apple. The kids cluster around my desk as they watch me quarter the fruit.

"Who sent all the apples, Miss Sheridan?" Artem asks, abandoning his Monopoly empire for the moment.

"Dr. Chance," I reply, keeping my tone light.

"Is Dr. Chance your boyfriend?" Mina pipes up. "My dad gives my mom flowers when he's sorry."

I place an apple slice on a napkin for her. "Sometimes, people give gifts because they care," I say.

"Then why is he sorry?" Bibi asks.

Mina nods sagely beside her. "Mommy says you don't have to accept an apology if you don't want to."

"That's very true," I concede, handing Bibi her share of the fruit. "How about you clean up the games while I cut apples to share with the rest of you?"

When the room has been restored to order, I pass out apples to each student just as the final bell rings. The kids dart from their desks, leaving a few scattered game pieces and damp jackets. With my hands braced against the cool surface of my desk, I watch them pile out of the classroom, their energy as relentless as the rain that taps against the windows.

"Quite the day, huh?" Tiffany's voice pulls me back to the present as soon as the door swings shut behind the last child.

"Always is," I reply.

"Heard you had some apples?" Her brow quirks up.

"What's up with the whole building talking about my apples?"

She leans against the doorframe. "Word travels fast around here. And apples are not just apples when they come with an apology note from Dr. Chance." She gives me a knowing look.

"Ah, so he's the talk of the staff room now?" I smile, but inside, I'm a quivering mess. I told him to manage the situation with Céline. And now, he has, or so he thinks. It feels foolish to believe we can just pick up where we left off. So I don't know quite where that leaves us.

"This was a heartfelt gesture," she points out, wrapping an arm around my shoulder in a sisterly side hug. "He's done what you asked, so at least hear him out, right?"

"I suppose," I concede. "I'm just feeling a little gun shy."

"Ah, you're braver than you think," Tiffany assures me. "Anyway, I've got piles of grading and a date with a software developer tonight. Wish me luck," she adds with a wink.

"Good luck," I call after her. "You deserve some fun."

Alone again, I turn to the task of tidying up the room. I stack chairs, collect stray markers, and corral the board games back onto their shelves. The rain continues its steady beat outside, a soundtrack to my methodical movements. My phone sits on the corner of my desk, silent and accusatory. I should probably text Chance back, but instead, I give it a wide berth, choosing to focus on the stack of spelling and math tests that demand my attention.

"Grading first," I mutter, sliding into my chair and flipping open the first test.

The red pen in my hand moves steadily, marking checks and crosses, tallying scores. The monotony of it is calming. By the time I reach the bottom of the pile, the sky has darkened.

"Okay. Time to face the music," I whisper, steeling myself as I reach for my phone. My thumb hovers over the screen before tapping out a message to Chance.

Me: Thank you for the apples.

It's polite, noncommittal, safe. I hit send before I can second-guess myself, and the familiar woosh sound feels like the closing of a chapter and the tentative turning of a new page, all at once.

Before I can even exhale the breath I'm holding, my phone erupts into a jingle, vibrating against the hard surface of the desk. Chance's name flashes across the screen, and my heart does an involuntary skip. I hesitate for a split second before answering.

"Lucy, hey. I'm glad the apples made it to you." Chance's voice is warm, familiar, tinged with something that sounds like hope.

"Hi. Yes, they did," I reply. "The kids enjoyed them too. We had quite the discussion about Dr. Chance and his apple delivery."

"Really?" He chuckles softly, and I can almost picture his smile. "I hope I'm still in their good graces."

"Of course. You're very much loved by your young fans," I assure him.

There's a pause on the line, and when he speaks again, his tone shifts. "Lucy, I can't thank you enough for your patience while I handled things with Céline. I remain very sorry that she showed up here, but I've realized so much, and I feel ready to move forward in a way I wasn't before. Everything is so much clearer, and I'd love the chance to explain."

My fingers tighten around the phone. "Okay," I whisper, feeling a tug at the corner of my heart, the one that still beats a little faster for him.

"I miss you. Could we go out for dinner?"

His words stir a longing inside me, a desire to dive back into the comfort we once had. I want to tell him everything, about the recent revelations concerning my father, about how every day has been a mix of confusion and clarity. But the memory of Céline's unexpected return stands like a warning sign on the path to reconciliation.

"Chance, I'm not sure that's the best idea," I start, my voice faltering. "You know, when we started this... I knew what it was. I was always the rebound, wasn't I? Just part of your process?"

"Lucy, it's not—"

"No, please, let me finish." I take a deep breath, gripping the phone tighter. "I need to protect myself too. I need to think about what's best for me."

He's silent on the other end, and I press my hand to my forehead, trying to quell the headache that's beginning to form. The classroom feels too big, too empty, echoing with the ghost of our conversation.

"Lucy, hear me out," he finally breaks the silence, his voice laced with a rebellious edge that isn't lost on me. "I have so much to tell you. Please. Let's not go to one of our usual spots. Let's do something different this time."

Oh, he's playing that card—the unexpected, the grand gesture. It's so like him to shake things up when the path becomes too familiar.

"I'm thinking St. Lawrence," he continues. "It's got a Michelin star. Quebecois cuisine at its finest. I can get us reservations. Maybe Saturday?"

My breath catches. *St. Lawrence.* The place is legendary, whispered about with reverence by food enthusiasts and critics alike. "Chance, I..." My throat tightens around the words. I want to say yes. I want to leap at the opportunity, to dress up and forget everything except the flavors set before us. But my heart, still tender from the week I've spent worrying about so many things, holds me back.

"Lucy?" His voice is softer now, tinged with concern.

I picture the restaurant again, the flicker of candlelight against fine china, the clinking of glasses, the murmur of conversation.

"Think about it," he says gently. "No pressure. I just... I can't just let this go—let you go. You are important to me. I've realized just how much. Let's just talk it through."

"Maybe," I whisper. I can think about it, yes. Weigh the pros and cons, imagine every possible outcome until my mind spirals into indecision. Or I could take the leap, let myself be swept into a night of indulgence and possibly mend what's been broken. "Okay. I'll think about it."

"Thank you. That's all I ask." He sounds relieved, hopeful even, as if my consideration is a victory in itself.

CHAPTER 30

Chance

The clock ticks past the end of Wednesday's night shift, but I'm still here, hunched over electronic medical charts on Thursday morning, determined to whittle down my backlog. I think I'm also determined to keep my mind occupied. Lucy hasn't confirmed whether she's accepting my invitation to dinner or not, so all I can do is wait. I force my focus back to the computer in front of me, and it's quiet for a moment, just the hum of the hospital and my clicking on the screen, until the double doors burst open.

"Dr. Devereaux!" Julie's voice slices through the lull, sharp and urgent. She's one of the nurses that's just come on for the next shift. My head snaps up. She's panting, face flushed.

"Julie?" I'm on my feet.

"It's a one-year-old female, unresponsive in her crib. She's breathing but just barely," she gasps. "Parents live close, drove her straight here."

Adrenaline spikes as I throw the chart I've been working on down on the desk and sprint to the room where the little girl lies, limp and frighteningly pale. Her chest barely moves, her lips tinged with a blue that sends a cold shiver down my spine.

"Talk to me," I command, even as I assess her vitals. No spontaneous heart activity. Cyanosis setting in.

"McGill forceps, now!" The tool is slapped into my hand, and I gently slide the tube down her tiny throat. One of the nurses, a blur at the periphery of my focus, starts bagging her, forcing life-giving air into lungs that have given up the fight.

"Has she been sick recently?" My voice is steady, clinical, as I look up at the parents—a mother and father clutching each other.

"No," the mother chokes out, tears streaming over cheeks pulled tight with distress. "She was fine… just fine…"

"Okay, okay." I nod, though my brain is racing ahead, cataloging symptoms, discarding possibilities. We'll get her stable first, then figure out the why. Because there's always a why…

"Any medications we should know about?" I ask, my gaze shifting from the child's face to her parents. They shake their heads almost in unison, their voices adamant as they respond. "She's not taking anything."

"Could she have gotten into something under a sink or on a bedside table?" I prod.

"No," the mother wails.

"Melissa," I say, directing my attention to the nurse at my side, who already has her kit prepared. "We need an IV, now." She nods, her hands steady as she searches for a suitable vein in the child's arm. My eyes flit back to the monitor.

"Got it," Melissa confirms. The small catheter slides into place, securing our lifeline.

"Let's check her glucose," I add, anticipation tightening my chest.

Melissa pricks the child's finger and reads the number

that flashes on the glucometer. "Blood sugar's twenty."

I curse under my breath. That's far too low. *Hypoglycemia.* It fits the puzzle, but we're far from done. "We need dextrose. Get me an eighteen-gauge spinal needle."

Nurses gently roll the baby onto her side, her tiny body so fragile. I take the needle, ready the dextrose, and administer it. It feels like forever, but only seconds pass before I'm listening to her lungs once more.

"Breathing sounds better," I murmur. Relief floods through me, but it's tempered by the knowledge that the day is just beginning. There are still answers to find, treatments to administer. But for now, this little girl's life is no longer slipping through my fingers like grains of sand. She's stabilizing, and that's a victory. "Let's get a blood gas, CBC, and chem seven," I announce.

The room moves in swift response, each nurse taking up her task with urgency but no sign of panic, a perfect reflection of our training. As they work, I turn to face the worried parents, who hover like anxious shadows at the edge of the emergency bay.

"Your daughter is going to be fine," I tell them, meeting their eyes with an assurance I've learned to muster. It's not a lie, but a promise I'm determined to keep. Their bodies sag with relief as they continue to hold onto each other.

Turning back to my patient, I scan the monitors, noting the numbers that indicate a battle being won. "Do either of you have a family history of diabetes type one?" I ask, peering over my shoulder at them.

They shake their heads, their expressions a mix of confusion and concern. "No, nothing like that," the mother says.

"Okay." I nod, processing this new information. "Nonetheless, it looks like she may be diabetic. We're stabilizing her now, and I'll summon our on-call pediatric endocrinologist. They'll be down shortly to get things set up and explain everything. Diabetes is very manageable, especially with early intervention like this."

After a bit of further discussion, the doctor arrives, and I step away from the relieved parents, leaving them in good hands. My mind is already shifting gears, and I pull out my cell. No messages. Then I spot Julie, her clipboard a shield against the onslaught of emergencies.

"Update?" I ask her.

"There's a rep from Prometheus Health waiting for you."

I nod. "Don't let them leave. What else?"

"Room two, woman with a broken femur waiting for ortho," she says, her eyes moving to the electronic board tracking the chaos. "And we've got an ambo incoming, firefighter with severe burns."

"Notify the burn unit. We'll need them on standby." The words are out before the weight of another critical patient truly registers. Like muscle memory, I tug on a fresh paper gown and snap on new gloves.

The ambulance bay doors rattle open, and the morning spills in with a gust carrying the acrid scent of smoke. The EMT meets my gaze, his eyes betraying the severity of what's inside the vehicle. "Thirty-year-old male, building collapse, extensive burns."

With a nod, I accept responsibility as he hands control of the gurney to me. "Let's move," I command. I brace myself for the next battle, ready to fight fire with science and willpower.

I scan the firefighter, taking in the expanse of white, charred flesh where his gear failed him, a stark contrast to the blistered and angry redness that speaks of second-degree burns on his hands, his face.

"Airway's clear," Melissa reports, her professionalism as unwavering, as if we're dealing with a sprained ankle instead of a man's life hanging by a thread. She's got an IV line in already. I'm thankful for her speed. It means pain management can start posthaste, and we can pump him full of fluids before his body gives up entirely on trying to retain moisture.

"Watch for respiratory distress," I instruct, hearing the rasp of his breath, the soot-stained wheeze that tells me his lungs aren't untouched. When he coughs, black mucus splatters against the gurney, a grim painting of what he must have inhaled.

"Got it, Dr. Devereaux," she replies.

The ambulance crew helps us wheel him to the elevator; our steps are swift but careful, a dance of urgency and precision.

"Prepare for intubation," I tell them, even as I feel the pull of fatigue in my limbs. It's been a long night. The elevator doors close, and I get him intubated. He's stable enough now for the burn unit upstairs, where real decisions will be made, where they'll chart out his future one graft at a time.

Once he's handed off, the adrenaline that's been fueling me ebbs away. My body slumps against the wall for just a moment, and then I head back downstairs.

Julie sees me coming down the hallway. "His name is Tom Lohman, and he's outside your office."

I nod and continue on until I reach my office. "Hi. I'm Dr. Chance Devereaux."

Tom stands. "Great to meet you. Sorry I haven't been by sooner. My wife and I just had our third child, and I took some paternity leave."

I shut the door behind us, and we sit down. "I'm glad you're here now. When I took over the ED six months ago, Eleanor Thompson didn't leave me any information on the study we're doing with you. I can't even find the contract. I'm hoping you can help me. I don't know what's going on."

"Absolutely." He pulls out his phone, and with a few clicks, he's emailed it to me. "The contract is pretty detailed. But the drug is being administered to some of your repeat visitors who are unhoused. I met with each of them and got their signed consent. The drug we're developing doesn't have to be administered on a regular basis. The first goal is boosting their immunity, as they have a higher risk of exposure to illness because of their lifestyle. The other component is a mental-health medication. It doesn't work like more targeted drugs because monitoring patients in this situation is nearly impossible. Instead, it's an antidepressant that releases over time, boosting overall outlook and energy. We've seen a lot of great response, and Mercy has been wonderful with the data."

I nod. "We've continued to collect the data but don't know where to send it, and it's pretty raw because I don't know what you're looking for."

"The person who took over for me during my parental leave didn't realize that was part of the job, and both Eleanor and I both left around the same time, so it was bad timing on all our parts. But that's okay. If you want to give me the data, we can compile it."

"I'd love a hard copy of the contract. And I'd also love any records you have about where the payments for the study are being deposited. I don't know where that money goes."

He nods. "I will have someone send you over the contract today. It was signed by the CEO of the hospital, and it pays one hundred thousand dollars twice a year."

My eyes go wide.

"From what she told me, Eleanor was using the money as bonuses for the nursing staff," Tom continues. "As you know, the ED is constantly short of nurses. She could have used the money to hire someone to compile the data, but instead, she was doing the compiling so she could keep the money for her team."

Thank goodness it was nothing nefarious. Why she left no record of this behind is a little confusing, but perhaps she had her reasons. "How much longer does the trial continue?"

"Three more years."

I nod. "I also want that money for my staff. If you don't mind compiling the data for the current batch and then perhaps someone can show me what you want from us. I can do it moving forward."

He agrees, and we talk a short while longer, making

plans for some training for me. He assures me he'll be by early next week to collect the data.

Once he leaves, I deal with a patient looking for opioids and refer her to a pain-management specialist. My shift is long over, but as I peel off my gloves, sticky with sweat and the day's grime, there's a prickling at the back of my mind, a voice that never quite quiets down. *You can do better.*

And I know it's right; there's always more to learn, another technique to master, another life to save. As I drag myself toward the locker room, each step feels heavier than the last, especially when I still have no response from Lucy. But that voice—it keeps me moving forward. It's the relentless pulse behind every choice I make, the insatiable desire to be better tomorrow than I am today.

CHAPTER 31

Chance

By Friday afternoon, I'm thrilled to say things are looking up. Lucy has finally texted to accept my invitation to dinner, and I can't stop grinning as I thumb the last emoji into my message back—a little chef's kiss because Saturday night is going to be perfect. Griffin swears St. Lawrence is a bastion of Quebecois delights and soft-lit romance, but this date is also going to be about more than just fine dining.

My phone hums with her response, a thumbs up emoji that sets another round of butterflies loose in my stomach. This is it, the perfect setting to repair our rift and then escalate things from casual to…who knows? I'm not sure how I can wait two more days.

My desk phone rings. It's the legal department.

"Chance, you got a minute?" William Long asks when I answer.

I tuck away thoughts of Lucy and focus on the here and

now. "Sure, William, what's up?"

"I reviewed the malpractice insurance," he begins, and I can hear the shuffling of papers over the line. "For the doctors volunteering at the safe-use clinics, we're missing a waiver of liability. They need to sign additional paperwork specifically for this work. It will mostly say they're doing this outside the realm of their duties at the hospital, and they're not covered by the hospital's malpractice insurance in that capacity. It's crucial."

"That offers us legal protection?" I probe.

"Exactly." There's the sound of a pen clicking. "Without it, any mishap could fall back on us — on the hospital."

"Got it. I'm sure I can get them to sign something if you can write up what you want," I assure him, mentally rescheduling my afternoon to deal with this new wrinkle. "William, can you meet me at Dr. Johns's office? We need to hash this out with him so he's comfortable. Let's try to get it done today."

There's a pause on the other end. "Actually, I'm due there in fifteen minutes," he replies. "We can talk about it then."

"Perfect," I say. This is my chance to set things right, to bridge a compromise everyone feels good about and make sure good work gets done. I hang up and immediately head to Dr. Johns's office with purpose in my stride.

The walk feels shorter than usual, or maybe it's just my newfound resolve quickening my steps. *Everything is coming together.* When I arrive, William is waiting, his expression serious but not unkind. We share a nod of mutual understanding; we're in this together now.

"Ready?" I ask.

"Let's do it," he responds, and together, we step into the lion's den, so to speak.

Dr. Johns's secretary gives us a knowing look as we pass her desk. William reaches for the handle before I do, pushing it open with a confidence I envy.

"Dr. Johns," William greets him as we make our

entrance. "Chance and I have been discussing the safe-use clinics..."

I follow his lead, stepping up beside him to present a united front.

"We've identified a potential issue with malpractice insurance, but we've also found a way forward that should cover the hospital legally," he continues.

The words hang in the air between us and Dr. Johns, who sits back in his chair.

"It's just a document we'd need each doctor to sign," I chime in, "noting that their volunteering is separate from their duties affiliated with the hospital."

The next move is his.

I stand firm, meeting Dr. Johns's wary gaze with determination. The lines on his forehead deepen, a clear sign of his discomfort with the situation.

"Dr. Johns, we're not trying to undermine your authority. But we have to consider the bigger picture. I can't afford to lose my staff, and their work at the safe-use clinic is important. It's also important to them, so if they're going to do this, we need to make sure we have the release."

He frowns. "Chance," he says slowly, "you know how this looks, right? Two against one. It's hardly fair." His hands grip the arms of his chair, knuckles whitening.

I nod. "I'm sorry you feel that way, but this isn't about fairness. We're working together to solve a problem, and we appreciate your support. Safe-use clinics are government sponsored. We know they make a difference. Volunteering is about saving lives. Every overdose victim we help at the safe-use clinics is one less emergency in the ED. And for those we can steer to rehab, it's a chance for a new beginning."

After a moment, Dr. Johns sighs. "All right," he concedes. "But I want it known that I'm not pleased with being cornered like this. This hospital operates on order and rules. You'd do well to remember that."

"Of course, Dr. Johns," I reply with a respectful nod.

"Thank you for understanding."

William explains a few details and the paperwork he'll put together, the conversation draws to a close, and I follow William out. As the door shuts behind us, I turn to him, realizing the safe-use clinics are the only topic we discussed.

"Wait, why were you scheduled to meet Dr. Johns today?" I ask. "Don't you have something else to discuss with him? Did we use up all your time?"

"Ah, that," he replies, waving a dismissive hand. "We'll reschedule. I don't want to hit him with too much at once. He needs time to digest today's developments."

"Fair enough," I say.

William walks beside me to the elevators, seeming a little stressed. I glance over at him, wondering about the burden of knowledge he carries.

"Can't say I envy you, having to navigate all these…legal pitfalls," I remark.

William lets out a half-hearted chuckle. "I think it's political, as much as legal. But it's in the job description. I've learned when Dr. Johns sets his mind to something, it's difficult to get him to adjust, but if you don't push too hard, he does better."

"That's a lot of managing."

"It is, but it's worth it." William smirks. "I'm also father to his granddaughter, and Cordelia and I will have another announcement soon."

I push the button to the elevator. "Are you expecting again?"

He smiles. "The kids will be about eleven months apart."

"Congratulations." I clap him on the shoulder. "That's big news."

"Thanks," he replies. "That's what happens when you marry a pediatrician. They want lots of kids."

The elevator arrives, and when I exit, I wave goodbye to William and opt not to walk into the ED. It's the end of the day, and the next shift is starting. I'm ready for a break. So instead,

I make my way across the street to Barney's. I push through the door to find Griffin and Kent already there, nursing their pints.

"Bonjour." I slide onto a barstool. The bartender nods and pours me a pint without me needing to ask.

"Chance, you look like you've just won the lottery," Griffin teases, raising his glass in a mock salute.

"Feels like it," I admit, taking a sip of the cool beer when it arrives. "Safe-use clinic volunteers are getting the go-ahead. With some additional paperwork, we'll soon have legal protection that keeps that work separate from the hospital."

"Cheers to that!" Kent raises his pint, and our glasses clink together in a satisfying chorus of solidarity.

We talk, laugh, and for a moment, the weight of responsibility lifts from my shoulders. But the absence of one person casts a shadow over the celebration. I wish Lucy were here. I want to share this triumph with her, to see her eyes light up with that fierce passion she has for making a difference.

"Missing your better half?" Griffin asks.

My thoughts must be obvious. "Something like that," I confess, a wistful smile playing on my lips. "But Saturday night's not too far off. We're going to dinner then."

"Then let's raise another round—for the clinics and for absent friends," Kent proposes.

"Absent friends," we echo.

Though that toast isn't exactly accurate. Lucy is so much more than a friend. I just have to convince her to share her heart with me.

CHAPTER 32

Lucy

The black fabric wraps around my body, the dress Janelle insisted I borrow clinging to every curve. She and Tiffany stand behind me, their eyes gleaming with approval in the mirror's reflection. "Lucy, you're going to knock him dead," Janelle says, adjusting the plunge of the neckline.

"Seriously. He won't even want to leave the apartment," Tiffany adds.

I laugh, but it's edged with nerves. "Well, that's definitely not on the menu for tonight…" My fingers fidget at the hem of the dress, then travel to the thong beneath. "I've spent my entire life making sure my underwear stays out of my ass crack, and now this thing seems to have taken up residence there." I roll my eyes at the ridiculousness of it all.

"Beauty is pain," Janelle says with a shrug, brushing out my curls until they fall in a perfect cascade around my face and down my back. Tiffany spritzes on some finishing spray, and I have to admit, the woman staring back at me looks better than she has in quite some time.

"Okay, deep breaths," I whisper to myself when the intercom buzzes, signaling Chance's arrival. I buzz him into the building, and the girls exchange knowing glances and hurry down the back stairs, leaving me to face him alone.

"Good luck!" Tiffany calls as the door clicks shut behind them.

"Thanks," I murmur to no one, grabbing my handbag and a coat to head downstairs.

"Hey," Chance greets me as I enter the lobby.

"Hi," I manage, feeling the flutter of a thousand butterflies in my stomach.

He steps closer, and for a moment, we're suspended in silence. Then he speaks, his voice soft yet clear. "You always look beautiful, but tonight…you're stunning."

Chance's hands are gentle as he helps me into my coat. His touch lingers just a moment longer than necessary, sending shivers up my arms. We walk in comfortable silence out to his SUV, the cool night air brushing against my skin.

As Chance navigates the city streets, the occasional streetlight casts a soft glow inside the vehicle, highlighting the intensity in his eyes. "I had a small victory today," he says, breaking the quiet. "With some persuasion and one of the hospital lawyers, Dr. Johns is now on board with the doctors volunteering at the safe-use clinic."

"Wow, that's amazing." This is such fantastic news, and no small victory at all. His dedication to making things better is relentless. "That will have such an impact. Good for you." His dedication to his work, to causes like these, it's part of what draws me to him, beyond the charming smile and easy laughter we share.

St. Lawrence restaurant looms ahead, its facade an understated promise of culinary delights. The hostess greets us with a smile and leads us to a secluded table in the small space.

The menu is a dance of exquisite flavors, each dish more

tantalizing than the last. I settle on fish, intrigued by the vegetables that come with it, while Chance chooses the duck.

"Did you have duck often when you were growing up?" I ask.

He shakes his head. "No. We had a lot of rabbit. My mother grew up in a small farming community, and she loves rabbit."

I try to keep my face neutral.

"She makes a wonderful six-pâtes," he continues. "It's a fantastic meat pie with beef, bison, pork, venison, duck, or rabbit with potatoes and carrots. She'll have to make it for you one day. I promise it's quite good."

I nod, and our comfortable chatter continues, though my nerves refuse to dissipate entirely. I know there are other topics on the agenda for us this evening.

We're halfway through our appetizers when Chance's demeanor shifts. He sets down his fork and meets my gaze squarely. "Lucy, about what happened with Céline... I'm sorry. I apologize that you had to see that. She showed up out of nowhere, and it took me by surprise. I could have handled things better." He looks up at me a moment, and when I nod, he continues. "However, while her appearance was difficult to manage, it was ultimately the best thing that could have happened. It helped me see so many things more clearly. My relationship with her is over. It hadn't been healthy in a very long time, and it's not what's right for me — or for her either. I explained that I was not going back to Montreal with her, now or ever, and I think she understands. I hope she does. But ultimately, it doesn't matter. I understand. I know that my path forward is here in Vancouver — with a job that matters to me and with you. You are the best thing about Vancouver, and my heart is here with you." His words are firm, decisive.

My heart skips a beat. He sounds more certain now than he ever has when speaking about her. I hardly know what to say.

"Look, when you and I started out, we were just friends,

and I appreciate that foundation. But then we became more, and somewhere along the line, something changed for me. I don't ever want it to change back."

His admission hangs between us, raw and revealing. I reach out, my hand covering his, needing to bridge the gap his vulnerability has opened.

"Thank you," I whisper. "That means a lot to me."

There's more to be said on this topic, but we're distracted as the server brings our meals. We settle in to eat, and the delicate taste of my fish lingers on my tongue as I answer Chance's questions about my class. "Farida has become quite the chatterbox," I say with a smile. "She's opened up so much, and that has to be in part because of your encouragement."

Chance nods thoughtfully. "That's fantastic to hear. And how's Aleksander doing?"

I sigh. "Not so well, unfortunately. His grandparents in Ukraine… Well, it's been tough news for him." I twirl my fork absentmindedly.

"Maybe I could stop by one day, hang out with him?" Chance suggests.

The idea warms me, but also sends a ripple of caution through my chest. "Let me think about it. His parents… They're all grieving." I murmur, not ready to untangle my reservations just yet.

Chance nods and redirects our conversation. "I feel like this was a victory today for the safe-use clinics, but Dr. Johns wasn't happy about the way it went down. He's threatened to end my contract early, and he could actually do that if he decides I'm not a team player," he admits, his brow furrowed. "It's funny because I really am a team player. I want what's best for my team. But I've never liked the politics of all of it."

I nod. "That has to be frustrating, but ultimately, he wants what's best for the hospital too. Hopefully, he won't get in his own way."

"Yeah, and we're managing. We've actually continued to reduce wait times by streamlining some processes." He takes a sip of water. "It's just the imaging and labs slowing us down. They're overloaded too, though. We're making progress, despite the hurdles."

I sense the underlying tension in his words, the drive to improve things no matter the obstacles. "You're doing amazing work. Everyone's swamped. It's not just you feeling the pressure."

He offers a half-smile. "I can always do better," he says.

It's not the first time I've heard him say something like that. He pushes himself so hard. I reach for his hand across the table, giving it a reassuring squeeze. The candlelight flickers between us, casting a warm glow on his determined face. "You're already doing better than you think," I assure him.

We continue chatting comfortably through dessert, and I realize I have to make a choice. Chance seems earnest and serious about wanting to pursue a future with me, and he's shared a lot this evening. Whether I have all the answers or not, if we're going to have any chance at continuing to progress in our relationship, I have to be open and willing to share too. So, once the last bite of crème brûlée is gone, I set my spoon down gently. "I have some big news as well."

Chance looks up, his gaze warm and searching. I tell him what I've learned about my biological father, how that's what was on my mind when I came over to find him with Céline, and how it contributed to throwing everything into question. I tell him about the building I now own and the identity that no longer seems real.

Chance is slack jawed when I pause a moment to breathe, and he reaches for my hand. "I can't believe you've been dealing with this on your own, that you had to sit with it while Céline blew everything up. I'm so very sorry. I am here to help you any way I can. How are you feeling?"

I blow out a breath. "I'm okay. It is a lot, and I still have much to sort out this summer—once I have some breathing room while school's out—but I've realized my dad is my dad, no matter what. He's been my rock my whole life, and that's not going to change."

"Of course," Chance agrees. "I'm so glad to hear that. How's he doing with all this news?"

I lean back in my chair. "Oh, you know," I say, trying to keep the mood light. "We could probably fill an entire week's worth of daytime talk show drama."

He smiles, his eyes crinkling at the corners. "That's not true. Lucy, you handle everything with grace."

"Doesn't always feel that way," I admit, shaking my head. "But you're right. Once Dad and I talked and determined that nothing in our relationship is going to change, everything got better. The rest is just details, right?"

Chance nods, and his compassion steadies my nerves.

The drive back to my apartment is a blur of city lights, and Chance's hand occasionally brushing mine on the center console. When we pull up outside my building, my heartbeat quickens. It's one thing to be brave over dessert; it's another to stand firm when saying goodnight. We still haven't figured out what we are, and I can't just jump back in like nothing happened.

"Thank you for dinner," I murmur, reaching for the door handle. "It was lovely. I'm so glad we were able to talk through all of this."

"Wait," he says. He's out of the SUV and rounding the vehicle before I can fully process my next move.

He opens the door and helps me out. Standing in the cool night air, Chance steps in close, his warm hands finding their way to my waist. "I had a great time tonight," he whispers, his breath tickling my cheek.

"Me too," I reply. My resolve wobbles precariously as I tilt my face up to meet his gaze.

His lips descend to mine, and it's like being struck by lightning—sudden, electrifying, and impossible to ignore. The kiss sears through me, leaving a trail of sparks and a yearning.

As we break apart, my breath comes in ragged pulls, and I clutch the front of his jacket for a fleeting second longer than necessary. "Goodnight," I manage to say, the words tinged with a regret that only fuels the fire he's ignited. But I want to take this slow. I want to be sure we understand each other.

"Goodnight." His voice is husky, filled with a promise that sends shivers down my spine.

He watches until I'm inside, and then he climbs back into his SUV and drives away. The taste of him lingers on my lips. Slowly, I make my way to my apartment, wondering if my heart will ever fully recover from everything that's been thrown at it this last week.

CHAPTER 33

Chance

The late afternoon sun throws long shadows across the linoleum as I push open the heavy door to King Albert Elementary on Tuesday afternoon.

"Good afternoon, Dr. Chance," purrs the school secretary. "Here for Lucy?"

"Guilty as charged," I admit with a smile, noting the twinkle in her eye. "Is it okay to go up? She's not expecting me."

"What a nice surprise. Go ahead," she says, waving me through with a playful wink. "But don't think I'll let you off so easily next time."

"Wouldn't have it any other way," I assure her, stepping past the main office and into the corridor lined with student artwork and educational posters.

I'm midway down the hall when, as if on cue, Artem barrels out of Lucy's classroom, his sneakers squeaking against the floor as he comes to a skidding halt in front of me.

"Dr. Chance!" His eyes light up like fireworks, and his surprise is almost comical.

I crouch down to Artem's level. "How is your sister feeling?" I ask. Artem and his mother and sister were in the ED the day after I had dinner with Lucy, and he recognized me. His sister had a nasty ear infection.

"Much better!" he declares. "I told everyone I saw you at the hospital and we did cool experiments."

"Our secret is out," I tell him with a wink.

"My sister's taking her medicine and feeling better," Artem adds. "Then we all had to eat these terrible vegetables. Mama says it's to keep us from getting sick too."

"Preventative measures." I nod. "That's smart. Your mom is taking good care of you."

Artem beams. "She says we're like superheroes now 'cause we're protected against germs."

"Absolutely," I agree.

Suddenly, we are not alone; a gaggle of curious faces spills into the hallway, surrounding us with a buzz of excited chatter.

"Is it true you can make volcanoes?" asks a little girl with pigtails.

"Can you really catch stars?" asks another, bouncing on the balls of his feet.

"Maybe not stars." I laugh. "But I can definitely show you how to make a volcano." My promise is met with cheers and claps, and for a moment, I feel like a superhero, not just a doctor who works in the emergency department.

"Did you bring apples again?" someone else asks.

"Not today," I respond, ruffling a few heads affectionately. "But maybe next time, okay?"

"Okay!" they chorus.

"I'm making the solar system," Artem says proudly.

"Sounds like you're on track to discover a new galaxy," I tease, standing up as more children join the throng. It feels good to be here, good to be a part of this. Then I see Lucy at the classroom door, and everything else fades into the background. We've only traded texts since dinner because I'm covering some night shifts this week, but I've missed her.

"I heard Artem and his sister paid you a visit in the ED," Lucy says. "I'm so glad everyone is okay."

"Yes, me too," I agree. "The ED is not where I want to see my friends." I smile down at the children. "I probably should have waited for the bell to ring, but I was discovered sooner than I thought. I heard you might need a ride."

Her eyes widen. "I could use one today. But give me just a few more minutes." She turns to the kids in the hallway. "Come on, everyone. We need to clean up before we can leave."

"Dr. Chance!"

I turn to see Kateryna, her face pinched in distress as she holds out her knee for inspection.

"Hey, what happened here?" I ask, shifting my attention to the tearful girl.

"I fell down," she explains, her voice quivering. "It hurts."

"Let's take a look." Carefully, I examine the skinned knee, noting the angry red abrasions but nothing that looks serious. "This is a brave knee. It tells a story of adventure and courage."

"Really?"

"Yes," I assure her. "Now, your job is to keep it clean. Can you do that for me?"

She nods. "Yes."

"Good. In a few weeks, you won't even remember you fell. It'll heal up nicely," I promise.

"Thank you," she whispers before scampering off.

I rise to my feet, and the kids shuffle back into the room, their energy subdued by the impending chores. I lean against the wall, watching the parade. Lucy catches my eye, a playful smirk on her face. "You're quite the Pied Piper. I'm pretty sure they'd follow you anywhere."

"Only if I come bearing gifts," I quip.

Before long, the ring of the school bell signals freedom. The students burst from the classroom, though a few linger, including Fatima, who approaches me.

"Dr. Chance!" She wraps her arms around me in a hug. "Thank you for the apples the other day. They were super yummy!"

"Anytime, Fatima," I say, returning her embrace. "Glad you enjoyed them."

She releases me and heads out, her backpack bouncing with every step. I wave goodbye to Ivan and Bibi as they make a beeline for the door, their voices already rising in excitement about some adventure awaiting them on the playground.

"Stay out of trouble, you two!" I call. Their figures disappear into the throng of departing students, but after just a few moments, I'm left standing in the nearly deserted hallway, the echoes of laughter and chatter gradually fading away.

Finally, a stillness settles over the hallway, and Lucy and I are alone. I follow her back into her classroom

"I have to say, I'm impressed," she tells me. "You remembered all their names. That's no small feat."

Heat creeps into my cheeks. Thankfully, I've always been good with names. "Well, they're important to you, aren't they? That makes them important to me too."

Lucy's gaze drops for a moment, and she smiles shyly. She's so endearing when she blushes.

I shift the conversation, revealing the tidbit of news I picked up last night. "When I saw Janelle at Barney's on my dinner break yesterday, she mentioned she was going to follow you to the mechanic this morning and give you a lift to school."

Lucy nods. "It's just an oil change and some new front tires. Nothing major."

"Can I drive you home?" The question tumbles out, revealing the reason for my visit.

There's a pause, a brief hesitation in her demeanor, before she nods. "Can you drop me off at the mechanic's instead? I need to pick up my car."

"Of course."

She collects her belongings, and together, we step out into the empty corridors of King Albert Elementary. As we exit the building, I hold the door open for her, and we walk side by side into the afternoon.

We make small talk as we drive to the mechanic, and when we arrive, the coffee shop next door sends the scent of freshly ground coffee wafting over the sidewalk. "Are you interested in a quick coffee?" I ask, pretty sure of the answer based on the way Lucy's eyes scan the menu board.

"Sure," she responds. "But let's not linger too long. The mechanic closes in a couple of hours, and I need to make sure I get my car."

"I promise I won't leave you stranded."

The barista prepares our orders—espresso for me and cappuccino for Lucy—and we move to the quietest corner of the shop. I feel a mix of anticipation and nervousness. This is more than just coffee; it's a chance to reconnect, to move our relationship forward on the path where I know it belongs.

We sit, the subtle clink of ceramic on wood punctuating our settling in. I take a deep breath, the steam from my cup rising like the thoughts swirling in my head. "Lucy, I've been doing a lot of thinking lately," I tell her, holding her gaze. "In case I wasn't clear the other night at dinner, I don't want to be just friends. I want more."

"You were clear," she says with a smile. "I've just been processing everything you had to say." She takes a sip of her cappuccino, her eyes never leaving mine. "Chance," she says softly, setting her cup down. "You often say you can do better. You push yourself really hard. That approach must help you a lot at work, right? And it probably did in school too."

Her observation catches me off-guard, but it's not inaccurate. "It has," I admit. "But you know, sometimes it pays to be a bit of a rebel, to make the system work for you instead."

"Like with the safe-use clinics?" She leans forward, putting her chin in her hand.

"Exactly," I reply, feeling a surge of pride. "My team was not going to give up, so we worked the system to get it done."

"Always finding a way to do better, huh?" Her tone is teasing, but there's an undercurrent of something else, something I can't quite grasp.

"Always," I affirm, though I'm aware that *better* is sometimes a moving target, one that shifts with perspective.

"Where does your always-do-better mantra come from?"

"It's something my mother ingrained in me," I confess, smiling as I think of her unyielding optimism. "She's always believed there's room for improvement, no matter the situation."

"And do you apply that to your personal life as well?" Her question hangs between us, challenging yet vulnerable.

I consider a moment, sifting through past experiences and choices. "Yeah, I do," I reply, nodding slowly. "We're constantly evolving, right? In self-discovery mode. Striving to do better seems…natural."

Lucy's expression shifts, shadows of something like pain flitting across her features so briefly that I wonder if I imagined it. But it's there, in the slight downturn of her lips, the furrow in her brow. She takes a breath, and when she speaks, her voice is laced with a cautious edge. "You were once in love with Céline, weren't you?" she asks.

I sense we've wandered into territory less sure than before. "Yes," I confirm, my throat tightening around the word. A memory, not fully forgotten, flickers in my mind's eye.

"Did you ever look at her and think…you could do better?" The words tumble out, and they hit me with an unexpected force.

"Well, yes," I begin, thinking of my realizations about our relationship. "She didn't have the capacity to consider my needs. She only…" I trail off as I look up at Lucy's face. She's not hearing this the way I intend to say it.

Lucy reaches out, her fingers grazing mine. Her touch is

gentle, but her words are heavy. "Chance, I think it's better if we're just friends."

I look into her eyes, finding a resolve there that tells me she's been mulling this decision for longer than the time it took to sip her cappuccino.

"I love spending time with you," she continues, and the warmth in her voice clashes with the coldness settling in my stomach. "But if you're always on a quest for something better...I'm not the someone you're looking for." She smiles sadly. "I'm not perfect, and I never will be. We can't be more than friends. I'm not sure I could survive if we became more, and then you wanted someone better."

The finality in her tone echoes around the quiet corner we occupy. My mind whirls, racing to find a way out of this. I want to argue, to tell her she's misunderstood, but she's already looking at the door.

She stands, slinging her bag over her shoulder, and I can only watch, paralyzed by the sudden turn of our conversation. She heads to the exit while I frantically search for something to say, some way to mend the rift that's just opened between us. Just when I thought we'd found a way forward.

"Lucy, wait—" The plea dies on my lips as she walks out the door without looking back.

I force myself to stand, moving to the window, where I can see her disappear into the mechanic's shop. I'm frozen, not sure what to do.

This is worse than what happened with Céline. So much worse. Lucy isn't just walking away; she's taking a piece of me with her, a piece I hadn't realized I'd given.

I stand there stunned, not sure what to do or where to go. After a few minutes, I watch her car emerge from the garage and pull into traffic, yet still I remain. The coffee shop fills and empties with different groups of customers, and I return to the table, rethinking our conversation. What it means. Whether it's true. When someone asks for the chair Lucy sat in, it finally breaks me from my thoughts, and I force myself back to my vehicle. I had expected a different outcome today.

I drive toward my home, stopping on the way to buy groceries for Ginny. I think she's been skimping on food to pay for heat, so I've been buying some extra things. When she does cook, she insists on feeding me, so it's the least I can do.

When I get home, I climb the stairs and knock on the door so I can put the grocery bags on the counter in her kitchen. Ginny's at the table, flipping through a magazine, but she looks up when I start unloading.

"More food?" she asks.

I shrug, avoiding her gaze. "I need to contribute if you're going to share all your meals." I smile, but there's a tremor in my hands as I open the cabinets to put things away.

"Something happen with Lucy?" Ginny asks after a moment.

I look over at her. She's sharp. She's always had a way of cutting straight to the heart of things.

"Yeah." I recount the coffee shop conversation, each word a weight that sinks me further into uncertainty.

Ginny listens quietly, and when I finish, she folds her arms, assessing me with a look that's part concern, part challenge.

"Chance, you're going to have to work for it," she says. "Getting past Céline was just the first step, it seems. But I've seen how you two are together. She's got real feelings for you."

I rub the back of my neck, tension knotting there. "I know, but she doesn't—"

"No buts," Ginny interrupts. "Don't give up. You need to fight for her."

I nod. "I don't know if that's what she wants. But I don't want to let her go."

"Then don't," Ginny says simply, as if it's the most obvious thing in the world. "Show her what she means to you."

I nod again, resolve starting to build. Ginny's right. I don't have to be passive. Look where that got me with Céline. There's no reason to just accept what Lucy says, especially when she has this all wrong. My ambition is nothing in the face of something real. She's what makes me better, inspires me to push forward and want more for my life. That's not something I'll ever want to replace.

CHAPTER 34

Chance

Later that evening, I step into the warmth of Kent and Amelia Johns's condo, a welcome reprieve from the rain and the cool breeze that skims off False Creek. Earlier today, I had hoped Lucy might come with me, but at least, this gives me somewhere to be this evening. Ginny was ready for me to storm the castle and charge right back over to Lucy's. But I need a minute to think through this. I want to have an answer for Lucy that will put her at ease, make her understand. And I don't know what that is yet.

The scent of rosemary and garlic greets me as Amelia ushers me into the dining room where Griffin and Tori Martin are already seated, beers in hand, chatting. Through the floor-to-ceiling windows, the city lights sparkle against the oncoming dusk, framing Science World in a halo of urban twilight.

"Smells amazing, Amelia," I compliment, and she beams

with pride.

"Hope you're hungry," Kent says, handing me a cold beer.

"Starved," I reply, my stomach seconding the statement with a well-timed growl.

After a few minutes, we move to the dining room and gather around the table, the clinking of cutlery a prelude to the feast. As expected, based on the scent, Amelia has outdone herself with Tuscan chicken, its creamy goodness perfect for a cold evening. Conversation flows freely, punctuated by laughter and the occasional toast.

As the meal winds down, Tori bumps my shoulder with hers. "How's Lucy doing?" she asks. "I thought she might be with you this evening."

I sigh and put down my fork, buying time to gather my thoughts. "Things have gone a bit off the rails," I summarize. I haven't done the best job keeping everyone up to date. "Céline, my ex-girlfriend, showed up here unexpectedly a couple weeks ago," I explain. "That was a whole mess, but it ended up being helpful, because it allowed me to close that chapter once and for all. I explained this to Lucy, and I thought she understood, but then after we got together a couple times, today she told me she thought we'd only ever be friends."

I pause, collecting the shards of that conversation with Lucy in the coffee shop. She walked away and never looked back. How can I put into words that she blew me completely out of the water? "She said something that really hit me, and she's so insightful, it kind of threw me for a loop. It made me doubt my own motivations for a bit, if I'm honest."

"What did she say?" Tori asks.

"Well, my mom is always saying, 'You could do better.' She's used that as an encouragement to me my whole life about everything—school, sports, personal goals... And Lucy thinks I must apply it in relationships as well. She's worried that eventually I'll decide I could do better than her. She doesn't want to risk her heart on that chance."

"Do you think that could happen?" Griffin asks.

"When she first said it, I had a bit of a panic, and I had to assess how I've made decisions in the past. But I didn't leave Céline because I thought I could do better." I stop myself. "Well, I suppose at the end of any relationship you always hope the next one will be better—a better match, a better fit." My thoughts swirl, but I know my heart is true, my choices valid. "I didn't cast aside something perfectly good for the next new, shiny thing. Céline and I had not been happy in a long time. Our relationship wasn't healthy, but I was tangled up in it. I stayed with her longer than I should have, but I came to Vancouver by myself after she changed her mind about joining me because I knew that was the right choice for me and what I needed to do. It had nothing to do with trading up, the way Lucy seems to think it does. I don't apply that mantra to any parts of my life in a shallow way, especially not relationships. I'm certain of that. But I don't know how to convince Lucy if she's latched on to that fear. I think it would just take time, and she's not willing to give me that. It makes her feel too vulnerable."

I push my plate aside, no longer able to stomach even Amelia's delicious meal. *How did I get myself into this?*

"Chance, how do you feel about Lucy?" Amelia asks, her voice cutting through the background noise. "Have you explained all this to her?"

"I tried, but she really threw me, and then she scooted out of there. And with the way she left things, I don't know how to—"

Griffin chuckles from across the table. "If you ask me, it sounds like you're in love with Lucy."

I rub the back of my neck. "I think you're right. I know I want to be with her, to see where things can go..."

They exchange knowing looks, their collective scoff sending a clear message. "You need to figure that out, buddy," Kent says, his tone leaving no room for argument. "What are you going to do?"

"I don't know how to get her to take a chance. If we could get back to dating, spending time together…" I trail off, unsure.

Their faces soften, empathy and encouragement mingling in their expressions. I'm a swirl of hope and doubt, but I know I want to try.

"I sent apples to her at school last week. That's what got us talking again, and we went to dinner last Saturday. But then today, things fell apart." I pause. "The kids loved the apples, though." I can't help the small smile that creeps onto my lips as I remember their joy. "I went by the school today and saw so many of them. They remembered me from when I'd visited before. I taught them about their hearts and took a bunch of old stethoscopes for them. Most of those kids are immigrants, their families are struggling. Getting to play doctor for a day, it meant something." I sit forward in my chair. "Those kids mean something to Lucy too. Maybe they're a way to show her I'm not going to find anything better than her."

"Chance, that's wonderful!" Tori says.

I'm not sure if she means my idea or that I just admitted Lucy is the best there is. But I did just admit it.

"What if we got a bunch of school supplies for the class?" Tori's suggestion sends a ripple of enthusiasm around the table.

Amelia's already nodding, pulling out her phone to jot notes. "We could get dry erase markers, pencils, regular markers…" She trails off, looking to me for more input.

"Glue sticks," I offer. "Fancy papers, watercolor paint packs…"

"Exactly!" Tori claps her hands together. "Let's make it a proper haul for them."

"Let's look online," Amelia suggests. "That will make it easy."

Within moments, both she and Tori are scrolling virtual shopping aisles, picking out colorful supplies.

"Wow, you guys don't mess around," I note.

"Neither should you." Tori gives me a pointed look.

"When it comes to Lucy or these kids."

"Right." I nod. She's saying more than just "buy school supplies," and I know she's right. Words aren't enough for Lucy. I need to show her she's important to me and I'm not just going away.

Two days later, there's a knock on my office door, and I find a pile of boxes waiting outside, an avalanche of school supplies courtesy of Amelia and Tori's enthusiastic online shopping spree. They've outdone themselves—stacks of dry erase markers, pencils, glue sticks, and watercolors in every hue imaginable. I smile at their generosity, knowing these supplies will spark joy. And hopefully, they'll pave a path back to Lucy.

Lost in thought and in piles of paperwork, when it's time, I make my way to the hospital cafeteria for lunch. That's when I spot it, the ice cream freezer, filled to the brim with an array of flavors. *It's perfect.* I picture the smiles, the laughter, the sticky fingers. It's more than just a treat. It's an olive branch, a way to show Lucy I care about her world, about the things and people important to her.

"Could you set aside some individual servings of ice cream for me to pick up tomorrow?" I ask the manager. "It's for an elementary class."

"Of course, Dr. Devereaux," she replies. "Haagen Dazs offers several flavors in the single-serving size, and they come with their own spoons."

"That would be great. Do you have about thirty?"

She nods. "Yep. Not a problem. It will be mostly chocolate and vanilla."

"That works."

As I head back to the ED to check in on the shift, a strategy forms in my mind. The kids are going to help me win Lucy over, whether they know it or not. With a car full of color and a cooler of ice cream, I'll bridge the gap between friendship and something more, show her I'm not just biding time until the next thing comes along. These thoughts buoy me through the rest of my shift, and then back at home that evening, I sprawl across my couch. My thumb hovers over the keyboard on my phone, hesitating just a moment before tapping out the words to Lucy that have been circling my mind since dinner last night.

Me: Sweet dreams.

A smile curves the corners of my lips as I imagine her reading the message, perhaps with a hint of a smile on her own face. The text is simple — no hidden agenda, just a heartfelt wish from someone who's come to care more than I ever expected to.

I hit send, feeling a pulse of anticipation. Tomorrow isn't just another day; it's a chance to step deliberately into her world, to be a part of something that brings her joy, to prove that's where I want to be.

I set the phone down and lean back. The cushions cradle me, but I'm too wired to sleep, too filled with the energy of possibility. I close my eyes, letting the excitement wash over me. This has to work. It has to be a start. It just has to.

CHAPTER 35

Lucy

Rain pelts the windows, relentless and unyielding. The kids are practically vibrating with pent-up energy, their usual outdoor hour stolen by the storm that blew through earlier this afternoon. I glance at the clock, the minute hand inching toward freedom. "Come on, everyone, let's tidy up," I tell them. "It's almost time to go."

Bibi, always the whirlwind, darts around with scissors in hand, a snowfall of paper scraps trailing behind him. I'm about to remind him of the dangers of running with scissors when Kateryna's voice cuts through the chaos.

"Miss Sheridan! Dr. Chance is here!"

Every child rushes to the window, noses smudging the glass, eyes wide with curiosity. Indeed, Chance is in the parking lot. As we watch, he runs toward the building, protectively holding a big box against the downpour.

Mina, ever the optimist, claps her hands together. "It

must be a puppy!"

I wince internally, praying she's wrong.

A few minutes later, a knock reverberates against the door, silencing the room for a heartbeat. Bibi sprints, almost tripping over his own feet, and flings the door open. Chance strides in, all smiles and calm. He places the mysterious box on my desk and produces a freezer bag from behind his back.

"Good afternoon, Lucy," he says, and I've barely had a chance to respond before he turns toward the class. "Have you all been good for Miss Sheridan?" he asks, brow arched.

A chorus of yeses fills the room, only to be interrupted by Anna's candid voice. "Nasrin hasn't."

I prepare myself for a frown or a stern look, but Chance merely smiles. "Tomorrow will be a better day," he tells the boy, and my heart swells a little as Nasrin smiles.

"If it's okay with Miss Sheridan, I have a treat for each of you to take home."

He looks over at me for approval, and my head is nodding before I've truly processed his words.

"Who wants ice cream?" he asks next, his voice becoming the catalyst for a small earthquake.

Twenty-five feet begin to stomp, and hands clap in joyous anticipation. Their energy now explodes into cheers and squeals. "Me! Me!" they chorus.

He reaches into the freezer bag and, one by one, distributes the frozen treats. I watch as Anna hangs back, a quiet observer amidst the frenzy. Chance notices too. He sidesteps over to her, producing a popsicle from another compartment in the bag. "I remember milk doesn't agree with you, so I brought you this," he says.

And Anna looks at him like he's just offered her a star from the sky.

"You need to eat those outside," Chance instructs, pointing out the spoons tucked under each lid. "So wait just a moment until the end of the day."

They scramble into rain gear and gather their things, and

then as the final bell rings, the children dash out the door, shouting thank yous as they go.

I can only shake my head. "Thank you," I say once the room has emptied. "This was the perfect day for a treat. The kids adore you."

"They're important to you," he replies, his gaze steady, "which makes them important to me." He points to the box on my desk. "That's for you, and there are three more boxes in my car."

I lift the flaps and peek inside to find rows upon rows of vibrant markers and pencils. "What's all this for?"

"You mentioned working extra hours at Barney's to afford school supplies," he says. "I thought this might help, as I know your time is precious. Feel free to share with the other teachers too."

The gesture leaves me momentarily speechless. It's not just the gift itself, but the thought behind it — the understanding of what matters to me — that touches something deep within. This man sees me, really sees me. And in this moment, the rain outside seems inconsequential compared to the storm of emotions brewing within me.

He waits patiently as I organize for a moment and prepare a spot in the classroom for the supplies. By the time we step outside, the rain has dwindled to a mist. Chance leads the way to his car, parked under the drooping branches of a willow tree. As he pops the trunk open, there's a chorus of giggles behind us. I turn to find Kayla, her cheeks smeared with chocolate ice cream.

"Ms. Sheridan," she lisps, "is Dr. Chance your boyfriend?"

A blush creeps up my neck. "No, sweetie, we're just friends," I assure her, but my voice is less convincing than I want it to be.

Chance winks at Kayla. "What do you think? Should I be Miss Sheridan's boyfriend?" he asks, and suddenly the air is filled with the high-pitched endorsements of fifth graders.

I shake my head with a half-hearted attempt at disapproval. "You don't play fair," I grumble as we move back toward my classroom, our arms laden with boxes.

"Never have." He chuckles, and the sound sends a warm shiver down my spine.

Back inside, I peel back the tape on each box, revealing stacks of crayons, glue sticks, and construction paper. My hands hover over the supplies, feeling the weight of his kindness. It's almost too much.

"Chance, this... I can't even begin to thank you," I stumble over the words, overwhelmed.

"Sure you can," he replies, standing close enough that I can smell the faint scent of his aftershave. "Go out to dinner with me."

I bite my lip, looking up at him. "Okay, but only if I'm buying."

He shakes his head, his expression serious now. "That's what a friend would do. And the answer is no, because I don't just want to be your friend." His voice drops lower. "I want more. I want it all. I understand your concerns, and I appreciate what you said yesterday at the coffee shop, as it gave me a lot to think about. But it's not true. May I explain?"

I huff and cross my arms, but I'm not feeling as resolved as I was when we picked up my car. He's been so kind. The least I can do is hear him out. So I sit behind my desk with a nod, and he sits on top of a student desk in the first row.

He tells me that he's considered carefully whether his mother's maxim applied to his personal life, and then he goes on to explain the soul-searching he did as things fell apart with Céline. In a way, he did leave her because he wanted something better, but he wanted it for himself and for her. He wanted a chance to grow and change, and they were never going to be able to do that together.

"You should never fear that I'll cast you aside because I've found something new and bright and shiny and better," he concludes. "Because you're the one whose shown me what's truly possible in a relationship—support, partnership, care." He holds my eyes a moment. "I want to provide that for you as well. We'll grow together, make each other stronger, find joy. You deserve all that you give to others, that you give to me. And there's nothing that could be better than that."

The world tilts slightly on its axis, and for a moment, I'm adrift in the possibility of it all. Then I nod because how could I not?

My pulse flutters, each beat a silent echo of Chance's confession. No one has ever been so direct, so boldly affectionate toward me. Suddenly, I want to lean into this feeling, to believe it can actually hold me up. "Let's get these put away," I murmur, rising from my desk.

Chance nods, letting me take the lead, and together, we organize the supplies into neat rows on shelves and in drawers. His presence is both soothing and an accelerant, and I'm acutely aware of every moment his hand brushes mine.

"Thank you," I say once the last marker finds its home. "For everything."

"Anything for you," he replies with a smile.

I gather my things and lock up the classroom, and we walk out into the afternoon. He follows me to my apartment, where we leave behind cars for the freedom of our feet.

"Too early for dinner?" I ask as we stand on the sidewalk.

"Maybe a bit, but it's the perfect time for a stroll," he counters, gesturing toward False Creek.

We set off, and walking beside Chance feels almost immediately natural. The air is crisp, carrying the scent of rain-washed streets and distant ocean brine.

"I've missed this," Chance confesses as we stop to watch a boat drift by. "Missed you."

"Me?" I can feel the color rise in my cheeks at his admission.

"Lucy, I was raised in a world of discipline and high expectations. Always looking, reaching for more." He hesitates, then looks at me, his gaze steady. "Like I said before, with you, I don't want more. You're the best thing that's happened to me, and I'll wait until you're ready. However long you need."

His words offer shelter, safety, a lighthouse guiding me home. Yet they also spark a flame within me. I'm always careful, but I'm not fragile. And I realize in this moment, as the city buzzes around us and the water laps at the concrete shore, that I am ready to stop waiting.

"Chance," I begin, turning to face him fully. "You don't have to wait."

His face breaks into a smile. "Will you come back to my place tonight?"

I smile coyly. "I wouldn't want to be too loud for Ginny."

He grins. "I don't think she can hear once she takes out her hearing aids."

I nod. "Okay then."

"Let's go back to your place, and maybe you can pack a bag—although you won't need clothes."

"Really? Why not?" I tease.

"Because I have every intention of keeping you sated and naked all weekend."

I cross my arms and tap a finger against my chin. "Hmmm..."

He leans in and licks from my collarbone to my ear. "Let's go before they call the police for indecent exposure."

I laugh. "Only if you promise—"

His searing kiss stops me. He pulls me in tight, and I can feel his hardness against my hip. "Whatever you want," he breathes. "As long as it's with me."

CHAPTER 36

Lucy

As we approach my building, I feel my heart pounding in my chest. I've pushed Chance away so many times, and he always returns. I can't quite wrap my head around what that means. When we reach the door, I fumble with my keys, trying to calm my shaking hands before unlocking my apartment.

Chance's hand covers mine, and I'm suddenly calmer. He turns the knob and opens the door, allowing me to pass before him. I'm grateful that my apartment is reasonably picked up.

We've come here so I can pack a bag, but the door is barely closed when he devours my lips with his own. My hands drift up his chest, craving the sensation of his skin. I can feel the strength of his muscles beneath my fingertips. I've longed for this man deeply and intensely, and I'm determined to move forward boldly.

Chance pulls my sweater over my head and cups my

breasts. My nipples stand at attention as he flicks them with his thumb. Then he squeezes, applying just the right amount of pressure, and I sigh into his mouth as he pushes me up against the wall.

He guides my pants to the floor. "I've missed you so much," he whispers.

His hand glides over my bare leg, and I melt into his touch, craving more of the fiery sensation building within me. I spread my legs, inviting him in and guiding his hand upward with one of my own.

His fingers glide over my panties, finding their way to my most sensitive spot. I moan as his skilled fingers circle my bundle of nerves. He knows exactly how to make me quiver. His finger slips inside, and he pulls away, his eyes filled with desire.

"You're so wet for me," he whispers. "It's driving me crazy." He teases my clit again before thrusting two fingers inside me. I whimper as he hits just the right spot. A few more strokes and I'm reaching the peak of my climax, unable to control the waves of pleasure that wash over me.

But Chance doesn't stop there. "I want to do this over and over again tonight," he says.

And I know I want it too, craving more of his intoxicating touch.

He gently removes my panties as I tremble. "Lean your elbows against the counter," he commands directing me toward the kitchen, and I oblige, turning to face him. Chance spreads my knees apart, exposing me fully. Before I can comprehend what's happening, he's sitting between my legs. His fingers curl inside me while his tongue teases my clit.

I cry out in pleasure, unable to resist another climax and unwilling to live without it. He strokes in and out with a steady rhythm while simultaneously sucking and licking. My body tenses as I feel another orgasm approaching, and I grip the counter behind me. Chance continues to pleasure me, and I savor every moment until I convulse in ecstasy.

When my vision clears and my senses return, Chance scoops me into his arms and carries me to my bedroom. "I think we should stay here tonight," he says with a playful smile. "And would takeout work for dinner? I promise to make it up to you another time."

I nod in agreement, and he gently lays me on the bed. As I look up at him, my heart pounds with desire…and still a little lingering fear. I've never been one to take risks, but I have to push forward. With Chance, I'm safe. He's given me no reason to doubt him.

He crawls over me, his eyes never leaving mine. "I want to make love to you," he whispers, and my heart skips a beat.

His body presses against mine, his warm skin and the hard lines of his muscles making me feel safe and protected. I wrap my arms around him, pulling him close as our lips meet in a passionate embrace. I can feel his desire, his need for me, and it only fuels the fire within.

As he trails kisses down my neck and chest, I arch my back, inviting him to explore further. His hands glide over my body, every touch sending shivers through me. I'm lost in the moment, in the intensity of our connection, and I let go of everything else.

"I'd like to see what you're hiding inside your pants," I tell him when we come up for air. He's still mostly dressed.

The corner of his mouth quirks, and he drops his jeans to the floor. His hard cock stands erect, and I want it deep inside me. He strokes it. "See how you affect me?"

He crawls over and positions himself above me. The passion in his gaze is overwhelming, and a new wave of desire washes over me. In one smooth motion, he enters me, filling me in a way that makes me feel complete.

He moves in a slow, deliberate rhythm, and I can feel the intensity building between us. He grips my hips as he pushes deeper. The feeling is incredible, overwhelming in the best way possible.

I wrap my legs around him as I beg for more. He

responds in kind, increasing his pace and taking me deeper with each thrust. Our bodies move in harmony, connected in a way I've never experienced.

He strums my clit as he pivots in and out, and I can feel myself reaching the peak of another orgasm. I cry out in pleasure, my body trembling as waves of ecstasy wash over me. He continues to thrust, matching my rhythm until I'm completely spent and he's groaned out his release as well.

When we finally come down from the high, I lie in his arms, breathless. We've shared something truly special, and I know this is the start of a path I've never been down before. He looks down at me, eyes filled with affection.

I reach up and trace my fingers over his face. "I've missed you too," I whisper, and he pulls me close, his lips finding mine once more.

This time, the kiss is slow and tender, a reflection of the emotions we've shared and the bond we've committed to build, that we're building already. We lie together for what feels like hours, enjoying each other's presence and the comfort of our embrace.

He brushes my hair back from my face. "I don't ever want to let you go," he whispers.

I look into his eyes, seeing the depth of his feelings reflected there. "I hope you don't."

CHAPTER 37

Chance

The predawn darkness clings to my bedroom as I hear the rustle of sheets. We finally made it to my place and we've spent the weekend together. Without opening my eyes, I know Lucy is slipping out of bed early this Monday morning. My chest tightens; I'm not ready for our weekend to end.

"Where are you going?" My voice sounds gravelly.

"I need to get ready for school. With the traffic this time of day, I'm not sure I'll be on time." She speaks in a practical tone that finishes the job of pulling me awake.

I prop myself up on my elbows and run my hand down her arm. "Can't you take the day off? We can enjoy a lot more of what we did all weekend," I say, joking but wholly hopeful.

She pauses, her conflict clear even in the dim light. "I didn't prepare for a teacher on call, so it wouldn't be fair to the substitute or the kids."

I lay back hard against the pillow, the mattress

absorbing the impact. She's always so practical, and she's as driven as I am. That's what this is, right? An irrational worry that this weekend was just a fleeting moment begins to gnaw at me.

"You don't have to leave with me," she says. "You can stay in bed as long as you want." Her silhouette is framed by the faint light sneaking around the curtains.

"I should go to the hospital," I mumble, shrugging it off.

But she's not buying it. "Chance," she presses. "Are you okay? I have to work. You know this." She sits on the edge of the bed.

"I know." I meet her eyes and force a deep breath. "Of course you do. And so do I. I'm just having trouble letting go of this bubble, just the two of us."

Her expression softens. "Me too."

I reach for her hand. "I want you to know — and this may seem fast — but I want you to know I love you."

Her eyes go wide. "You do?"

"Yes." I nod. "I have no hesitation about how I feel."

She leans down, and her mouth finds mine. When we break apart, she looks at me and smiles. "I love you too."

Suddenly, I can breathe again. "I'm going to go up and check on Ginny before I go to the hospital. It's the only way I can be sure she eats."

"You always care for everyone around you. What do you do for you?"

I chuckle. "I think last night I did something for me at least twice."

She blushes. "I had a lot of fun this weekend. But this is all new."

I realize I'm putting a lot of pressure on her. "I'm sorry. I don't mean to be greedy with your time."

She shakes her head. "You're fine. I want to see you tonight. How about Barney's? I'd like to check on my dad."

"I think that's perfect."

Her head tilts to the side. "I know you always strive to

be better. To continuously improve everything around you. But I don't expect you to be perfect. We won't be perfect. Because I'm not perfect, either. We'll both make many mistakes. But we can do this together."

Her words strike a chord deep within me. We're both flawed, beautifully human, but we have a chance at making this work.

A little while later, she's ready for school, and I'm ready to face the day. It's funny how a few words can lift weights off your chest, weights you didn't even know were there.

"See you at Barney's after work?" I ask, and Lucy's nod is all the confirmation I need. I walk her to her car, and her scent still lingers on my skin, a reminder that this weekend was so much more than a dream.

After a quick shower and a change of clothes, I climb the stairs to Ginny's. When I knock on her door, it swings open almost immediately.

"Chance! What a pleasant surprise," she exclaims, stepping aside to let me in. "I haven't seen you all weekend," she adds with a smirk.

"Hope I'm not disturbing your morning," I say, nodding to the paper and mug in her hands. I'm not touching that other comment.

"Never," she replies. "You're always welcome here, you know that."

She steps back and ushers me in. I follow her into the kitchen.

"Sit down, sit down," Ginny insists before bustling over to the stove. "I'll make you some breakfast. It's the least I can do since you've bought all my groceries."

"Really, Ginny, you don't have to—" I start, but she cuts me off with a stern look that brooks no argument.

"Chance Devereaux, you will eat and enjoy it," she commands.

"All right," I concede, taking a seat. "But just so you know, helping you is never about getting something in return."

"Of course not," she calls over her shoulder, "but nobody leaves my house hungry."

I watch her move around the kitchen, cracking eggs into a bowl and whisking them vigorously before pouring them onto a hot pan.

"Coffee with a splash of cream and a sugar, right?" Ginny asks, reaching for a mug.

"Spot on," I reply.

"Good." She slides a steaming mug across the table to me. "Drink up. You'll need the energy."

I wrap my hands around the warmth of the cup, letting the simple act of being here, with Ginny, anchor me after the emotional rollercoaster of the weekend.

"Thanks, Ginny," I tell her, and I mean for more than just the breakfast.

When she brings over the plates, I fork a hefty bite of scrambled eggs into my mouth, the rich taste mingling with the savory notes of sausage.

"Lucy and I are back together," I say between bites, happy to say it out loud.

Crinkles form at the corners of her eyes as a smile stretches across her face. "That's wonderful! She's a special girl."

I nod, appreciating her approval.

She then launches into the story of her past, recounting the passionate saga of her relationship with her late husband. "...and I told him, 'This is your last chance. If we're doing this, it's for keeps,'" she says with a fiery glint in her eye. "And would you believe it? We never parted again until he passed — forty-eight glorious years."

"Sounds like you two really figured it out," I muse.

"Chance, don't make our mistakes. Don't start a cycle you can't break. Know what you want with Lucy, and go after it with everything you have," she advises.

I nod. It's easy to forget that every couple has their struggles, even my own parents, who seemed to sail smoothly through life. "My folks probably had their rough patches too," I confess. "But they made it look so easy."

Ginny gives me a knowing smile. "They worked it out before you even knew there was a problem to fix."

"Guess they did," I agree, feeling a newfound appreciation for the unseen efforts love requires.

The rest of breakfast passes in companionable silence. I stand to leave, plate clean and stomach full. "Thanks for the talk, Ginny. And the breakfast."

"Anytime, dear," she calls as I step out the door.

The day at work is a blur—signing papers, treating patients, the hum of hospital routine—but my mind is a record stuck on Lucy, replaying our moments together and counting the moments until I can see her again. And the good news is that we found where the money from Prometheus was being deposited. It's going into the payroll account and payroll tells me it has gone to nursing bonuses. I'll leave it there and continue the practice.

I'm flanked by Kent, Griffin, and Tori as we arrive at Barney's. Amelia is already there, sitting next to Lucy at the bar. They all turn as we walk in.

"Hey, guys!" Lucy greets us, her eyes meeting mine with a spark of something private and joyful.

"Be right back," she says, tugging gently at my sleeve, guiding me away from the group.

"Sure thing," I reply, curious but happy to follow her lead. "Guys, grab a table," I call to my friends over my shoulder.

I follow Lucy through the dimly lit corridor to the back office. The door creaks open, and we step into the cramped room, illuminated by the soft glow of a desk lamp.

"Chance," she says, her voice laced with a hesitant excitement, "are we... I mean, are you my boyfriend?" There's a vulnerability in her gaze that swells my heart with affection.

"Absolutely," I say. "I want us to be exclusive, just you and me."

Lucy's lips stretch into a wide, brilliant smile. "Good," she breathes. "I want to tell my dad. Like, right now."

"Let's do it," I agree.

We navigate through stacks of liquor boxes and pallets loaded with bar supplies before reaching the door marked *Private*. Inside, the room is a chaotic collection of Barney's innards—cases of beer form makeshift walls and boxes of napkins and disposable cutlery crowd the floor. But none of that seems to matter as Lucy approaches her father, who's buried under paperwork at his cluttered desk.

"Dad," she says. "I want to tell you something." She pauses to give him time to look up. "Chance and I are together. I wanted you to know first."

His weathered face breaks into a smile that quickly turns misty. "Lucy girl, that means everything to me," he murmurs, his voice thick as he rises to give her a hug.

She takes his hand. "You'll always be my dad."

He turns and offers me his hand.

"Thank you," I say, realizing the gravity of being let into their world.

Declan's grip is firm as we shake. His eyes, clouded moments ago with emotion, now sharpen into a focus that pins me in place. "Chance," he says, "I've got old friends, the kind who owe me favors. Members of the Irish mob. If you ever step out of line with Lucy, I make one call, and… Well, let's just say everyone's promises are kept."

I swallow hard, trying to gauge whether this is fatherly bluster or a genuine threat veiled in half-jest. The hint of steel in his tone suggests it's no laughing matter. Yet there's a twinkle in his eye that leaves me doubting. "Understood, sir," I manage.

"All right then." He claps me on the shoulder, a rough gesture that somehow conveys approval.

I'm searching for something else to say when Lucy tugs at my arm. "Come on. Dad's gotta work, and so do we," she says, pulling me back toward the laughter and chatter of our friends.

Kent, Amelia, Tori, and Griffin are clustered around a table, beers in front of them, waiting for our return. I catch the collective lift of their eyebrows as they see us approaching hand in hand.

"Guys," I start, feeling a rush of something like pride swell within me, "I want to propose a toast." I raise my glass high, catching the light in the golden liquid. "To Lucy, who's absolutely perfect in every way that matters." I turn to her, seeing a soft blush coloring her cheeks. "We're officially together."

The words hang between us, simple but heavy with meaning—a new beginning built on the rubble of the past.

The table erupts into happy gasps and hearty chuckles; Kent shoots me an incredulous look, one that mirrors Griffin's expression of bemusement.

"Man..." Kent shakes his head with a wry smile. "You've been with us all day, and you didn't drop even a hint?"

"Well, it wasn't the time earlier," I note. "And a few things were still falling into place." I wink at Lucy. "Inside the hospital, I have to be your boss," I admit. "But here..." I pause, my eyes traveling around the table to each person who has become more than just a colleague. "Here, I consider you friends."

It's Griffin who breaks the brief silence that follows. He lifts his glass once again. "To friendship," he declares, and the sentiment rings true and clear.

"To friendship," I add agree. *And the foundation it provides for so much more.*

EPILOGUE

Lucy

I zip my makeup bag, the tidy conclusion of the last four whirlwind months.

"Lucy, you ready?" Chance's voice carries down the hall, tinged with urgency. The forecast promises a snowstorm, and Chance, ever the planner, is hellbent on outrunning it to Griffin's cabin.

"Coming!" I call, hefting my overnight bag over my shoulder. Its weight feels less significant than the decision still hanging in the air of this apartment, its key now cold and heavy in my pocket. Though we've yet to consolidate our lives under one roof officially, my presence has permeated his space in Ginny's basement unit, my things scattered among his belongings. I turn off the lights, the apartment darkening around me, and hurry up the stairs.

"Snow's picking up," he says as I emerge, the words almost visible in the chilly air. He's holding open the door, urgency written in the lines of his face, the excitement in his eyes. This trip is a stolen week away from the pace of our daily lives. "Let's beat the storm," he urges, grabbing my bags.

I nod, pulling my coat tight around me as we step out into the biting cold. Snowflakes swirl, a dance of white against the encroaching gray sky — a beautiful adversary. Chance locks the door behind us, and I watch him, this man who defies the very upbringing that shaped him. Meeting Chance's parents over the Christmas holidays felt like deep diplomacy, all steps measured and moves calculated. Yet there was an authenticity to their spartan home, where space breathed free of clutter, that spoke volumes about the childhood that shaped my rebel — my Chance. Where his parents' world is orderly and restrained, Chance embraces chaos, seeks the unpredictable. I love him for it, and I'm coming to find that his rebel heart in some ways mirrors my own.

Or maybe it's that he inspires me to embrace the unknown, the offbeat. After at first largely ignoring the information I've received about my biological dad being Jimmy O'Connor, I've finally started planning a trip to Ireland. Chance has been supportive and is even going to go along, letting Janelle off the hook. I haven't remotely decided what I'm going to do with a building and all that money, but I hope things will be clearer after I meet the lawyer I've been putting off. With Chance by my side this summer, I'll go see what needs to be done.

We hustle to the car, its engine already humming a warm welcome. "Ready for this?" He grins, his hand finding mine, interlacing fingers that seem designed to fit together.

"Always," I reply, squeezing back.

As Chance navigates the streets, I watch the city blur past, the snowflakes now racing us to some unseen finish line. "Griffin's place, huh?" I muse, picturing the cabin nestled in nature's embrace, a stark contrast to his usual high-society haunts.

"Only the best for you," Chance says with a wink, and I

can't help but laugh. I don't need the best. I only need this — the thrill of the drive, the anticipation of seclusion, and Chance by my side.

As we merge onto the highway, the cityscape gives way to open road, and I lean back, letting the hum of the tires lull me into a peaceful state. The road unwinds before us, a ribbon of gray slicing through a world that's increasingly white. Snowflakes, in their erratic ballet, tap against the windshield, and Chance keeps his eyes on the road, a focused intensity that makes me feel safe despite the weather.

"Is Griffin going to be there?" I ask, breaking the silence that has settled between us.

Chance spares me a brief glance, his brow furrowing slightly. "He'd better not be," he mutters.

Two hours later, we ascend the final stretch, the cabin emerges, a fortress of solitude perched regally on the hillside. Silver Lake stretches out below, its frozen surface a flawless mirror reflecting the stoic pines that stand sentinel around it. My breath catches at the sight; the expanse of natural beauty is overwhelming.

"Who cleared the snow?" I gesture toward the immaculate driveway and walkways as we pull up.

"Griffin's place comes with all the bells and whistles, heated concrete included," Chance informs me.

I shake my head. Of course, Griffin would have heated concrete. We step out of the car, the air crisp. Chance types in the code Griffin provided, and the front door swings open.

"Wow," escapes my lips as we enter. The interior is grander than I'd imagined, the walls stretching up to meet wooden beams that cradle the ceiling high above. The windows frame the lake, turning it into a living painting that shifts with the light.

Chance wastes no time, shrugging off his coat and moving to the hearth. His movements are efficient as he builds a fire from logs that look like they've been waiting just for us. I set about unpacking the groceries we brought.

Flames soon spring to life under Chance's care, chasing away the chill.

"Fire's ready," he calls over his shoulder, and I admire the way the firelight plays across his face, highlighting his strong jaw and the determined set of his lips.

"Perfect timing," I reply, joining him by the fireplace.

Chance wraps his arms around me and nuzzles my neck, peppering kisses. "I think you're wearing too many clothes."

It's hard to concentrate when he does this. "Here in front of the window?"

His fingers slip under my sweater and into my bra as he plays with my nipple. I shiver with anticipation.

"I think your body wants us to have sex here in front of the fire and the windows."

I turn around, and our lips meet in a searing kiss.

He steps away from me, both of us breathing hard. I understand the desire that thrums between us, and I'm more than willing to oblige. As he takes a seat in the leather chair, a shiver of excitement runs through me. With a smile meant just for him, seductive and brimming with promise, I reach for the hem of my sweater. The fabric grazes my skin as I lift it over my head, the cool air of the cabin peaking my nipples beneath the thin lace of my bra.

Turning away, I give a little push at my waistband, sliding my jeans down to reveal the curve of my behind. His sharp intake of breath tells me how much he enjoys the view.

"Turn around." His voice is a caress, a velvet touch that sends a shudder through me.

I comply, and the sight of him—his arousal so evident, straining against his pants—makes my body clench.

"You're fucking beautiful," he says, each word a stroke against my already heated skin.

He rises, shedding his clothes with an impatience that mirrors my own. Pants, boxers, and sweater are discarded in swift succession, revealing the man I've come to adore in all his raw masculinity. As he strokes himself, the blatant need in his gaze ignites something primal within me.

"See what you do to me?" he murmurs. Chance retakes his seat, every line of his body taut with expectation. "Come here," he commands, and I cross the distance on trembling legs, drawn to him as surely as the flames are drawn to the night.

I lower myself onto the plush rug, my hands and knees sinking into its softness. The heat from the fire dances across my bare skin, but it's his smoldering gaze that truly warms me. His eyes hold a heavy lust, darkened to the color of a storm-ravaged sea.

"Come closer," he growls, gravel in his voice.

I crawl forward, each movement deliberate, fueled by the anticipation.

"Lucy, suck my cock."

His command is raw, edged with need, and my core clenches. My breaths come shallow and quick, and I gaze up into his hungry eyes. His cock stands before me, engorged and leaking with desire—desire for me. It's a heady thought.

I lean in, inhaling the musky scent of his arousal before my tongue darts out to lick up the slit, gathering the glistening bead of precum. Its salty tang mingles with the heat of the fire, igniting my senses. With care, I trace my tongue along the underside, feeling him tense and swell even more under my ministrations.

Finally, I take each of his balls into my mouth, one at a time, sucking gently as if they hold the essence of his passion. And perhaps they do, for Chance leans into the chair, his head thrown back, eyes closed, lost in the sensations I coax forth. There's no mistaking the deep satisfaction on his face, the way his chest heaves, the way his fingers grip the armrests.

In this moment, there's nothing else—no snowstorm outside, no cabin around us—just Chance and the silent language of our bodies. He's here with me, fully present, and I know without a doubt he's loving this.

His gaze finds mine, and the intensity in his eyes is a force that draws me deeper. My lips encase him, and I take him in, feeling the velvet steel of him against my tongue. He groans, his hand finding my chest, slipping beneath the lace of my bra. A pinch of my nipple, sharp and sweet, sends electric thrills spiraling through me, straight to the heat between my legs. My core clenches, craving more, but this isn't about my pleasure. It's about his unraveling.

I hum around him, my pride swelling as much as he does in my mouth. I adore the way he loses himself when I'm worshipping him with my lips and tongue. Yet even amidst this surge of power, there's an edge of frustration. He never allows me the satisfaction of completion.

"Enough," he suddenly commands. "Lie back on the rug."

Obediently, I pull away and recline on the plush fabric, the fireplace doing little to quell the chill that forms with the absence of his skin against mine. I part my thighs, the sheer fabric of my panties barely concealing the evidence of my arousal.

He positions himself between my legs, his fingers tracing the damp silk, teasing me through the barrier. "You look good enough to eat." His words are a promise that stirs a desperate moan within my chest.

"Yes, please," escapes my lips.

His fingers have barely grazed me, yet I'm teetering on the brink, ready to shatter under the weight of my own desire. Chance knows exactly how to ignite my body. And right now, I am aflame.

With a decisive movement, Chance tears at the side of my panties. The sound of fabric giving way sends another jolt of anticipation through me. His fingers then dance over my most sensitive spot, circling with an expertise that has me gasping as I arch into his touch.

"Come here," he says, his voice thick with desire.

He shifts, lying back on the rug, and motions for me to straddle him. I position myself, feeling warmth emanating from his body, the heat from the fire now a mere backdrop to our own burning intensity. Lowering myself, I guide his eager mouth to my waiting flesh. The moment his tongue meets my skin, a shiver courses through me, and I lose all sense of place and time. It's just his mouth, his hands, and the waves of pleasure rolling over me.

Distracted by the sweet torment, I lean forward, taking him into my mouth. His taste, mingled with my own arousal, is intoxicating. I savor him, drawing him deeper, listening to his moans that blend with mine. He doesn't hold back, and within moments, my body convulses around the crest of the climax he's skillfully coaxed from me. As I shatter, he licks me clean, each stroke of his tongue both soothing and igniting the aftershocks of my release.

Before I can catch my breath, he pulls away, and with gentle firmness rolls me onto my back. The soft rug cushions me as he positions himself at my entrance. I look up into his eyes, finding them alight with something fierce and tender all at once.

Then he enters me with one hard thrust, filling me completely, claiming me in the most primal of ways. "I love you," he breathes out, the words hitting me as hard as he does.

He sets a punishing pace, in and out, as if each stroke could convey the depth of his feelings. His breath is heavy and ragged. He's close. Then, his hands find my breasts, fingers pinching my nipples in a rhythm that sends electric shocks straight to my core.

"Chance," I gasp, teetering on the brink once again.

"Lucy..." He groans, his voice breaking on my name.

In perfect synchrony, we reach the peak. We moan together, a duet of climax that echoes in the vastness of the cabin. My vision whites out as waves crash over me, his name a silent prayer on my lips.

I'm still catching my breath, the heat of our passion dissipating into the cooler air of the cabin, when Chance's arms envelop me. With infinite care, he reaches for a blanket draped over the back of the nearby couch and wraps it around my spent body.

He moves away for a moment, scrambling to find his pants. I watch him, a smile playing on my lips; even in such mundane actions, there's an urgency I find endearing. But then he's back, wrapping me once again in the warmth of his arms.

"Lucy," he whispers, and time seems to hold its breath.

There in his hand, clasped gently between his fingers, is a solitaire diamond ring. Its simple beauty catches the light, casting prisms across the walls, as if the room itself is coming alive.

"You are everything to me," Chance says. "You're amazing in every way, and there will never be anyone better for me." A vulnerability flickers across his face, a silent plea for me to understand the depth of his conviction. "I can only hope to be as worthy a partner for you. But I promise to try. Lucy, will you marry me?"

The question hangs in the air as shock ripples through me, followed by an undertow of joy so intense it threatens to sweep me off my feet. My heart hammers against my ribs, a wild thing seeking escape, as a single word forms on my lips.

"Yes."

It's more than affirmation; it's a revelation, an acceptance of our intertwined souls. Yes to Chance, yes to love, yes to a future filled with the beautiful unknown. And as I say it, the world shifts, aligning itself to the new path we have chosen together.

Thank you for giving me your spare time and the opportunity to entertain you. I hope I met your expectations. I would love a review. Reviews point other readers to books. After you so kindly did that, you are the master of your own destiny. If you'd like to read about Lucy and Chance's visit to Ireland, check it out here. But if you're more interested in what's next, you can read this sneak peek:

DOCTOR TYRANT

Christian

The first ray of dawn slips through the blinds, casting a warm glow on Lillian's bare skin as she eases out from under the sheet. Her silhouette is a familiar dance of curves and grace — a performance I never tire of watching. She doesn't look back as she pads softly toward the bathroom, confident and unhurried. The sound of the shower is a subtle reminder of our uncomplicated arrangement. Lillian Bryant, no strings attached. It's exactly what I need — no emotional entanglements to muddy my already chaotic life.

With the bed now empty beside me, I prop myself up against the headboard. I find my phone on the nightstand, its screen lighting up to reveal a barrage of emails. Each one demands attention, but it's the calendar reminders that weigh heaviest — a triple bypass at ten sharp, followed by implanting a heart monitor late afternoon. A marathon run in scrubs and sterile gloves. I can almost feel the dull ache that will settle into my feet by evening. Running a hand down my face, I suppress a groan. Surgery requires precision, control, qualities I've honed over countless hours in the OR. But today, anticipation gnaws at me.

But there's no time for distraction. I swipe through my inbox, mentally preparing for the long day ahead. I am Vancouver's most sought-after cardiac surgeon. And I'm not a narcissist. I just know I'm the best.

The doorbell chimes, and I click over to look at the security camera feed on my phone. A woman stands at my doorstep, a stranger. Probably lost. I ignore the persistent ringing. She'll figure out her mistake soon enough.

Shifting my attention back to my messages, a smirk forms as a spicy text from Cinnamon pops up — an image of her perfect breasts. They're a little more than a handful, round, with small, light pink nipples.

Cinnamon: Something to look forward to after your surgeries.

Me: See you tonight.

We're fire together, and she always knows exactly what I need—a distraction, a release.

Cinnamon: Expect me at eight.

That's followed by a string of emojis—handcuffs, blindfold, paddle, and a red kiss. Looks like tonight's menu will be particularly hot. Kinky even. Good. I need something to clear the cobwebs and keep the shadows at bay.

The doorbell intrudes once more. An irritated sigh escapes me as I tap the intercom button. "What do you want?"

"Delivery for Christian Bradford." The woman's voice is assertive and unwavering.

I frown. "I'm not expecting any deliveries," I respond.

"Sir, you need to accept this personally. I can't leave until you do." Her tone brooks no argument, but I'm not one to bend easily.

"Look, I'm busy," I insist. "You must be mistaken."

"Dr. Bradford, I am not leaving this doorstep until you come down," she fires back, an edge of determination in her voice that irks me.

"Fine," I snap. I toss the covers aside and swing my legs over the bed. But then I watch as Lillian emerges from the steam-filled bathroom, swirling the lingering mist. She's a vision of composed elegance in her business attire, a stark contrast to the disarray of bed linens we've left behind. Her dress—a tailored navy number—hugs her figure with an understated sophistication that suits her no-nonsense disposition.

Just as she's fastening the clasp on her pearl necklace, that incessant doorbell chimes again.

"Can you get that?" I ask, gesturing vaguely downstairs. "I should start getting ready." My tone is casual, but my mind has an undercurrent of urgency as I mentally run through the day's surgeries again.

"Sure," Lillian replies with an easy smile. "It's probably your summons to court. Maybe someone's suing the miracle-working heart surgeon." Her laughter tinkles in the air, a playful jab at my expense.

"Ha-ha," I respond dryly. "There's nothing going on that could lead to that." Although I have to admit, her jokes are part of what makes this arrangement so refreshing—no strings, just shared moments of levity and lust.

"See you next time, Christian." She leans in, pressing her lips to mine.

"Next time," I confirm, breaking away. She's already a distant second to the meticulous rhythm of surgery that awaits me.

With a final glance at her retreating figure, I step into the shower, letting the hot water cascade over me, washing away traces of perfume and passion. Steam rises around me, fogging up the glass, enclosing me in a world where there's only the steady beat of water against tile.

The shower door slides open abruptly, jolting me back.

"Christian, you need to hurry up," Lillian's voice cuts through the mist. "There's a package, and it's kind of insistent."

"Insistent?" I frown, raking a hand through my hair. "Just leave it on the bed, Lillian. I'll be out soon."

"No, really," she insists. "I've got to head out, and it seems...important."

"Fine, almost done," I call, though I take a moment longer than necessary. The steady pulse of water calms my pre-surgery nerves, and I'm not ready to face whatever awaits outside this sanctuary.

Finally, I shut off the faucet, the echo of droplets trailing off as I wrap a towel around my waist. A clean shave is next, the razor gliding in familiar strokes over my jawline, methodical and calming.

Eventually, I emerge from the bathroom, and my gaze lands on the bed—and freezes. There, nestled in a car seat atop my scattered bedding, is a baby. A soft pink bonnet crowns her tiny head, and a plush brown teddy bear stands guard at her side. She slumbers peacefully, oblivious to the turmoil her presence stirs within me.

"Eight months, maybe?" I murmur, trying to gauge her age as I inch closer. She's so small, so vulnerable. I stand there, uncertain, my mind grappling with questions I can't begin to answer. A bag sits beside the car seat, its contents undoubtedly tied to the child before me.

I stare down at her, feeling the weight of responsibility press upon me like never before. This wasn't part of today's plan—or any plan, for that matter. And yet here she is, breathing softly, a new life in my stark bachelor's world.

I pace back and forth, feeling the thud of my heart against my ribcage. "Lillian?" I call, voice laced with disbelief. The silence that greets me is as heavy as the air before a storm. I fumble for my phone, and in moments, her number is ringing through the speaker.

"Hey," Lillian answers, her tone breezy, nonchalant.

"Did you see this...this baby?" My words trip over each other, hoping this is some kind of elaborate prank.

"Congratulations. It's a girl." She chuckles, but there's no humor in her voice. "The woman who left her said there's a letter for you in the bag."

"Can you come back? Please, I need help with this."

"Sorry, Christian, but no way. I don't do kids. They're too much work." Her finality stings more than the dead connection that follows.

I hang up, my hands shaking as they reach for the mysterious bag. With a forced steadiness, I tear it open, and papers spill onto the bed. I snatch the first one I see—a birth certificate. Addison Hearst Bradford. My name is printed, bold and accusing, on the father's line. The mother is Taylor Tull Hearst.

> *Christian,*
>
> *I understand that what I am about to share with you will come as a great shock, but I must ask you to read through this letter in its entirety.*
>
> *My name is Erica, and Taylor Hearst is my sister. Taylor and I have always been close, and she spoke of you often. When she asked me to babysit Addison this last time, I didn't hesitate. I'd done it many times before. Taylor told me she would be back soon, but she never returned. Despite my efforts, I can't locate her.*
>
> *You are Addison's father. Taylor always intended to tell you, but life and circumstances got in the way. Addison is a beautiful baby girl who deserves to know her father. Enclosed with this letter, you will find her birth certificate, a list of her doctors, and a picture of her with Taylor.*
>
> *Caring for Addison has been an immense joy, but also an overwhelming responsibility. I have a job and a life that makes it difficult for me to provide the care and attention Addison needs and deserves. I cannot do this any longer.*
>
> *I want you to know that Taylor loved Addison very much. She always intended for you to be a part of Addison's life. I know this is a lot to take in, but I believe Addison needs you. She needs her father.*
>
> *Please, take care of her. She is an amazing little girl, full of life and potential. She deserves to grow up knowing that both of her parents love her deeply.*
>
> *I understand that this is sudden and difficult, but I hope you can find it in your heart to step up and be the father Addison needs. If you have any questions or need to discuss this, please do not hesitate to contact me.*
>
> *Sincerely,*
> *Erica*

The room is spinning.

"Taylor..." I whisper the name, trying to summon a face, any memory from the haze of my past relationships — no, that's too strong a word. *Encounters*. Nothing comes.

Addison stirs in her car seat, her fussing a sharp contrast to the numbness spreading through me. I'm anchored to the spot, clutching the letter and the birth certificate. This can't be real, yet here she is — my daughter.

That word is foreign on my tongue, and it tastes bitter.

My hand trembles as I dial my mother's number. The phone rings twice before she picks up, her voice as calm and collected as ever.

"Christian, darling, what a surprise. What can I do for you?" Her words are like silk, smooth and unruffled.

"Mom, I need you to come over. Now," I say, struggling to keep my voice steady.

There's a pause, and then a sigh. "It's Thursday. You know I have my spa day, sweetheart. Massage, facial, mani-pedi...then my hair appointment. It's my regular Thursday."

"Mom, please. This is important. I never ask for your help, you know that. But I need you here, quickly." My words rush out, pleading.

Another sigh, heavier this time, resonates through the phone. "All right, Christian. I'll be there as soon as I can."

"Thank you," I breathe out, relief momentarily easing the tightness in my chest.

As I end the call with my mother, my thoughts race to the hospital. Today is supposed to be a marathon of surgeries, responsibilities I cannot simply abandon. With shaky fingers, next I dial Joanne Kim, my office manager and scheduler.

"Joanne? It's me. Listen, I need you to get the on-call doctor to start the triple bypass at ten. I'll be there as fast as I can, but I don't know when that's going to be."

"Is everything okay?" Joanne asks.

"Something's come up. Just handle it, please," I say, trying to maintain composure.

"Understood. I'll take care of it," she responds

efficiently.

"Thanks, Joanne." I hang up and glance back at Addison, sleeping innocently in her car seat. She's still there. At least she's asleep.

I need to figure this out. And fast.

I stand frozen, my gaze locked on the tiny figure. Addison's delicate features tell a story all their own, one I struggle to comprehend. Her eyes, although shut, slant gently upwards. As I study her, the single crease across her palm and the pronounced gap between her toes leave a silent, undeniable declaration — she has Down syndrome.

A surge of confusion washes over me. This can't be right. I can't be her father. I'm always meticulous, never without protection. The very notion that she could be mine sends my mind reeling, searching for any lapse in memory, any forgotten encounter that might explain this impossible scenario.

Taking a deep breath, I force myself to calm down, to focus on what lies before me. My fingers, steady now, pick up the note again. A photo flutters out, landing softly on the bedspread. Taylor and Addison reads the elegant script on the back of the photo. The woman radiates a familiarity — the kind I'm drawn to — yet her face evokes no spark of recognition.

I scrutinize the details in the letter, a trail of Addison's short history. She was born at Mercy Hospital, my own workplace — a detail that adds a surreal edge to the unfolding drama. Michael Khalili was the OB, and his name implies a complicated birth. Cordelia Johns, her pediatrician, and Davis Martin, her pediatric cardiologist — all names synonymous with excellent care within the hospital's walls.

Relief flickers briefly, knowing Addison has been in capable hands, but it's quickly chased away by a stubborn certainty. She can't be my child. This must be a mistake, an error that brought her to my doorstep. I need to confirm this somehow.

Yet as I look down at the sleeping baby, her chest rising and falling in peaceful rhythm, I can't help but feel a strange pull, a connection that defies logic and precaution. Who is this little girl, and how has she found her way into my life?

A whimper cuts through the silence, and I freeze. In an instant, Addison's cries escalate, ripping at my composure. She's loud, insistent, and I'm out of my depth. My hands shake as I reach for the car seat, rocking it in a desperate attempt to soothe her. It's futile. Her distress grows, and with it, my panic. I don't know what to do.

"Christian!"

I barely register the door swinging open or the click of high heels across the hardwood floor. My mother, Madeline, strides in, a vision of composed luxury. I can't make out her words over Addison's cries. With an exasperated sigh, she scoops Addison up, giving her a pinkie to suck on. I stand there, useless, as she expertly changes the baby on my bed. I can't bring myself to step any closer.

"Christian, you must have formula or breast milk somewhere," my mother says.

"Uh, right." I fumble with the bag, tipping its contents onto the bed. Two cans of formula and a bottle emerge among a jumble of baby items. She takes charge, instructing me on the mixture—two scoops, six ounces of water. "All I've got is tap," I mumble.

"Tap water will do just fine," she says, and I can hear her patience thinning. When I return with the bottle, I hand it to Mom. She takes it from me, but shoves Addison into my arms before handing it back. "You've got to learn."

Addison squirms against me, her small form a foreign weight in my arms. I tip the prepared bottle toward her, but it crashes to the floor.

"Christian!" There's more than a hint of reprimand in her voice now. She retrieves the bottle and thrusts it back into my hands. "Hold it properly."

I want to tell her I don't know how, that this isn't my life, but the words won't come. So I just nod, my throat tight, and tentatively hold the bottle to Addison's lips, praying she'll be quiet, praying I can somehow manage.

My hands shake as she latches on, drawing from it with a ferocity that belies her small size. She finishes with a final, greedy gulp, and a burp bubbles from her lips. My mother, with deft fingers, unfurls a clean diaper.

"Once she's done eating, you may need to change her again," she says, her voice a mix of command and compassion.

I can't even begin to process the thought of changing a diaper. "I—I don't even know how," I admit, feeling the weight of my helplessness.

"Life is full of surprises," she replies with a wry smile. "Now, tell me, where did this little one come from?"

I recount the morning—the persistent doorbell, Lillian's departure, the package left behind. With a sigh, I point to the letter resting on the nightstand, its words still echoing in my head.

Mom picks up the letter, scanning it with eyes that have seen much in their time. Her brow furrows slightly as she reads. After a moment, she looks up at me, her expression unreadable. "Christian, do you recognize the girl? Taylor Hearst?"

I hesitate, searching the archives of my memory, but still, no clear image forms. "I'm not sure," I confess, the uncertainty gnawing at me.

She offers me a knowing smile. "You should get a DNA test, just to be certain," she advises. "But honestly, look at her... I'm quite sure she's yours."

I stand there, the bottle still in my hand, looking down at Addison's peaceful face and wondering how my life has shifted so suddenly. There's a vulnerability in her slumbering form that tugs at something deep within me, something I hadn't known was there.

"Get a DNA test," my mother repeats gently.

"Mom, what am I supposed to do if she's mine?" My voice cracks as the weight of potential fatherhood bears down on me.

She looks at me, her gaze piercing. "Christian, you'll be

her father, and you'll have to care for her." Her voice has an edge of iron, a reminder that some things in life can't be shrugged off or sent to voicemail.

I reach out, trying to pass Addison into her arms so I can escape to work, to normalcy. "Can't you just watch her for today? I've got surgeries—"

She steps back, hands raised in refusal, shaking her head. "No, Christian. This is your child. You need to be responsible for your actions. We had this conversation when you were fifteen."

Her words sting, but I know she's right. "Then what am I supposed to do?"

"Find a nanny, and quickly," she says, already moving toward the door, her presence receding like the tide pulling away from the shore. "You have room here for Addison and her nanny."

"Mom!" But she doesn't turn back. After a moment, I hear the front door open and close.

I'm alone now, save for the tiny human being whose steady breathing fills the suddenly cavernous room. With trembling hands, I lift Addison, still swaddled in her pink blanket, and settle her back into the car seat. She stirs slightly, a soft sigh escaping her lips as she nestles in.

"Okay, Addison," I whisper, more to myself than to her. "We're going to figure this out together."

The quiet is profound, broken only by the rhythmic sound of Addison's breaths. My heart clenches, a strange mix of fear and something else. But I can't place what it is.

I pull out my phone, the screen lighting up with unread emails and messages, all ignored for now. I do a search for local nanny services, my fingers clumsy and uncertain. There's a whole world I need to navigate now, and it's one I never prepared for. *What am I going to do?*

To Pre-Order Doctor Tyrant Click Here

THANK YOU

There are so many people who make this possible. Thank you, my reader, for giving me the chance to do what I only dreamed possible. I am forever grateful.

Thank you to my husband and soul mate who is my first reader and my amazing husband (who isn't a doctor). You're my inspiration and the yin to my yang. The peanut butter to my jelly. The generous and kind father to our children. I love you.

Thank you to my developmental editor, Jessica Royer Oken who makes my words shine.

Thank you to Courtnay, Linda, Iris, and Nancy who find all those pesky typos that try to burrow and stay behind. And thank you Diana for being that final set of eyes.

BOOKS BY GRACE MAXWELL

Men of Mercy
Doctor of the Heart (Paisley & Davis)
Doctor of Women (Nadine & Michael)
Doctor of Sports (Eliza & Steve)
Doctor of Beauty(Laine & Jack)
Men of Mercy Box Set

Mercy Medical Emergency
Doctor Delight (Tori & Griffin)
Doctor Bossy (Amelia & Kent)
Doctor Rebel (Lucy & Chance)
Doctor Enemy (coming October 2024)
Previously released as *A Doctor for Valentines* in "Love is in the Air, Vol 3"
Doctor Tyrant (coming February 2025)

Printed in Great Britain
by Amazon